BENEATH DC

A BRANDON HALL MYSTERY 3

JOHN THEO JR.

Print Edition
Copyright © 2020 John Theo Jr.
All rights reserved.

Published in the United States by CKN Christian Publishing, an imprint of Wolfpack Publishing, Las Vegas.

CKN Christian Publishing
An Imprint of Wolfpack Publishing
6032 Wheat Penny Avenue
Las Vegas, NV 89122

christiankindlenews.com

Paperback ISBN: 978-1-64734-697-3
Ebook ISBN: 978-1-64734-696-6

BENEATH DC

In loving memory of Nicholas Jole.

SPECIAL THANKS TO

Jim Prendergast, who patiently answered all of my military questions over the years.

And this is the condemnation, that light is come into the world, and men loved darkness rather than light, because their deeds were evil. For everyone that doeth evil hateth the light, neither cometh to the light, lest his deeds should be reproved.

- John 3:19-20

ONE

On this particular April night, I was perched on the tin roof of my parent's log cabin, dressed in mossy oak camo, wearing dark face paint. The view looked out over the 500 acres of pastures, forest, and ponds my family called home. A slice of paradise we used to raise cattle. The red hue of the setting sun cast a romantic aura over the grazing cattle. It looked like a scene from an epic movie from the likes of Cecil B. Demille. We named the farm *Twenty-Three-One,* after the Psalm of the same number. *The Lord is my shepherd, I shall not want.* The Lord had lived up to that promise through many tough times for our family.

As gorgeous as the view was, I wanted nothing more than to go home, shower, and go to bed. I had been up since five AM, but this was a rare occasion when my stubborn dad asked for help. My parent's chicken coop was located within a large fenced garden. This allowed the chickens the ability to free range and also fertilize the plants, but an animal was sneaking in and killing the chickens. Dad was on a mission to identify and shorten that animal's life span.

I turned to my dad next to me with his flintlock rifle resting across his lap and whispered, "Your birthday's coming up."

"And?"

"And how about you let me buy you a rifle that brings you into the nineteenth or early twentieth century?"

He looked at me with something akin to shame as I held onto my smaller .22 caliber lever action rifle. Dad held up his massive rifle with a muscular forearm and whispered, "This is a real gun. Something your ancestors used to defend their homes, and—"

"Provide food for their families," I finished the statement I'd heard dozens of times before.

Dad held back a grin and motioned for me to be quiet. He whispered, "I've faced off against some cunning humans in my time in the military, but nothing as insidious as this fox."

"How so?"

"He avoids any trap I set. In fact, the last one I set he flipped it over as if to taunt me. This here's personal."

"You sure it's a fox and not a coyote, bobcat, or even a hawk?"

"There's holes under the fence which tells me it's a four-footed predator, and it's too small for a coyote or bobcat. Besides, there's only one animal this sly."

About fifteen minutes later we heard the fox before we saw it. The animal entered a hole under the fence my dad had left unfilled. It was a petite, gorgeous, red fox, maybe ten pounds. Dad and I put our earplugs in at the same time. He held up his massive rifle and aimed. I prepared for the thunderous boom the antique flintlock would bring. After a long pause, Dad lowered the rifle.

He pointed and whispered. "Rascal made it inside and is hiding behind that peach tree in the corner of the garden."

I could see the fox's fluffy auburn tail poke out from behind the tree and rest on the corner of the raised garden bed Mom had asparagus growing in. "It's like he knows we're watching him," I whispered.

Dad nodded. "You have a shot?"

"Negative," I whispered.

The chickens inside the small coop were making a racket. They knew a predator was nearby. The fox periodically stuck its pointy nose out from behind the peach tree and sniffed the air before ducking back behind the tree. Dad raised and lowered his rifle three more times as the animal teased us. I looked over at Dad and shrugged my shoulders as if to ask, *what's the plan?*

Dad raised the flintlock to his shoulder a final time and whispered, "I'm gonna bark 'em."

"You're gonna what?"

"Just get ready to shoot."

I followed my orders and knew to ask questions later. The boom of the flintlock almost knocked me off balance. Suddenly, the wood from the raised garden bed exploded into the fox's hind-end forcing him out from behind the peach tree. The impact was so powerful that it shot the fox upright almost on his two hind legs. If I had stuck an umbrella under his front paw, he would have looked like he stepped from the pages of a Beatrix Potter novel. I wasn't going to get a better shot. If I missed, my old man would never forgive me. I took the shot and a moment later Dad clapped me on the back.

Mom came rushing out of the back door of the cabin beneath us. "What is going on out here?"

The only thing I saw on my father's makeup-covered face were his white teeth set in a smile. "I forgot to tell your mother what we were doing?"

"Sorry, Mom," I said, shouldering my rifle and starting to climb down the ladder. "We had to get rid of that critter that was killing your chickens."

Mom walked into the garden and proceeded to shout at us for ruining some of her asparagus. After apologies from both of us Mom went back inside.

As we picked up our quarry, I said, "What did you mean by bark 'em?"

"Your ancestors never had multiple firearms for hunting like you softies do today." Dad held up his flintlock. "They hunted both small, and big game, with the same rifle. The problem is the ball from this rifle would devastate small game ruining both meat and pelt. So they'd hit the bark above, or next to, the squirrel, possum, or raccoon. The concussion would kill the animal, leaving everything intact rather than a pile of mush. I knew the fox was a too big to kill with barking, which is why I said for you to be ready."

"So you're barking knocked the fox out from behind the tree so I could finish the job."

"Just the one-two punch we needed."

"You never cease to impress me, old man."

His two-word reply was quintessential Dad. "I know."

It didn't take much persuasion from my mother to get me to stay for dinner. Just a whiff of her barbecue chicken and grilled asparagus was all it took. After I washed up, I texted my wife Annie to come over and join us with our two daughters Emily and Addison, but they had already eaten. Mom, Dad, and me sat on their back porch, watching the last rays of the sun disappear behind the tree line. The silence was soon interrupted with a muffled thump, thump, thump that brought me back to my time in the Marines. From the sound, I knew it was a military grade helicopter. The noise grew louder as a

Blackhawk helicopter came into view and passed directly overhead.

My dad raised his mason jar of sweet tea up as if to toast the chopper. "Big brother is on the move."

"That's a strange choice of words," my mother said.

"Dad recently purchased a tinfoil hat," I said. "He now thinks everything's a conspiracy."

"You don't find it odd how low it's flying and that it's at dusk?" he said.

"I never thought of it," I said, realizing his powers of observation were sharper than mine. "Where do you think it's heading? Fort AP Hill?"

"No, they were heading northeast. Probably Fort Pickett." He thought for a moment before adding. "There's also Fort Belvoir, Fort Detrick, and don't forget Fort Meade. Then again, there's bases we don't even know about."

"Top secret places," I whispered to Mom.

She giggled.

Dad half chuckled. "You of all people shouldn't joke, Brandon. You've personally lived through some strange times."

He was right. Recently, my life had gone from slow to hypersonic. First, a domestic terrorist group attacked my home. Then I had a shootout with two psychopathic criminals in the Great Dismal Swamp, and a second shootout at my friend's house down the road. It was nothing short of a miracle how I was still alive.

"I've seen some unusual activity lately," Dad said. "Choppers flying at dusk, and my military contacts in DC are on edge. Spiritually, there's something afoot in this country."

Mom picked up Dad's hand. Her petite fingers all but disappeared when he closed his hand over them. "Take therefore no thought for the morrow: for the morrow shall take thought for the things of itself."

Dad finished the passage from the Gospel of Matthew. "Sufficient unto the day is the evil thereof."

I patted Dad's shoulder and kissed mom on the top of her head. "It's past my bedtime," I said.

"I have peach cobbler for dessert," Mom said.

I patted my belly. "If I stay, I'll end up having multiple servings."

"How about I save you a piece and you come by tomorrow?"

"You baby him too much," Dad said.

Mom lightly smacked Dad on the shoulder. "You shush," she said. "That's my baby."

I walked over to my four-wheeler and fastened the lever action rifle to the front handlebars before starting it up. I started to drive away but stopped when I remembered the one thing my wife told me to confirm.

I called back. "Can you two still watch the girls tomorrow?"

Dad leaned forward in his chair and placed his free hand behind his back in a mock gesture. "Gee, twist my arm some more watch those two angels."

"You guys are the best," I said.

Dad replied, "We know."

Driving back through the wooded trail that led to my farmhouse I thought how blessed I was to have both of my parents alive, healthy, and living on the same property as me. Annie's parents had both passed away and she had only a scattering of relatives throughout Virginia and North Carolina. My parents knew this was sensitive subject and treated her like the daughter they never had. Coming out on my home's side of the trail, I could see dark shapes of the cattle scattered throughout the pastures, which provided the majority of income for my family. It wasn't enough to make all the bills. I supplemented this with private investigating work and periodic scuba diving jobs. Most of the PI work was insurance fraud and the dive jobs were through the local sheriff's office.

Overhead, the clear night sky had started to reveal some of her majesty. Nowhere on the eastern seaboard south of Maine was there a nighttime viewing like this. An unintended consequence of living in a farming community was that it kept high-rises and excess light pollution out of the area. Above me, Ursa Major, the Great Bear glimmered with innumerable other specks of light. It was unfathomable to think that God had named each star.

I stopped the four-wheeler in front of the old, wrought-iron fence surrounding the family cemetery plot. Every headstone inside the space was thin alabaster revealing ages from long ago. All except one. A single new thick grey headstone stuck out from the rest. In the dim headlight from the four-wheeler I could still read, *Jonah Hall, March 12, 2015- August 10, 2017. Beloved son and brother. Now resting in the arms of our Savior.*

Much of my heart was buried in that red clay cemetery plot. It seemed like only yesterday that my wife's car was hit by a drunk driver along Route 501. Annie survived but my son did not. Since then, God had healed our brokenness, but there would always be a hole in my heart in the shape of my infant son. I started the four-wheeler back up and drove into the barn. No sooner had I stepped onto the side porch of our house than my twelve-year-old daughter Emily rushed out to greet me with a hug. Her pet collie, Fescue was right behind her.

"Daddy's home," she announced.

I lifted Emily up and my back tightened at the tall girl who used to be my chubby baby. "A hug from my daughter never gets old."

"Are we still gonna watch that Jimmy Stewart western?"

"Winchester Seventy-Three?"

She nodded. "I have the popcorn ready to go on the stove."

I placed her back down. "I'm convinced your mother gave birth to an eighty-year-old woman when you were born."

Emily smiled whenever I said this. She really

was an *old soul*. She preferred old black and white films and classic books to their modern-day equivalents. Inside, Emily went into the living room to play with Fescue. Annie worked at the kitchen table on her laptop. Our infant daughter Addison crawled along the kitchen floor, trying to make her way over to the counter where a blueberry muffin rested out of her reach. She reached the cabinets and climbed upright. I picked her up and kissed her. The moment I moved away from the counter she cried out. Not until I broke off a piece of the muffin was she content to sit in my lap across from Annie.

"How's things?"

"Addison wouldn't go down for her afternoon nap," Annie said, "and now I'm behind on all that I wanted to get done."

I looked over to see what Annie was typing. "Working on your blog?"

"No."

"Poetry?"

"No."

"Updating your profile on an online dating website?"

Annie finally gave me a forced smile. "I'm trying to project our bills for the month."

"How are we looking?"

Her smile faded. "If it were a normal month, I'd say we'd be okay, but it's not a normal month. Emily needs to go for her eye checkup, your tractor needs that part, and we should have never upgraded the Jeep."

"We have two kids," I said. "My old truck's great but we both agreed we wanted something newer, with four doors, for a family vehicle. Besides it's not even new; it's like five years old."

"It's still a car payment where we didn't have one before. We should have prepared better."

"I won't argue," I said, "but that won't change our current situation."

Annie wrote some numbers on a piece of paper and continued to alternate between the computer and the paper. I cleared my throat to try to get her to speak.

She threw down the pen. "What?"

Emily came into the kitchen and turned on the stovetop burner for the popcorn. I handed Addison to her. "Take your sister into the living room and prep the movie. I'll take care of the popcorn."

"Okay," Emily said, watching us both intently.

After she left the room, I leaned over to Annie and whispered. "I don't want Emily to worry. We need to pray."

As if to counter my whisper Annie spoke loudly, "Prayer won't pay these bills, Brandon."

I stepped away from her and walked over to the stove to shake the pot the popcorn was in. Emily had her mother's *panic gene* and I wanted to protect her from our financial troubles that had nothing to do with her. I wanted my children to have as innocent a childhood as we could give them. In the pot, the crinkling cooking noise of the oil was followed by a single kernel pop.

After a long pause I said, "I'm doing the best I can, Annie."

The baby started crying from the living room, and I could hear Emily shushing her.

Annie got up and walked over to the stove. "I'm tired of going hand-to-mouth, Brandon."

The popcorn in the pot started to erupt. "We're better off than most."

"It's not that," she said. "I need security."

"There's no such thing as security outside of God," I said, trying to keep my cool. "Everything's a façade. My buddy JT had close to two million dollars in the bank when his wife up and left him for his business partner and his life crashed around him. He was as financially secure as they come." Annie didn't seem moved by the story. I started to quote Matthew 6:20, "Store up for yourselves treasure in Heaven. Do not worry about—"

"We need more money," she interrupted.

"I'm working multiple jobs," I barked. "What do you want me to do?"

"I know," she said.

I collected myself and lowered my voice, but I knew from Addison's crying from the living room that it was too late. "We're not rich, Annie, but we are wealthy in the truest sense of the word. We'd be wise to spend time pondering our blessings."

I left the stove and kicked open the screen door and headed back towards the barn. Emily called after me, but I didn't respond. Behind me I heard the smoke alarm go off from the burning popcorn, which made the dog bark, and the baby cry.

TWO

I FELT HORRIBLE THAT WE AIRED OUR FINANCIAL problems in front of my daughter. Emily didn't need this stress. She'd already had to deal with the loss of her baby brother at a very young age, and since then had always been hyper-sensitive. I was so angry with Annie for airing these problems the way she did, and for piling on to my guilt. I didn't need her to lecture me about providing. I was fully aware of our friends working in big cities who took their families on fancy vacations, but I couldn't even pay our bills.

Whatever exhaustion I had felt was now gone. I had excess energy to burn and tried to re-focus it on something productive and started to clean up the barn's workbench. A couple times throughout this process a wrench was thrown against a random wall. Eventually, I got the place organized. Next, I finished writing up a bill for some PI work I did for a local insurance company. I submitted the bill via email but knew this corporation was slow to pay. They had the money, but the invoice had to clear a bunch of middle management before it would be approved. If I was lucky, we'd see the money in net thirty days, but more than likely it would be net sixty.

I wandered into a messy storage room in the back corner of the barn. It had once been a farm manager's bedroom back when my great granddaddy ran the place as both a cattle and tobacco farm. I had lined the walls with shiplap and fixed the sink. It needed more work but would make a nice guest suite. I sat on the futon and called my cattle broker, Rick. I had a couple dozen cattle a few months short of going to slaughter. If I were to sell them now, I'd take a hit due to their lower weight, but as the saying goes, a bird in hand was worth two in the field. I got Rick's voice-mail and told him to call me to move up the date of pickup.

When I turned around, Annie stood at the entrance to the room. Part of me wanted to stay mad but I could see that she was on the verge of tears. "Yes, how may I help you ma'am?" I said, knowing the two words she was going to say.

"I'm sorry."

I went quiet. There was some truth that came out when she was upset. I tried to stay angry but couldn't withstand my wife looking so sad.

"Brandon, I said I was sorry?"

"I forgive you."

"Do you?"

I stood up to face her. She was dressed in jeans and a tee-shirt but looked beautiful with her dark brown hair in a ponytail. "Of course, and I'm sorry for losing my cool. Just note for future reference that I don't ever need help feeling like I'm not doing enough. I struggle with the fact that I can't give you all a better life."

"I wouldn't change places with anyone," Annie said, now crying. She tried to collect herself but failed. "I have the best life of anyone I know. We live on a beautiful farm and I'm able to homeschool our daughter, and we've never gone without food. I know we are wealthy in the truest sense of the word. It's a lack of faith and my sin nature."

"It's fine. I'm sorry I lost my cool as well. We're good."

"You sure?"

I leaned in and kissed her cheek before pulling her in for a hug. "Don't worry. It's forgotten."

"Why'd you call Rick?"

"I'm going to move up a pickup date on some of the cattle."

"I thought we were gonna wait another few months so we could get more money."

"We need it now," I said.

Annie grabbed my chin and forced me to look at her. "We'll be fine. I'm sorry I've panicked you."

"But—"

"You're right," she said. "We need to trust God."

"Okay, when Rick calls back, I'll tell him to hold

off." I pointed to the room. "You know we could put a small fridge and microwave in here and rent it out?"

"Let's just wait for now."

We walked back to the house, hand-in-hand. I found Emily playing with Addison on the living room floor with Fescue. The three of them rolled a tennis ball back and forth. Fescue was doing a better job than Addison. I nodded to Annie as if to tell her we needed to talk to our daughter about what happened.

"Emily?" Annie said, but Emily did not look up. My wife repeated her name.

"What?"

I spoke up. "Your mother just wants to say how sorry she is, and finally admit that I'm always right and she's always wrong." Annie laughed and Emily smiled.

"We're sorry for arguing like that in front of you," Annie said.

"Are we going to lose the farm?"

"No, baby," Annie said, reaching down to sit between Emily and Addison. "We just have to tighten our belts for a few months is all."

"You guys can have my savings in the bank," Emily said, "and you don't need to pay me for my chores and—"

I turned away not wanting my daughter to see me tear up. After a few deep breaths I had collected myself and leaned down to kiss Emily's head. "I don't deserve a daughter like you. We'll be fine."

"God has been faithful," Annie said. "He doesn't change, and his promises don't either."

Emily nodded and seemed to have a peace about her now. I was convinced that children needed to hear from their parents not to worry.

"It's too late to watch the movie isn't it?" Emily said.

"How about I let you stay up a little late tonight and we watch the first half?"

Emily clapped her hands and rushed into the kitchen. "I'll make some more popcorn."

"Sounds good, baby."

Forgiveness from a child was one of the best reset buttons in the world.

THE NEXT MORNING, I was up at sunrise. The meteorologist forecasted three days of clear skies and I wanted to use the dry weather to hay the pastures. If rain hit before I could roll the cut grass into bails it would ruin the hay and the cows would be short on food for the winter. There was a cool breeze on the cusp of a morning chill that was my favorite temperature to work in. Dad was in one of the pastures on the back of his horse, Savannah. He looked tall and stoic in the saddle. Like he was pulled from a John Wayne movie. As much as we both liked westerns, I knew his heart was stuck in the 18th century. I passed by in the tractor and waved. When I saw his flintlock rifle resting across his arms, I knew something was wrong, and shut the tractor down.

"What are you hunting now?" I said, stepping from the cab of the tractor.

Dad pointed to the clear blue sky. "There?"

I couldn't see much of anything. He handed me a pair of antique brass binoculars hanging from the horn of his saddle. I focused, and what I thought was a large buzzard, turned out to be a small black drone.

"That thing has been flying around here for the past hour," Dad said. "It's driving me nuts."

"Don't shoot it," I said, handing the binoculars back up to him. "It could be some military thing."

"Or some joker trying to peep in on your wife while she's changing."

The drone came a bit closer but was still hundreds of yards away. Dad lifted the rifle, but it was as if it saw him and moved out of range.

"Dangit," he said, lowering the rifle.

"I think there are laws stating we don't own airspace over our property, so if you shoot it—"

"Okay," he said, ignoring me to lift the rifle back up to a shooting position. A moment later there was a boom as the flintlock rifle fired. The horse under my dad moved a bit, but Savannah was either used to my dad shooting from the saddle, or deaf from him doing so.

"Thanks for the warning," I said, sticking my finger into my ear as if to stop the ringing.

"Blasted thing moved," dad said, "or I'm losing my touch."

The drone drifted up and was soon out of sight.

"That would've been a hard shot for a scoped rifle," I said.

Without a word Dad nudged Savannah and they trotted back towards his cabin. I spent the rest of the morning in the pastures. The rhythmic sound of the tractor had a peaceful relaxing beat to it. When the temperature rose, I turned on the air conditioning in the tractor's cabin. Farming was hard work, but I had it much easier than my forefathers who did this same job with a team of horses. At lunch I found Annie dressed in an evening gown, making a sandwich in the kitchen.

"You look nice," I said, kissing her on the cheek.

"Just trying on a few dresses for tonight." Annie must have seen my confused look. "We are still going tonight?"

I snapped my fingers. "Ah, Senator Schilling's dinner party."

"How do you always forget this stuff, or do you block it out of your memory on purpose?"

"Sorry, I was in my own world haying the pastures. I definitely want to go."

"You do?" Annie looked surprised.

"Of course," I said, getting a bottle of water from the refrigerator. "It's a free date night."

"It's a once in a lifetime opportunity to be invited

to a senator's party and you see it as a free date night?"

"Is that bad?"

"I'll never understand how your brain works."

"Most people struggle to understand geniuses," I joked, grabbing half of her turkey sandwich without asking. "Rumor has it, Senator Schilling may announce his retirement tonight."

"You really think he's calling it quits?"

"No idea, but we don't know any other politicians. We better go to the party as we'll never be invited to an event like this again."

"You mean a free date night."

"Yeah, that's what I meant."

"The sad thing is you're not kidding," Annie said. "And you're welcome for the sandwich."

"Love you," I said, kissing her cheek.

Back in the pastures, I watched Emily throw sticks into the main pond, with Fescue running in after them. Periodically, the dog would go under the fence and chase some of the cows. The animals paid little attention to the collie who then ran back under the fence and jumped up and down until Emily threw the stick again. I was jealous of how much energy both Emily and the dog had. Emily threw the stick one more time before waving to me. I blew her a kiss. I would never leave my children a large monetary inheritance but hoped they would look back on their childhood on the farm with fondness. After haying most of the afternoon I cut out early to shower and get ready for my free date.

When I entered the house, Annie was dressed in a different black evening gown. I whistled. "You look gorgeous. I'd never have guessed that body gave birth to three children."

She blushed. "Not bad for thirty-four, huh?"

"I'd never guess you were a day over thirty-three and a half." She gave me a stern glare. "I'm just kidding," I said. "You look more like a college undergrad."

"That's more like it," Annie said. "Okay, follow me. I've laid out your clothes."

I owned two suits. One was a double-breasted black suit I assumed I'd be buried in someday. The other suit was a cheap blue pin stripe for the rare occasion I met a PI client in a business setting, or when I had to testify in court for an insurance fraud case.

Annie held up the black suit, a black tie, and starched white dress shirt. "Black tie means tuxedos, but this will have to do."

"There's no way I was gonna rent a tux for this," I said.

After a shower and touch up trim on my beard I called from the bathroom, "Annie did you machine wash this thing?"

"Your suit? No."

"Dang it, the pants seem a tight. You sure?"

"Honey, suits are dry clean only. Even your polyester ones. Did you ever stop to think it's you."

I looked down at my gut and sucked it in so I could close the top button on the pants. There was once a time where I had a six pack of abs, but I had been reduced to more of a two to four pack now. I made a mental note to hit the treadmill some more and ease off the sweets. Stepping out I felt naked without my cowboy boots on. I forgot how much I disliked dress shoes. The only dress shoes I owned were a cheap twenty-dollar pair of wingtips covered in dust.

Annie fixed my hair and pulled me closer using my beard as a handle to kiss me. "You look handsome."

"You look hot," I said, kissing her back.

She turned around and lifted her dark hair. "Can you do the top button on my dress."

"Sure," I said, starting to undo the back zipper.

"Brandon Hall."

"What? You look too good in this dress. I feel the need to get you out of it. Just for a minute."

"Addison's about to get up from her nap, and Emily could come downstairs any second?"

"So, lock the bedroom door."

She turned around and pushed me away. "Later, stud. We're gonna be late."

We dropped Emily, Addison, and Fescue at Mom and Dad's before heading out to Clarkesville where Senator Schilling owned an estate. I usually detested fancy events, but it was a beautiful drive along route 58, and it had been a while since I had last seen my friend.

My path crossed Senator Schillings when he hired me to investigate the death of his son who had been an aspiring race car driver. I was able to prove that Drew Schilling's death wasn't a racing accident, but homicide. This allowed the senator the ability to have some closure with the loss of his only son. Since then we had become friends and would catch up whenever he was at his Clarksville estate.

THREE

THE SMALL QUAINT TOWN OF CLARKSVILLE WAS dotted with boutique stores, and overlooked Buggs Island Lake, the largest lake in Virginia. Senator Schilling's plantation style estate was located a few blocks behind Virginia Drive near downtown. The long gravel driveway was lined with magnolia trees and small paper lanterns with candles in them. It looked like a historical movie set. The white ante-bellum home was lit with electric candles in every window. Annie's gasp reminded me that she had never been to the plush estate before. To the left of the main house a massive lawn where valets dressed in tuxedos parked expensive vehicles. The space was littered with Land Rovers, Mercedes, BMWs, as well as antique cars.

A valet approached the Jeep with a confused look on his face. "Good evening," he said. "Are you a guest?"

"No, employee," I said, turning to Annie with a grin.

He pointed to the house. "Staff were told to be here over an hour ago and to drive in the rear entrance. And why aren't you wearing a tuxedo?"

"I'm kidding," I said, noticing that he did not seem amused.

"I'm so embarrassed," Annie whispered under her breath, but loud enough that I could hear.

"Sorry, we're guests," I said, starting to feel a bit embarrassed myself.

"Name?" he said, looking at a clipboard.

"Brandon and Annie Hall."

He nodded when he saw our name. "Okay, let me take your car."

I stepped out and left the Jeep running. "Here," he said, handing me a ticket.

Before he drove off, I tried one last time to be funny. "Don't scratch the paint."

The guy didn't look amused and tore off as another employee stepped up to take the next car in line behind us, which happened to be a Mercedes.

Annie said. "Please get this out of your system before we go inside."

"No one has a sense of humor around here."

"Did you ever stop to think you're just not funny?"

"Not really," I said, approaching the massive front door.

Another older tuxedoed gentleman smiled when he saw my beautiful wife, but winced when he looked upon my attire. "Welcome to Senator Schilling's home. People are gathering in the library as well as out back."

The interior of the home was like being transported back into multiple eras at the same time. From the 1800s up to the 1930s. The foyer ceilings were at least twenty feet high and the floor was a bright white Carrara marble. A wrought iron elevator ascended through the middle of a grand spiral staircase up to a second story landing. Another gasp escaped Annie's mouth, but she didn't say anything.

"Place is a dump," I whispered.

"I know you've told me how nice it was but—" she stopped herself.

"I know. I know."

We entered a library that looked like a museum. It was lined with floor to ceiling wooden bookcases packed with leather bound antique first editions. All the furniture had been removed from the room since the last time I had been there. Ornate folding wooden chairs now lined the perimeter of the space along with a mahogany bar in front of the fireplace.

Most of the library was filled with older men and women who could probably trace their lineage back as far as mine but had families that prospered better than the Halls. Tuxedoed young men and women in black cocktail dresses walked around with silver trays of champagne. We approached the bar. The beers displayed behind the bartender were from all over the world. The same with the wine and champagne. We both opted for a sparkling water with lemon.

French doors opened to a back porch lined with hanging lights and glass lanterns filled with candles. At the end of the porch was a buffet line where chefs dressed in white served filet mignon, grilled chicken, and fish. The backyard was peppered with small bistro tables and a clamshell path I had once walked down with the senator to discuss his son's case. In the middle of the yard Senator Schilling stood taller than those around him. His salt-and-pepper hair, tan complexion, and bright smile made him appear as if he should be in the movies instead of politics. He wore a shiny tuxedo that looked hand tailored. He saw me and Annie and excused himself.

He came over and kissed Annie's hand. "Nice to finally meet you Missus Hall. Needless to say I can tell your husband married up."

"I won't argue that point," I said.

"How're you doing, Brandon?" he said, shaking my hand with a firm politician's grip.

"Can't complain, sir."

"Your home is stunning," Annie said, looking around.

"This property has been in my wife's family for

five generations," he said. "Out of our three properties this is my favorite though."

"I can see why."

"Speaking of which," I said. "Where's Missus Schilling?"

"Here I am," came a woman's voice in a rich old southern accent. A woman with a huge smile and auburn hair stepped from the porch to approach us. She looked like a twin sister to Raquel Welch and held a martini in her hand.

"Mister Hall," she said. "Who is this gorgeous woman you've brought into my home that has cut me to the core?"

Annie shook her hand. "Annie Hall, ma'am. I'm in awe of your property."

Mrs. Schilling waved her hand like it was no big deal. "Feel free to roam around if you'd like." She refocused her gaze on me and reached out to shake my hand. "How have you been Brandon?"

"Fine thank you." She didn't let go of my hand and seemed like she were trying to pull me in closer. It was the strangest handshake I'd ever experience. I pulled away and pretended to scratch my opposite arm like I had an itch. "Thank you again for inviting us tonight."

"It's my pleasure," she said. "It's nice to have some normal people here among these vultures."

The senator placed his arm around his wife. "Margaret's a bit melodramatic but not wrong in her assessment."

Mrs. Schilling added, "The groupies around DC are not much different than Hollywood groupies, except their net worth."

A waiter came by with some hors d'oeuvres wrapped in bacon. Annie helped herself to one. Mrs. Schilling seemed bored and looked past us to smile at someone. A moment later she was gone. Senator Schilling shook his head as if he didn't approve of some aspect of his wife.

A young male aide with blond hair came up and whispered something in his ear. The senator turned me and shook my hand again. "A donor needs to speak with me. Promise you won't sneak away. I'd like to think I have one friend here."

I looked around the packed yard. "You have plenty of friends here."

His smile faded and he leaned in to whisper, "My wife was wrong. They're not vultures, but sharks. Don't leave, okay?"

"We'll be here," I said. Once the senator left our side I turned to Annie. "Let's go see how the other half live."

"I don't think it's the other half," she said. "It's more like the one percent."

We each got a plate of food and sat at a bistro table. As we ate, random people would come over and chat me up as if I were some rich lobbyist who could help their career. I enjoyed watching their expressions change when they learned I was a cattle farmer from Nathalie. Ten-seconds was the average amount of time it took the person to find an excuse to move on and find another target. Annie was horrified at how much I enjoyed it. Soon, we walked arm-in-arm down the back clamshell path under the starlight.

"Are you sorry you didn't marry one of these men instead of a dirt-poor farmer?"

"I know you're fishing for a compliment," Annie giggled. She pulled me closer. "Remember, money isn't everything. These people seem…" she paused as if she were choosing the right word.

"Shallow?" I offered.

"Not shallow, but hollow. They have everything money can buy but seem empty inside."

We reached an old brick garage and brick perimeter wall and turned around to walk back towards the house. Tucked away in the far corner of the backyard was what looked like a shiny RV with a sign on the outside which read, *Rest Rooms*.

"I'm going to the little boys' room," I said.

"I'll meet you on the back porch," Annie said.

Inside the mobile RV were marble counters, air conditioning, and a valet handing out fancy paper towels. I checked and didn't have any cash on me to tip him. I shrugged my shoulders as if to say, *I'm sorry*. He rolled his eyes and handed me a towel. I laughed out loud at the irony. Even the young twenty-year-old bathroom valet was looking down on me.

Outside, I was greeted by Mrs. Schilling who

seemed surprised to see me at the rest rooms. The martini was gone from her hand, but in its place was a glass of champagne.

"Mister Hall, what do you think of our little party?"

"A little low-brow compared to what I'm used to," I joked.

She laughed a little too loud. "You are hilarious, Brandon."

"I'm kidding," I said. "The last party I attended was a barn raising for an Amish neighbor."

She reached out and touched my forearm. "I've been to one too many of these parties and they are a bore."

I politely broke contact with her, using my arm to survey the property. "The place looks amazing."

She re-touched my forearm again. "Have you taken a tour of our home?"

"Just the downstairs and grounds. It's gorgeous." I started to look for Annie to rescue me from the uncomfortable situation.

Mrs. Schilling upended what was left of her drink and tightened her grip on my forearm. "Why don't I show you the rest?"

"Maybe later," I said, looking for my wife.

"I'll be here for the next week, if you want to stop by." She started to rub my forearm with her thumb and forefinger.

I was ignorant when it came to many things in life, but this was a pretty clear signal she was looking to add a notch to some blue-collar headboard.

I leaned in and whispered. "Thanks, Missus Schilling, but I love my wife." I feigned a left and right glance like I was being watched and added with a whisper, "And I fear my wife."

Mrs. Schilling giggled and seemed emboldened. "You're nothing like the people I know, Brandon. Still, the invite remains."

I nodded and did a mock bow like we were in a medieval court and skedaddled like Joseph from Potiphar's wife. I found Annie on the back porch. She was surrounded by two early twenties frat boys who probably worked for a hedge fund in DC. When Annie saw me, her eyes widened as if to say, *get me out of this situation.* I stopped behind the duo to watch the scene play out. It reminded me of two prowling lions hunting what they thought was a limping female wildebeest on the plains of the Serengeti.

One of the young men pointed to his buddy. "Lance here's going to pull in seven figures this year."

Annie smiled, showing tremendous restraint. She was clearly unimpressed and uncomfortable. I walked around the two boys and came up to stand beside Annie.

Annie pointed to the two young men. "Lance and Trevor here were telling me about their work in the financial sector."

I shook both their hands. Both guys had weak handshakes. "Hedge fund managers?"

"Yes, sir."

Annie looked impressed at my guess.

The one named Trevor held up his fancy beer and pointed to my chest. "What do you do?"

"I'm in the oil business," I said.

"Really?"

"No," I snorted. "I'm a cattle farmer." To their credit both guys tried not to laugh. I added, "Now if you boys don't mind, I want to make sure my wife gets some water. Can you believe she's four months pregnant? Looks amazing, doesn't she?"

Annie's eyes widened, but she didn't give away my joke. Both the guys looked disgusted at the same time and walked away without another word. Within moments I watched them descend upon another woman.

"That sure cleared them out," Annie said. "This place is—"

"Horrific," I added. "I just had an equally awkward interaction with Missus Schilling leaving me feeling dirty."

"What do you know about her?"

"I've only interacted with her a couple times. She seems to be broken from the loss of her son."

"She's a beautiful woman," Annie said.

I linked my arm through Annie's. "She doesn't hold a candle to you."

"I think I had my fill of this place," Annie exhaled. "I want to go home to our quiet life on the farm."

"Wow, I'm the one who usually pushes to leave

parties early." I looked around the crowded yard and saw lost souls dressed in thousand-dollar tuxedos and dresses. I quoted Matthew six twenty-one. "For where your treasure is, there will your heart be also."

"Amen," Annie said.

Back inside, we found Senator Schilling talking with a group of elderly men. Several of whom smoked thick fancy cigars. The senator saw me and excused himself.

"You're not leaving, are you?" he said.

"I have a curfew," I said, shaking his hand.

"We appreciate the invitation," Annie said.

The senator turned to Annie. "Do you mind if I steal your husband for a few minutes before you leave?"

"Sure," she said. "I'll wait out on the back porch."

A handsome middle-aged man with a full head of grey hair stepped over and put his hand on the senator's shoulder. "Sir, I apologize for interrupting. My name's Sterling. I work for—"

"Can you see I'm in the middle of a conversation?" the senator snapped. His tone was guttural and angry.

"My sincere apologies," the man known as Sterling said. "I just stopped by to pay my respect. I work for—"

"I know who you work for," the senator said, turning to face him.

Annie and I exchanged glances. It was getting

awkward real quick. I motioned for her to step to the side. "Excuse us," I said. "We'll wait over at the bar."

"No, Brandon," the senator said. "Mister Sterling was just leaving."

"My employer," Sterling said, ignoring the senator's comment, "wishes to build bridges not tear them down, Senator."

The senator poked Sterling in the chest. "You tell your boss that it's impossible for him to build a bridge over my dead son's grave."

The packed room went silent.

"My employer had nothing to do with your son's death, sir. A terrible loss but—"

"He funded those radicals that killed him," the senator said, baring his teeth. "I'm going to connect him to Drew's death if it's the last thing I do."

The man known as Sterling nodded and turned to leave. "As you wish, Senator. Farewell."

As Sterling walked towards the front door the senator shouted, "Tell your boss to make sure he shows up at the hearing."

Moments later the patrons in the library went back to their conversations.

A young man I hadn't seen before approached the senator. By his earpiece I could tell he was security. "Everything okay, sir?"

"Nice of you to show up, Mister Jones. That man Sterling is not allowed back here. Ever."

The young man nodded. "Sorry, sir. Somehow he got on the list."

The senator regained his composure and waved his hand as if to dismiss the employee. "It's fine." He turned back to me and Annie. "My apologies. You know what, why don't you both join me?" The senator looked around the packed library as if to try to find a private area. "Let's step into my office just off the kitchen."

FOUR

ANNIE AND I FOLLOWED THE SENATOR THROUGH THE foyer and down a hallway. We passed several male and female employees with trays of food. The senator said hello to each, most of whom he knew on a first name basis. It was ironic that the one individual who had the most grounds to be a snob, seemed to be the most humble. We passed a massive kitchen on the left and continued on passing a larger caterer's kitchen. The senator stopped in front of double glass-paned French doors.

"I feel like I'm being ushered into the principal's office," I said. "I'm not in trouble, am I?"

The senator laughed and opened the doors. "You're fine. Just wanted to chat for a second before you two escape."

We entered a plush office with a massive Betsy Ross flag draped behind a mahogany desk. Framed copies of the Constitution and Bill of Rights were mounted on either side of the flag as if to remind Old Glory not to get too big for her britches. To the left was a fireplace with two leather couches facing one another across a coffee table sprinkled with travel magazines. The senator motioned for us to take one of the couches before sitting opposite us. He reached down and opened a wooden humidor on an ornate stand filled with fat cigars.

"Would you like a cigar?"

"No, thank you, sir."

The senator removed a sterling silver cutter from the inside pocket of his tuxedo as well as an antique gold lighter. He snipped the end off the cigar. After it was lit, he blew out a perfect smoke ring.

He showcased the cigar like it was a model plane. "Cubans. One of the only things in history to come out of a socialist country that is superior to anything you'll find in a capitalist market." He took another puff of the cigar. "I'm sure you're wondering why I snagged you before you left?"

"I'm curious, for sure."

He leaned forward and turned to Annie. "I want to offer your husband a job."

"Brandon? Why?"

The senator laughed. "Let me back up a minute. I'm making an announcement before the end of the party tonight that I'm retiring."

"I'd heard rumors," I said, "but didn't know how true they were."

"I just don't have the fight in me any longer. DC is

too corrupt. The Constitution is all but shredded. Congress just spends like a drunken sailor, leaving us trillions in debt. I like the new administration, but I think it's too late. The country's on life support except no one in Washington knows, or cares."

Annie spoke for the first time. "That's quite pessimistic, sir."

"You're right, and I'm sorry. I'm not a glass-half-empty sort of guy, but when your personal life is a mess it's hard to find the strength to fight the day-to-day battles in your professional life."

"You mean since your son's passing?" I said.

"Not just that," he spoke with the cigar between his teeth. "My wife's about six months overdue from going into a rehab program. My daughter's struggling at UVA, and to tell you the truth, I'm just tired."

"I understand," I said, and I did.

"There's one thing I want to do before I retire. Based on the guy I just threw out you might guess what that last item on my professional bucket list is?"

"Expose Gaspar Schultz for the globalist he is?" I said.

The senator gave me a thumbs up. "Me, and a few of my colleagues who haven't sold out yet, cornered him into testifying at an upcoming hearing about the stock market hiccup last year where the plunge protection team had to intervene." The senator must have seen the confused look on our faces and added, "The plunge protection team is a group created in the late eighties to monitor the stock market and intervene when it dips too low, and prevent another a Black Monday like we saw in eighty-seven. And by intervene, I mean manipulate the market, but don't get me started on that rabbit trail."

"You think Schultz had something to do with this hiccup as you call it?"

The senator nodded. "He's that powerful, and not happy that the country turned away from most of his communist candidates he's propped up over the past few years. The man hates this country, liberty, and the free market, and has spent billions trying to pervert it towards the socialist utopia he wants. It's nothing short of a miracle that we got him to testify, but while he's there I want to pull the veil back and bring to light his other evils."

"Such as?"

"Trafficking, drugs, arms, you name it. The guy is a devil." The senator sat back looking at the Cuban cigar in his hand as if it were hypnotic. "If I can do this in my son's memory—" he stopped himself. "It will make everything worthwhile."

"Forgive me, sir," Annie said, "but how does my husband fit into this?"

"I'd like to offer your husband a job to act as my personal security detail until this is over."

I turned to Annie and shrugged my shoulders. "I'm honored you think so highly of me."

"I know you're busy with the farm, but think of this as another PI job, just a bit longer. I've been getting some threatening letters and emails and I'd feel better if someone I trusted were watching my six."

"I don't think—"

"It would be twenty-five grand a month for at least a four-week contract. This would cover me for a period of time before, and after, the hearing. I'd take care of a hundred percent of your expenses, including a rental car, apartment, meals, and give you a stipend to spend however you see fit to do your job, so that a hundred percent of that pay would go to your family's savings."

I looked at Annie. Both of us were trying not to look surprised at the generous offer. "I don't know what to say, sir."

"As you can tell by my security detail, they're not top notch." He chuckled and flicked the cigar ashes into a marble ash tray next to the couch. "Even though they charge top dollar."

"What about Capitol and DC police?" I said. "Aren't they investigating the threats?"

"The civil discourse in this country has descended into anti-intellectual temper tantrums. Metro Police and Capitol Police are overtaxed dealing with threats to politicians. Just last month, someone mailed an envelope of white powder to my office. It wasn't anthrax, just baking soda. Still, it scared everyone who works for me. Then one of my counterparts across the senate aisle had an angry intern who doxed me."

"Doxed?" Annie said.

"It's a term for when your political enemy releases your personal address to the public. Since then my brownstone in Alexandria has been egged, spray painted, and one night a crowd rallied in front of the house for hours beating on the front door. I wasn't home, but Margaret was pretty shaken up."

"Why would people do this?" Annie said.

"I'm very fiscally conservative, but liberal on social issues. This has allowed me to walk unscathed for a long time in my career as a politician. However, last year I came out as pro secure border, which has triggered a lot of people. The left claims diversity, and tolerance, only if you agree with them." There was a long pause before he added, "So what do you think about the job?"

I looked to Annie. "I'm not sure what to say, sir."

"I have a garden unit apartment under my brown-stone in Alexandria where you'd stay. I'd sleep better knowing you were onsite."

"Do you think some of this could be tied to Gaspar Schultz testifying before congress?"

The senator pursed his lips. "The short answer is, yes."

Annie reached out and held my hand. "Forgive me, but my husband's not trained in this area."

"Your husband's a veteran with some combat experience along with a proven PI background that I'm more than satisfied with. Besides, in a place like DC loyalty goes further than experience. It's a rare currency up there." The senator shook his head like he was embarrassed. "I'm convinced even my closest staff would sell me out if it benefited their careers."

"Then why do you employ them?"

"Quid pro quo," he said. "Politicians use employees to get ahead, and the employees use the politicians to build their careers. It's effective and efficient but promotes backstabbing like crazy. People call DC a swamp, but I'm not sure that's the correct metaphor. It's more like a vast polluted ocean where everyone swims with an open wound. It's not a matter of if, but when, a shark smells blood and bites you."

"I understand," I said.

"If the price is too low I can—"

"No," I almost shouted. "That's not it." I tallied it in my head. That would cover paying for all our current bills, paying off the Jeep, and allow us to put some money in the bank. Over the years we had touched our savings too often and it was almost depleted. This job offer was too good to be true. "Can me and Annie talk about this?"

"Of course," he said, crushing the expensive cigar in the ash tray with two-thirds of the Cuban still unsmoked.

The senator walked us out the front door and stood while we waited for the Jeep to be brought around. When the valet got out, the senator hugged Annie and shook my hand. "Let me know what you decide."

"I will, sir."

I turned to the valet holding our key and realized I still had no money. I turned to Annie who didn't have her pocketbook.

"Hold on," she said, getting into the Jeep. She took five dollars she kept for emergencies in the ash tray and gave it to the valet.

"Sorry, we don't valet much in Nathalie," I said, opening the passenger door for my wife.

The first ten minutes of the drive home were quiet. The only sound came from an AM station playing classical music, which complimented the gorgeous night sky. Annie cleared her throat.

"Yes, dear?"

"Are we going to talk about this?"

"About what?"

Annie chuckled. "Don't play dumb. The job offer?"

"Oh, right. I totally forgot."

"Sure, you did."

"What are your thoughts?" I said.

"I don't want you to take it."

"It's good money and would pay off all our debt and more than replenish our savings. Can you even imagine?"

"There's more to life than financial security."

"Singing a different tune about financial security now that your gorgeous trophy-husband might have to go away for a few weeks."

"Oh shush."

"We should at least pray about it."

"I already did," she said, "and I don't have a good feeling."

"Well, let me pray about it and we can reconvene tomorrow."

It took a little over an hour to reach home. The house was dark and empty. Devoid of noise.

Annie turned on the kitchen light. "The place seems so different with the kids at your parent's house."

"I know," I said, trying to get my uncomfortable dress shoes off as quick as possible.

Within minutes my suit was back in the closet where it belonged. I looked over at my dirt stained cowboy boots next to my worn jeans and wrinkled button-down shirt draped over a chair, and remembered how well they fit. When I worked on the farm it was like wearing a hand tailored outfit just for me. Like many things in life, it was time and toil that made them fit so well. Annie stood in front of her wrought iron floor mirror, removing one of her earrings. She had yet to take her dress and high heels off and stood about at my height of five-foot-nine. I wondered if she were trying to savor the moment of make-believe a bit longer.

I walked up and started to rub her smooth pale shoulders. "Sorry I can't give you a better life."

"The party was fun, but I love the life we have together. I wouldn't trade it for anything."

"Are you sure?" I said, kissing her neck.

"Yes, I'm sure. What are you doing?"

"Just trying to help you out of that stuffy cocktail dress." Annie giggled. I changed my voice to sound as if I were a rich blue blood with marbles in my mouth. "Did I ever tell you that I'm a hedge fund manager?"

"Oh really?"

"Yes. I will make seven figures this year, so you must sleep with me."

Annie's giggle left and a serious look came over her. She kissed me and whispered that she loved me. I whispered the same.

The next morning, I joined Annie on the front porch with a cup of coffee, a bowl of oatmeal, and my worn Bible. The morning sky was transitioning from red hues to a bright blue. We talked and prayed about the job offer from Senator Schilling.

Annie paused at the 23rd Proverb. "It reads here not to kill yourself for riches."

"I don't think the senator's job is for riches. Just to get us over a hump."

"I still don't want you to go."

"That's a one hundred and eighty degree turn from the other day."

"I told you I was wrong."

I grabbed my phone and put it on video. "Can you repeat what you just said so I can have it on record. You said you were...what was the word you used?"

"Wrong," she laughed, "and you're rude. Shut that thing off. I look horrible in my bathrobe."

I put the phone down. "You look beautiful. And so it's a no-go on the job?"

"That's my opinion. What's yours?"

I looked out over the pastures. A large group of cattle stood by a small pond. "I guess I agree."

Annie reached out for my hand. "We'll get through this."

After breakfast, Annie went to pick the kids up at my parents while I walked into the barn. I did a quick workout of pushups, sit ups, and a two-mile run on the treadmill. I made sure to stretch for a few minutes at the end. My joints weren't what they used to be when I was in the Marines. I now had a Rice Krispies body where things tended to snap, crackle, and pop. In the barn office I sat at the computer with a second cup of coffee and placed an online order for some number two diesel to be delivered for the tractors. A half hour later I rode out towards the wooded section of the property on the tractor with the brush hog attachment on the back. We kept the forest section in place for hunting, but saplings were starting to migrate from the woods into the pastures and needed to be tamed.

After brush hogging for an hour I spent the rest of the day haying. I worked through lunch but broke off for an early dinner. Annie had grilled steaks along with corn and vegetables. I brought Addison's high-chair out onto the porch so we could eat dinner overlooking our piece of paradise. The days were getting longer, and there was still enough sun for me to go back out and work after dinner if I wanted.

"This view never gets old," I said. Emily came out and plopped down in her small rocking chair. "Where have you been baby girl? Mom was calling you?"

She held up her hand. It had a scratch mark on it. "Fescue nipped me."

"That's odd," I said. "She's never done that before."

Annie looked at the scratch. "Go wash it and put some antibiotic ointment on it."

When Emily came back outside, I said. "Fescue's a good dog. Did you do something to provoke her?"

"She's been sleeping most of the day. I was trying to get her to go play and she growled and bit me."

"Maybe she's not feeling well," I said.

Emily looked nervous. "Should we take her to the vet?"

"If she's still not feeling well tomorrow then I'll call the vet."

Emily seemed to relax now that we had a plan. "Are we still going to the race tonight?"

"Up to your mom."

"Colt texted and said he left us four tickets at the gate."

"I like anything free," I said.

Emily squealed. "This is gonna to be so much fun."

A springtime tractor-pull and lawnmower race at the local fair grounds wasn't most American's idea of a fun Saturday night, but for the Hall family, it was a redneck theme park.

"We can't stay until the end." Annie said, "Addison needs to get to bed at a reasonable hour."

After dinner the four of us piled into my 1976 Ford F250 pickup truck Emily named *Hazel*. Annie knew better than to ask why we weren't taking the newer Jeep. For an event like this we had to show up in an American made pickup truck. Every Hall family member had on their cowboy boots, and jeans. Even Addison had on slip-on soft cowboy boots I picked up at the local farm supply store in Halifax. The drive to Cluster Springs Raceway was just over a half hour. We parked at the fairgrounds located behind the racetrack next to hundreds of other American made trucks decorated with American flags and patriotic stickers.

"Ah, my people," I said, unfolding Addison's pop stroller.

The tractor pull competition was just ending. People had started to line the fence surrounding a nearby dirt racetrack. Inside the track, Colt Burnell and his three brothers Wyn, Moss, and Wes, stood by a fire engine red lawnmower dressed in mossy oak overalls. Their dad had been a firearms fan and named each of his boys after gun makers Colt, Winchester, Mossburg, and Smith and Wesson. All four brothers sported full beards and healthy mid sections within their overalls. I propped Addison up on the top of the fence and she seemed to enjoy all the different colored racing lawnmowers.

Emily gave my waist a hug and looked up with a dimpled smile. "Did I ever tell you that you're the best Daddy in the world?"

I knew it was a ploy. "What do you want?"

"Could I get a funnel cake at the concession stand?"

"No," Annie said. "We just ate, and you know we are pinching our pennies right now, honey."

Emily lowered her head. "Sorry, I forgot."

I handed the baby to Annie and checked my wallet. I had a wrinkled five-dollar bill I had found on my work desk earlier, which I gave to Emily. "Here."

"I feel bad," Emily said, handing it back to me.

Annie looked to me as if to say, *it's your call.*

"Come on," I said, grabbing Emily's hand. "Let's go together, but I want the first bite."

On the way I saw my buddy Tollers dressed in his sheriff's uniform. He came up to Emily and picked her up from behind. She squealed until she turned around to see who had her.

"Ma'am, I need to see your ID," Tollers said. "I think you were just about to cut someone in line, and I have to give you a ticket."

Emily laughed. "You scared me, Uncle Jimmy."

Tollers put her down and gave me a light punch in the shoulder. "What's up?"

"You cutting out of work to hang with us?"

"Nah, just passing through to make sure everything's okay."

Tollers' beard, like mine, had started to grey. Jim and I grew up playing baseball together. Tollers received an athletic scholarship to Duke where he proceeded to blow out his arm sophomore year. He dropped out and came back home to recover, and within a few years he joined sheriff's department. Around town he was still referred to as *Fast-Ball Tollers.*

"Why don't you stick around for a race or two?"

As if in response to my request Tollers' radio chirped. He rolled his eyes. "Duty calls. I'll see you at church tomorrow."

Back at the fence the crowd had grown. The first race was about to start. Colt was in this heat with four other modified lawnmowers. He was by far the heaviest driver of the bunch with his beard sticking out from the bottom of his helmet resting on his belly.

A man dressed in camo held a megaphone up to his mouth and a starting pistol. "Riders on your mark, get set—"

The pistol fired and Colt's mower took off like it was fueled with nitrous oxide. Within seconds he was a full length in front of everyone else. For a big burly guy, Colt was able to lean into the turns like a nimble gymnast. A few laps later he had won his heat. We stayed for a few more races but had to leave when the lights came on over the track. By the time we got back to Nathalie the only illumination was a sliver of a new moon and dim light from Hazel's old halogen headlights. No matter how many times I pulled into our property there was something special about doing so at night. It felt like we were all alone in the world and the heavens seemed to touch the earth.

I shut the truck off and looked in the back seat. Emily leaned against Addison's car seat. Both of them asleep.

"Precious," Annie whispered.

I got out and picked up Addison from the car seat. One whiff and I knew her diaper needed to be changed, and I immediately handed her to Annie. "Take the baby and I'll get Emily."

Annie cradled the sleeping baby. "She's so cute." A moment later, Annie's smile faded, and her nose wrinkled. "Brandon, you're so rude."

"You know the rule. Whoever's holding her gets the diaper duty. Besides, I gotta wake the princess."

By this time Emily was yawning. I took her hand and escorted her out of the truck. Part of me wanted to carry her inside like I had done so many times in the past, but she was getting too big. She walked up to the front door and wandered in after Annie and the baby. All three headed upstairs to the kids' bedrooms. I stayed in the kitchen, prepping the coffee maker for the morning. As I ground the coffee beans, I could hear Addison's high-pitched wails from being woken to have her diaper changed. I smiled, trying to think of a way to make Annie laugh when she came back downstairs with the dirty diaper.

Suddenly, there was a scream. It wasn't Annie or the baby.

It was Emily's.

FIVE

My hand dropped under my shirt where I kept my appendix holster that held my nine-millimeter Smith and Wesson. Emily's second scream was blood-curdling, convincing me a burglar was in the house. I ran up the stairs with images of a past gunfight on my property flooding my mind. Annie met me outside Emily's room holding Addison.

"What's wrong?" I shouted, rushing into Emily's bedroom ready to pull the gun.

My daughter pointed to the opposite side of her bed and began to cry hysterically. I rushed around her bed expecting to find a dead body. What I found was a body, but not a human one. Fescue lay dead with her tongue hanging out the side of her mouth.

"Oh baby," I said, removing my hand from the gun and using it to reach out for Emily.

Emily collapsed into my arms and started sobbing uncontrollably. I started to cry as well. I felt bad for

Fescue but devastated to see my daughter this upset. Annie shrieked when she saw the dog but collected herself. She must have known her shock would feed Emily's hysteria. Addison was also crying, but for different reasons. I motioned for Annie to take the baby into her room.

"Come on," I said, picking up Emily.

I carried her out of the bedroom and down the stairs, taking each step with caution. I placed Emily on the couch and sat with her for the next few minutes as her sobbing slowed to crying and eventually sniffles.

"I'm sorry, baby," I said, stroking her shoulder-length dark hair. "I'm so sorry."

"What do you think happened?"

"I don't know," I said. "Maybe she was bitten by a copperhead, or a brown recluse, or black widow spider."

Annie came down to join us on the couch. After a few minutes I walked over to the small bookshelf where we kept a handful of DVDs. I chose *It's a Wonderful Life*, one of Emily's favorite movies.

I showed her the movie. "I'm gonna put this on for you while I go take care of Fescue, okay?"

Emily nodded still sniffling. I dimmed the lights and went back upstairs as the credits rolled for the old black and white movie.

Annie followed me to the top of the stairs. "What are we gonna do?"

"Get me an old blanket and I'll take Fescue outside."

Fescue was a great dog for the short time we had her. She had never shown any signs of sickness and was always up for playing with my daughter. My heart broke for Emily who now had another tragic memory added to her short life. The first was the loss of her baby brother. Then there was the time she came home to her bedroom riddled with bullets from the shootout on our property. She had also been at the scene when a friend's child had been abducted in Richmond, and now the loss of her adored pet collie.

I checked Fescue all over for bite marks but didn't see any. Her teeth and gums looked fine and her skin had some flexibility which meant she was hydrated. She looked like a healthy dog.

I covered Fescue with the blanket. "Thank you for being a loyal friend to Emily," I whispered. I carried the dog downstairs. Emily started to get up from the couch when she saw me. "I got this, baby. You stay there."

Outside, I placed Fescue down by the large oak tree near our porch and went to the barn. I grabbed a spade shovel and headed back out to the oak tree. Far out in the pastures I heard a few strange moos from the cattle as if they knew what had happened to their canine peer. I buried Fescue at the base of the oak tree she played around so often. I'd find a stone and mark it the next day and let Emily say something over the grave.

Back inside, Emily rested her head on Annie's lap. On the television screen a young George Bailey, played by Jimmy Stewart, wanted to get out of the fictional town of Bedford Falls and travel the world. Having watched the movie a hundred plus times I knew that George would soon have to give up his dreams of leaving town to stay and run his late dad's business. Instead, he'd hand over his life savings to his younger brother Harry so he could go off to college. The sacrifices George made would soon be compounded by tragedy, culminating in a spiral of self-pity.

I motioned with my hands like I was scrubbing my hair to let Annie know I was going to take a shower. When I got out of the shower Annie sat on the edge of our bed.

"How's Em?" I whispered.

"Sleeping," she said. "What do you think happened to Fescue?"

"Only thing I could think of was a snake bit her, but I didn't see any signs."

"Where'd you bury her?"

"Under the oak," I said. "We can let Emily say goodbye tomorrow."

Annie wiped a tear off her cheek. "I feel so bad for both Fescue and Emily."

"Me too."

Back in the living room the third act of the movie was about to start. George Bailey had just been shown what the world would be like without him. He stood on the bridge and called out to God that he wanted his life back. Immediately, the snow started to fall showing the audience that George had returned from the sacred world and was back in the secular world. George was now ready to face his problems head on. He had realized how rich he truly was. Romans 8:28 came to mind, which said that God was always at work for those who loved him, and He could turn tragedy around for good.

At times I felt like George Bailey from Act I. Like I missed out on things my friends had. Fancy vacations and new homes, but more often than not I felt appreciation for the life God had given me. Like George Bailey from the end of act III. I was married to the love of my life and we had two healthy girls. I worked for myself outdoors doing something I loved. Although money was tight, I truly felt like I had a wonderful life. No, a blessed life. I covered Emily in a blanket to let her sleep on the couch. I shut off the television just as the entire town surrounded George Bailey in a cocoon of love and support.

THE NEXT MORNING, I was the first one up. I dressed and headed out on to the porch with a bowl of oatmeal and cup of coffee. The air was cool, but I could tell by the humidity it was going to be a warm sticky day. In the distance a few cows lay in the main pasture. Not an uncommon sight. I scanned back and forth and noticed more lying down. No, all of them were in on the ground. The bowl of oatmeal fell from my hand shattering on the stone path just off the porch. I dropped the mug as well and started to sprint towards the fence line. I hopped over the fence and ran as fast as I could into the main pasture. In the distance I saw a UTV approach from the trail that led to my parent's cabin. Dad jumped out and ran to meet me at the nearest cow. Scattered throughout the pasture hundreds of cows lay dead or dying. Faint moos fell from some of their mouths. The heifer in front of me lay with its large tongue hanging out of its mouth.

"Dear Lord, what happened?" I said, trying to register what I saw.

"This ain't good," Dad said, with a surprising amount of calmness to his voice.

I lifted the head of the dead young heifer. "I don't know what we're gonna do—"

Dad rested a hand on my shoulder as if to calm me down. I collected myself but still needed his help to get up. It was as if all the energy had left me. Dad half carried me around the pasture so we could inspect the dead, and dying, cattle. Buzzards circled overhead while flies started to collect around the dead. The dying ones panted for breath as if they were having asthma attacks. Every animal was the same as the next. Dead, with their tongues hanging out of their mouths, or dying with heavy breathing. So many things went through my mind.

Was the farm safe? Were Annie and the girls in danger? Was this natural, or did someone do it deliberately? And finally, how were we going to make our bills?

"I've never seen anything like this," Dad said, looking over the pasture which was now a graveyard.

"What are we gonna do?" I repeated.

"First things first," Dad said. "Who's in control?"

It was a rhetorical question, but he wanted to hear me say it out loud. "God," I said.

Dad put his arm around my shoulder and started to pray. "Father, we know you are always at work for your children. Whatever hardship is coming our way I pray you give us what we need to face it. We lift this devastation up to you and ask that you show us how to proceed. We pray all this in Jesus name."

We both said, "Amen."

"Thanks," I said. "I needed that spiritual slap in the face."

"It's gonna be okay," he said. He must have read the anxiety on my face. "Take a breath, son. Go to worst case scenario?"

"We lose the farm?" I said, trying not to break down in tears in front of my dad.

"Wrong," he said. "We lose the farm, and we all live to see another day. Think about what your momma went through with the cancer scare? Think about the shootout that happened on this very property? The shootout at the Eldridge's? Those things were far worse than what we're facing."

"But the farm, Dad? I know how much you want to pass it on, and keep in the family-"

Dad waved his hand. "I'm over it. The farm is a thing. I care about your mom, you, Annie, and the girls. If we have to go live in two RVs I don't care anymore as long as we're together."

I looked over at the family cemetery plot. Jonah's headstone stuck out from all the older stones. I wanted to vomit at the possibility of losing the farm and leaving it, and the cemetery, in another family's care.

Dad squeezed my shoulders as if he knew what I was thinking. "It'll be okay, Son."

I reached up to tussle his full head of hair which barely had any grey in it. "Thanks."

He smiled. "We gotta call the authorities. They'll probably want the CDC to come out as well as the FDA and FSIS." He stopped for a moment to scan the area. "Only thing that could do this is food, or—"

"Water," I said, remembering Fescue. "It's the water," I repeated.

"How are you so sure?"

"Fescue was playing in the pond the other day and died last night the same way."

"What? How's Emily taking it?"

"She was a mess last night, but—" I caught my breath.

"But what?"

"Emily was nipped by Fescue yesterday," I whispered.

"Did the dog break the skin?"

"I don't remember," I said, starting to sprint back towards the house.

Every step I took my feet felt heavier. It was like I wore lead shoes. "Please God, not Emily. Please Lord."

I burst through the screen door into the kitchen. Annie was pouring a cup of coffee and jumped back startled. "What's wrong?"

I sprinted past her into the living room to where Emily's still pale form lay on the couch. I fell to my knees and said her name? She didn't respond. I pleaded, "Emily, wake up baby please?"

A few seconds passed before her beautiful dark eyes fluttered open. She yawned. "Why are you shouting, Daddy?"

I cradled her in my arms, tears pouring down my cheeks. "I just wanted to remind you how much I love you is all."

"Okay," she yawned again, "but you don't need to yell."

"Let me look at your hand," I said pulling the Bandaid off her cut. The nip mark was red but didn't look infected or swollen. "Did you clean this like mom said?"

"You told me to, so I did."

"Thank you for listening," I said, placing the back of my hand on her forehead to confirm it wasn't warm.

Dad burst through the kitchen door and Annie jumped again. "What is going on with you two?"

"Emily?" Dad said.

"She's fine."

"What's wrong?" Annie said.

"Annie, you're gonna need to sit down."

MOM JOINED us at our house as we broke the news to Annie and Emily. My daughter was still in shock from losing Fescue and didn't seem as upset as Annie about losing the herd. I knew why my wife was a mess. She knew we could lose the farm.

Dad went out to meet the first officer who showed up. Once Annie had calmed down, I went out to join them. Within an hour the farm was full of law enforcement. Tollers showed up dressed in plain clothes and parked his sheriff's cruiser at the entrance to the farm to keep local newspaper reporters out. I moved the tractors out of the barn and set up a makeshift command center in the middle space. By mid-morning a male and female government official showed up from the CDC. I had to pull paperwork on feed and the few organic pesticides I used on the property for them to review.

"You've got to go check the ponds," I repeated over and over.

"How are you so sure it's the water?" The male

CDC officer said, bending down to inspect a dying cow.

"Our dog was playing in it the other day and she died last night."

"Where's the dog?"

"I buried her in the yard."

"We'll need to exhume the animal and do an autopsy."

I asked him to give Emily a look and he confirmed she was fine. Historically, the words *government* and *efficiency* were not synonymous, but I was impressed with these two individuals. Within a few hours they confirmed the water was contaminated. The main pond had an inflow and outflow to other parts of the property and was already almost clear of the poison, but the other ponds scattered around the property had sitting water which still contained the poison. Dead fish now floated over the surface of the watering holes.

The female CDC agent dressed in a clear plastic face mask and white paper throwaway onesie came over and lifted her mask. "At this point we'll place a neutralizing agent in the ponds which should clear it up."

A male police officer came up to her. "A lot of us men fish in the area. I know the main pond has an outflow."

"It just feeds other ponds on the property," I said, "and doesn't make its way to anything major like the Bannister River."

"If it's the poison I'm thinking," the agent said, taking off the paper overalls revealing a business suit beneath, "then it's got a short half-life." She rolled the overalls into a plastic bag before using disinfectant on her hands. "Most of the poison was already absorbed into the ground, which is the best water filter in the world. How deep is your well?"

"Three hundred feet," I said.

"Your drinking water will be fine. This farm is how big?"

"Five hundred acres."

She nodded and turned to the officer. "We'll check the neighbor's property and see if they have any water sources."

Tollers came up to me while Dad was on his cell phone. "This contamination seems deliberate."

"I agree," I said.

"There was a case I read about years ago," Tollers said, "where two neighbors were arguing over property lines and one dumped nitrates into the other's water source to kill their cattle."

"Any people mad at you lately? Neighbors?" the agent said.

"Besides my parents, our nearest neighbor is a ninety-year old widow a mile down the road who wouldn't hurt a fly."

Dad placed his hand over his cell phone. "Brandon, tell them about the thingy?"

"The what?"

"The thingy I tried to shoot out of the sky the other day."

I turned back to Tollers and the agent. "Dad's a bit of a tinfoil hat conspiracy theorist."

"Tell them," Dad repeated.

"We saw a drone over the property the other day, and Dad must think that's how the poison was released."

The agent raised her eyebrows like she couldn't believe I said something that crazy. "That's quite a theory, Mister Hall. If true, the person who did it has some serious resources and motive. Know anyone like that in Halifax County?"

The only person I could think of was the globalist billionaire Gaspar Schultz whose path I indirectly crossed a few times. Maybe I had become a thorn in his side whom he wanted to terrorize? I pushed the thought out of my mind. I wasn't that important.

"I don't think so," I said.

"What are you gonna do?" Tollers said.

"I don't know."

Dad put his cell phone away. "I got good news and bad news."

"Always the bad first," I said.

"Sorry, I gotta give you the good first, or it won't make sense. I never told you and Annie, but I kept an insurance policy on the herd."

"Livestock insurance? Why didn't you tell me this?"

"Because you would have insisted that you pay for

half of it and I know things are tight for you right now." I started to say something, but Dad cut me off. "Your mom and me don't have little mouths to feed and I have my military pension to supplement my part of the farm income."

"So, what's the bad news?"

Dad extended one finger at a time. "Livestock insurance covers attacks by wild animals, natural disasters like floods and hurricanes, and even loading and unloading accidents. It doesn't cover disease."

"What about intentional poisoning?"

"There's nothing in the policy about poisoning, but there is verbiage about deliberate harm caused by another party which it will cover. I'm optimistic, but payout wouldn't happen for a while as they will need to do an investigation."

"To see who poisoned the cattle?"

"No. To make sure we didn't do the poisoning."

The agent must have read the dumfounded look on my face and filled in the blanks. "You hear about people torching their own cars and homes all the time to get an insurance payouts. Same thing here."

"It's sad that people would do that to a herd of animals."

"So there's hope," Dad said, pulling me aside so we were alone. He lowered his voice to a whisper. "But while we wait for an answer, your mom and me want to help you guys out."

I held up my hand. "We'll be fine, Dad." I knew we

were in deep trouble, but I didn't want to make it my parents' problem. I was a grown man now.

"Don't be stubborn, Son."

I chuckled. "That's funny coming from you."

"It's not wrong to take help when you need it."

Senator Schilling's offer floated back to my mind. "I just turned down a contract job that I may still be able to take. It could carry us through this."

"Okay," he said, "but I'm here if you change your mind."

SIX

BACK INSIDE, ANNIE AND MOM GRILLED BEEF hotdogs for everyone on the property. Annie and I didn't have a chance to talk much, but every once in a while we made eye contact and it was clear she was worried. I worked the rest of the day to collect carcasses with Dad, using the two tractors we owned. The government officials took samples from all the cattle and removed a couple full carcasses as well as Fescue to send off to a lab. I made sure Mom took Emily to her house before they dug up the dog. The rest of the cattle were buried in a mass grave we dug near the edge of the farm where it met the forest section of the property. Around dinner Emily brought Dad and me out bottles of water and sand-wiches. She wanted to drive in the cab with me, but I told her no. The morbid sight of dead cattle being dumped into a ditch wasn't a memory I wanted her to have.

Before I got back in the cab, she asked. "What are we gonna do, Daddy?"

"We'll be fine."

"I'm not a baby anymore you know?"

"Gramps had an insurance policy on the cattle. We'll be fine."

"Are you sure?"

I repeated my father's pep talk. "Who's in control?"

"God."

"He's got this."

It was late when I came back into the house. Annie waited for me in the kitchen. She had a Bible open in front of her and I could tell she had been crying.

"Emily and the baby go down okay?" I said.

Annie nodded. "What's the plan?"

"Did my mother tell you about the insurance?"

"She did, but she also said it's not a guarantee."

"We gotta have faith."

"Who would do this to us?"

"I don't know," I said, kissing the top of her brunette head.

"What about the PI case you worked. The one where the guy went to prison for the insurance fraud?"

I shook my head. "The work I did for that case was behind the scenes stuff. I never had to testify, and he never knew I was involved."

"Then who?"

"I don't know," I said. "All I know is I need to take a shower."

"What are we gonna do in the meantime?" Before I could mention the offer from Senator Schilling she blurted out. "You're not taking that contract job."

"It's for a month. Four weeks," I said, as if the different way of expressing time away from home would sound better. It didn't and Annie dropped her head in her hands.

After the shower I crawled into bed. Annie was still awake and whispered, "I don't like the idea of you being away that long."

"I've already thought about it," I said. "Maybe after a week or two I can come home on weekends? Maybe I can get someone to fill in for me during those days?"

"Who, Tollers?"

I nodded. "I mentioned it to him when he was here today. He said he's even willing to drive up to DC."

"I still don't like it."

"It's a short-term contract, sweetie."

"And if the insurance refuses to pay out for the cattle?"

"We'll deal with that problem if it comes up."

I drafted an email to Senator Schilling from my cell phone and let Annie read it before I pressed send. It simply read, *Would like to take the job if it's still available?*

Annie nodded off while I read for a bit from the

Psalms as I was still jacked up from the stress of the day. King David was dealing with far worse than me when he wrote some of the Psalms. It was encouraging to read of another man calling out to God in desperation. Before I shut off the light, I checked my cell email. Senator Schilling had sent back a thumbs up emoji along with a note that his assistant would email a simple contract over by morning.

The next morning, Annie was up before me and had checked my email and already printed out the contract the senator's assistant sent. It was straight forward with agreed upon pay.

She whistled. "Oh my word."

"What?" I said, leaning down next to her with a cup of coffee.

"Look at your additional perks," she said, pointing to a long list of bullet points. "Included in your package is the address of a garden unit under his brownstone that you'll be staying in. There's a code attached to this contract to get you inside. You'll find a key and a credit card on the kitchen counter in the apartment. The key is for the unit's deadbolt and the credit card for meals, gas, and anything else you need. Get this, the senator's giving you a line of credit at his tailor. He wants you to pick up three suits, five shirts, and five ties as well as new shoes prior to meeting him. There's also web link to a leasing company who will give you any car you want."

Annie's tone went from excitement to somber

when she read the next section. "His lawyers are getting you proper permitting to carry your firearm which is next to impossible in DC with their strict laws." She looked up at me. "Do you think you'll need it?"

"Don't worry," I said. "DC is locked down tighter than my wallet when I take you shopping. It should be safe."

Annie didn't laugh at my lame joke. "Senator Schilling's assistant left her information in case you had any questions." She paused before saying, "Uhg."

"What?"

"He's sending a driver down to pick you up tomorrow. For some reason I thought we'd have more time together before you left."

"That stinks."

"Emily's gonna be devastated."

My stomach tightened like someone had just punched me. I forgot about my two daughters still asleep upstairs. The thought of not seeing them for one day, let alone many days, made me feel sick. I took for granted the life I had on the farm, and the blessing of being able to see my wife and children throughout the day. Even though my days were much longer than friends who worked in cities like Danville and Raleigh Durham, I still had periodic breaks that allowed me to see them whenever I wanted.

I packed a duffle bag with workout clothes and toiletries. Annie followed me around our bedroom like I was about to sneak out without saying goodbye. I placed dress shirts and khakis on the bed. Annie swapped out a couple shirts she didn't approve of before folding everything. She was somber, like a mother about to send her son off to war. I reminded her it was temporary, and she reminded me it could be permanent if I wasn't careful. I had no witty comeback for that remark.

Annie was almost done folding a shirt when she balled it up and threw it across the room. "I feel like I'm living in a nightmare and can't wake up!"

I walked over and sat down next to her on the bed. "This is the hand we're dealt right now," I said. "I hope it's just a season we're going through."

"What is?" came a voice from the doorway.

We both looked up to see Emily holding Addison. Emily's dark eyes were a beautiful almond shape but were filled with tears ready to fall out depending on what I said next.

Annie wiped her eyes. "Bring me the baby."

Emily did as she was told. "What's wrong?"

"Your dad needs to go up to Washington DC to work a side job until the insurance check comes in for the cattle."

"I'll be working for Senator Schilling," I added, as if the famous name might cheer her up.

"It's an exciting opportunity," Annie said, trying to do the same.

"Then why are you upset?" Emily said.

"I'm just gonna miss your daddy, but he's just a few hours away."

"How long will you be gone?"

"Couple weeks," I said. Emily came over to the bed and fell into my arms, sobbing. "Maybe I can come back on weekends," I said, trying not to get upset myself.

Annie walked around the room jostling Addison who was the only one who seemed happy. "We can go visit dad as well."

Emily perked up. "Really?"

"Sure," I said. "I'll take you and your mom out to a nice restaurant, so make sure you wear a fancy dress."

Emily seemed less upset. Annie placed the baby down and she crawled over to Emily who picked her back up. "Come on, Addison. Why don't I put you in your jogging stroller and we go over to Grammy's and see if she'll make pancakes."

"Let me change the baby and put on some sweat-pants on and I'll join you," Annie said.

Once everyone left, I went into the back of our walk-in closet and opened an old sea chest. Inside was piled with gear, guns, and ammo. It was good that Annie wouldn't see me pack this gear as she would freak out. I pulled out a large black rucksack covered in MOLLE straps. This would be my *go-bag* I'd keep in the vehicle. The bag would hold everything I might need for an emergency. I placed my compact Smith and Wesson M&P shield along with four spare mags in a front pouch along with a box of hollow point nine-millimeter ammo. In the top pouch I placed a multitool, but then drew a blank. I wasn't sure what else to pack?

Someone whistled behind me. I turned to see Dad. "I hope you're packing the right stuff for your job?"

"Annie told you about the side job?"

"Yup."

"Will you be okay on the farm by yourself?"

Dad shrugged. "Nothing for me to do other than continue to hay the pastures until we can get more cattle."

"You'll keep an eye on the girls?"

"Of course," he said, walking over to peer into my backpack. He shook his head. "I think you need to prepare better.

"I'm going to DC, not downtown Baghdad."

"Open your eyes, son."

"But—"

"I feel like everything that's happened in the past is all connected." He repeated, "Check your gut."

"You think our cattle dying has that Gaspar Schultz written all over it, don't you?"

"You don't?"

I shrugged my shoulders. "What's your thought on a motive?"

"Evil doesn't need a motive. With that said, your past work has indirectly crossed this wicked man's path. Maybe you've become a nuisance? Annie said the new job could somehow be tied to him as well."

"Dad I'm sure-"

"Son, please do me a favor. Just check your naivety at the door. Trust God and never fear, but I want you to go into this contract job expecting a worst-case scenario." He paused for a moment before adding. "Correction. Don't expect it, but plan for it." His final word was spoken in a broken voice. "Please."

"I will."

After Dad left, I refocused on the bag in front of me and the assortment of gear in the sea chest. I added a full-size mag light flashlight and an LED headlamp along with six glow sticks. A stainless water bottle with water purification tabs taped to the outside. A pair of black shooter gloves. Two throw-away rain ponchos. Zip ties, two pairs of zip hand cuffs, a windproof lighter, hand sanitizer, a pair of two-way walkie talkies with spare batteries, a small roll of duct tape, and an expandable baton.

On the outside of the bag I strapped a Ka-Bar fixed blade knife on one side and an Individual First Aid Kit to the other side via the bag's MOLLE straps. The IFAK was a holdover from my time in the Marines. It held a tourniquet, quick clot blood stoppers, a chest seal, combat gauze, along with other smaller items like tweezers, Band-Aids, aspirin, anti-histamine tabs, and antibiotic ointment. Before shutting the sea chest, I took one last look at what was left. I had a Glock 19, a Smith and Wesson .380 Annie sometimes carried. Under the lid, I had mounted an AR-15 and a twelve-gauge shotgun. I grabbed the

Glock, two spare mags and added it to the bag. I said a quick prayer that I would need none of this gear.

After lining all the packed bags on the end of the bed I sat down to review the contract which had a photocopy of a credit card number waiting for me in Alexandria. I had unlimited stipend for anything to do with the job. Using Annie's laptop, I looked up a few more items I could use. One was a thin Kevlar vest the I could have the senator wear under his suits. The other was a Kevlar blanket I could keep in the rental car. Before I pressed the purchase button a fictional conversation popped in my mind of how I'd explain this to Senator Schilling's assistant who would ask for copies of my receipts. To anyone in the business world it would seem like a reckless purchase. I decided to hold off on purchasing the additional gear for now.

The next step was fun. I got to pick out the rental car of my choice. I logged on to the leasing website and found all high-end vehicles. Range Rovers, BMW's, Mercedes, Audi, and Porsche were the primary choices, but nothing seemed to jump out at me. Dad's warnings still rang in my ears and I looked at my options through a, *worst case scenario lens*. Would I rather the safety of a heavy SUV, or speed to get out of a bad situation. In the military, nine times out of ten we went with safety, utilizing heavy reinforced vehicles like Humvees. On rare occasions we did employ fast vehicles like dune buggies.

Another factor to consider was weather. It was

spring and snow was not an issue, so the need for a 4x4 vehicle was off the table. Ultimately, I opted for speed rather than size. I wanted something with a stick shift, but the vehicle would need to be four-door as I'd be driving the senator around. America, in its laziness, all but purged manual transmissions from its car culture replacing them with automatic, and Tiptronic transmissions. The only four door stick-shift sedan I could find was a year-old black Audi A5, which I ordered.

After a quick workout, I found myself in front of a bathroom mirror, staring at a man who seemed to be aging by the day. Forty was fast approaching, but in my mind, I was still twenty-one. My sore knees rebuked this optimistic mindset. Regardless, something had to be done with my disheveled hair and beard. In DC I wouldn't be able to roll out of bed, put on a ball cap, and jump on a tractor. This contract job was in the nation's capital, a land of short haircuts, Brooks Brothers suits, and Hermès ties. Although I had no desire to blend in up north, there was a need to.

Electric clippers took my beard down to a five o'clock shadow. From there, I finished bringing it down to the skin with a razor. My sink was filled with hair, and the skin under the beard had gained a few more lines since it last saw the light of day. I continued with the clippers on my head and took it down tight. After cleaning up the mess in the sink I rinsed off in the shower.

SEVEN

When I walked into the kitchen the girls had just returned from their walk. Annie turned and gasped, Emily pointed at my face and giggled, and Addison started to cry. I picked up my infant daughter and kissed her which seemed to scare her more. She finally stopped crying when Annie took her.

"It's daddy," I kept repeating. Addison seemed to understand, but still wouldn't let me hold her.

Annie, Emily, and I sat in rocking chairs on the porch, looking out over the empty pastures while Addison played with one of Jonah's old toy trucks in the grass. This would be the last time we'd be together as a family for a long stretch of time. I tried to take a mental picture of the girls.

Emily got up to play with Addison. She held Addison's hands and helped her take a few steps.

Once or twice she let go for a split second and Addison wavered but stood upright.

"Look dad," Emily said. "She's almost taking a step."

"I see," I said before turning to Annie. "I'll be crushed if she takes her first steps while I'm away."

"Emily didn't walk until after she was a year old," Annie said.

"What about Jonah?" I said, hesitant to even bring up his name. "How old was he?"

"Nine months," Annie said, shaking her head. "Just be in the moment, Brandon."

"You're right," I said.

Watching my oldest child play with Addison made my heart melt. At twelve-years-old, Emily had already solidified her personality. She was outgoing, adventurous, and smart. There was also an introvert side to her that loved to sit in her room on rainy afternoons and read all day. On one hand, I could see her taking over the farm, but I could also see her leaving to go to the coast as she loved the sea. I never got to see Jonah's personality develop. From the short time he was with us we saw a lovable mischievous boy who liked toy trucks and cars. In my mind I thought he would one day grow up to become a mechanic, an engineer, or even a race car driver. Watching Addison play in the grass, I longed to find out the type of child she'd become. All I knew so far was she liked to be held, ate well, and slept well. A happy baby who spoke a handful of sentences like, *more bubba pease.*

Annie reached for my hand. "Are you sure it's safe for us to stay here?"

"It's fine," I said. "The government tech said the neutralizer they placed in the ponds should have done its job by now. Everything else from the soil to the grass has been tested and is fine. Please just keep an eye on the baby, and don't let her wander."

"She's rarely out of my sight," Annie said.

"And when she is," Emily added, "I watch her."

I texted a group of friends including Tollers, JT, Colt, and Pastor Dale. They had all heard about what happened and had reached out to me with emails and voicemails. I brought them up to speed on the farm situation, as well as having to go to DC for side work until we got things squared away. I asked them to check in on the girls and keep the family in prayer. Between my parents and church friends the farm would have more than enough eyes on it. All of them texted back asking what else they could do to help, including monetary help. It was an amazing gesture as most of them were paycheck-to-paycheck middle class guys like me.

The rest of the day was quiet. I topped off both tractors with diesel, greased the fittings, and pressure washed the outsides. For dinner I grilled chicken and corn, and we ate on the porch, watching the sun set over the empty pastures. The absence of animal noises created a melancholy feel that the farm never had before. In my gut, it felt like the calm before some proverbial storm. The last time I felt like this was driving down to the Dismal Swamp for the case of a missing girl. That night ended up in a shootout leaving one man dead.

The emotions and memories from that event made me want to call Senator Schilling and tell him I had changed my mind about the job, but the Dismal Swamp incident was a different time. A different job. I knew with all the police and government presence around DC my contract job should be uneventful. Before bed, I logged on to the concierge driving service to see when the driver would pick me up the next morning. I requested they show up prior to the arranged time of seven a.m. if possible. I didn't want a big goodbye and would rather sneak out before anyone was awake.

At five thirty a.m. I was dressed in khakis, a button-down shirt, and my workout sneakers. My cowboy boots and jeans didn't belong in a fancy city and would be left behind along with my two cheap suits and shoes. I'd pick up a pair of shoes when I went to the tailor in Alexandria. I made a travel mug of coffee and sat on the porch with my bags as I read from the Bible. My reading gravitated towards the book of Exodus where the Israelites journeyed out of Egypt. The Israelites, being freed from their bonds of slavery, traveled into the desert. *And the LORD went before them by day in a pillar of a cloud, to lead them the way; and by night in a pillar of fire, to give them light; to go by day and night.* Like the Israelites, I was also about to embark on a journey away from all that I knew and prayed that God would guide my steps with something as clear as a pillar of fire.

I made one last pass through the house and checked on both Emily and Addison who were fast asleep. Both were restless sleepers like their mom. Addison lay on her back in her crib with her arms open. While Emily was on her stomach with her legs sticking out from a disheveled afghan blanket. I fixed blankets in both bedrooms and gently kissed each daughter before checking on Annie. My wife also had one leg sticking out from under the blankets. I didn't kiss her as she was a light sleeper.

At six-fifteen a dark sedan pulled into the gravel driveway. The young man who stepped out looked to be early twenties and was dressed in a black suit and had slicked back dark hair.

He shook my hand with a firm grip. "Good morning Mister Hall. My name's James."

"Please call me Brandon," I said, tossing one of my bags in the backseat. "Nice to meet you."

James opened the trunk and placed my other two bags inside. For the first half hour of the drive we talked sports and current events before he started asking more pointed questions like what kind of work I had waiting for me up in the DC area.

"I have a contract job for a month," I said.

James smiled in the rearview mirror. "Contract work, huh? I bet you're an assassin for the CIA or something? I drive a lot of people around DC and I can tell when I pick up CIA and FBI guys. They're very hush hush like you."

I laughed out loud. "What you call being hush hush I call nerves. I'm a farmer who's nobody of significance, but I appreciate the sentiments, James. My wife will crack up when I tell her what you said."

He looked back in the mirror and grinned as if to say he didn't believe me. Annie texted and scolded me for not waking her up before leaving. I texted back saying that it would have been too hard to say goodbye face-to-face. I ended with a promise that I'd call later.

There was very little traffic heading out of Halifax County and I nodded off somewhere north of Richmond. Eventually, the rhythm of the car slowing down, and turning off the highway woke me. I was shocked to see over an hour had passed.

"Good morning," James said from the front seat.

"Sorry I fell asleep," I said. "That was rude."

"No worries. We're almost there."

At the bottom of the ramp were signs directing us to different parts of Alexandria. We headed towards old town. Adorable brick storefront shops, restaurants, and pubs lined the aged streets. Concrete sidewalks gave way to sections of old hand-laid brick which accented the stunning antique architecture. If the cars were removed, and lampposts changed to gas lights it would easily pass for the early 19th century. However, the beauty was contrasted with a congestion that was suffocating. I liked open pastures and not being able to see my neighbor. These people lived in apartments on top of one another.

Ten minutes later the car came to a stop. James got out and opened my door. "Here we are," he said, moving to open the trunk.

I shook his hand, realizing I had given Emily my last five dollars. "Uhm, James you're gonna kill me."

James seemed to know what I was talking about. "No worries, Mister Hall. I'm not supposed to accept tips."

"Wait," I said, taking out a blank wrinkled check I kept in my wallet. "Can I write you a check?"

He was trying not to laugh. "It's not necessary—"

"You don't want to upset a CIA assassin now do you?"

James chuckled. "I guess it's okay."

After James left, I looked down at a piece of paper with Senator Schilling's address. It matched the number on the massive stand-alone brownstone in front of me. The complex was three stories high with a roof deck. Wood shutters, that had long ago been pinned to the brick siding, accented tall antique glass windows. A six-foot high wrought iron fence surrounded the entire home with a strip of about eight feet of grass between the fence and the home. Not the size yard I was used to. On one side of the home was a narrow driveway with a parked Mercedes SUV. Large granite steps led up to a massive oak front door with gas lanterns burning on either side of it. Next to the door was a mounted bronze plaque which read 1867.

To the right of the granite stairs was a smaller set of stairs descending towards a basement garden apartment. My home for the next month. At the bottom of the stairwell was a brick patio decorated with potted flowering plants and a bistro table near a small wall-mounted gurgling fountain. I punched in the pre-assigned security code into a keypad next to the glass-paned apartment door. A moment later it unlocked with a click.

Inside the garden unit apartment was an open concept with a tiny galley kitchen and a small living room with a couch, coffee table, and flat screen television. An alcove provided a small bar height table with two seats. The place smelled of pine cleaner and was spotless. There was a muffled sound of running water I assumed came from someone doing laundry in the main residence above. Three doors were spread out in the space. The first was an empty coat closet. The second led to a bedroom with a modest dresser and queen size bed. I walked back into the living area and tried the third door and was greeted with a waft of steam from the bathroom. Someone was in the fogged-up glass shower.

"Hello?" I said, stepping back into the privacy of the living space.

The water turned off and there was movement inside the bathroom. The sound of a thick glass shower door opened and shut. My stomach tightened. Somehow, I knew who it was going to be.

Margaret Schilling stepped out dressed in a bathrobe that stopped just short of her tan knees. She rubbed a monogrammed towel on her wet hair. "Well, hello again, Brandon. I almost didn't recognize you with the haircut. You look handsome without that scruffy beard too."

I raised my hand as if to say *hello*. "What are you doing here, Missus Schilling?"

"I live here, and please call me Margaret."

"That's not what I meant?"

"My bathroom's being remodeled and I needed a place to shower. I hope you don't mind?"

"My guess is your brownstone above us is what... thirty-five hundred square feet?" She jacked her thumb up to signify my guess was too low. "Four thousand square feet?" She jacked her thumb up again. "Five thousand square feet?"

She smiled. "I would never settle for less."

"So, at five thousand square feet I'm assuming you have more than one full bathroom?"

"I walked into that one didn't I," she said with a devilish smirk. Margaret took a step towards me.

"So why are you here?" I repeated.

She raised her eyebrows as if to ask why I had asked a stupid question like that. "I wanted to spend some time to get to know you." She must have read confusion on my face. "Don't you find me the least bit attractive, Brandon?"

Margaret Schilling was very attractive with her tan skin and bright smile. Still, I replied, "I'm sorry, I don't."

She stopped her advance and looked confused. It was as if she had never heard someone rebuke her before. Margaret reached into the pocket of the bathrobe and pulled out a slim silver cigarette case and matching lighter and proceeded to light a cigarette. She took a long drag and blew the smoke in my face.

"That stuff will kill you," I coughed.

Margaret walked towards the door. "Everything dies, Mister Hall. Including contract jobs."

"Please shut the door on your way out, Missus Schilling."

The door was slammed so hard I thought the glass panes would break. I looked towards the ceiling and said a silent prayer of thanks to God for providing me a way out of the awkward situation. The Biblical story of Joseph and Potiphar's wife ran through my mind again. How she threw herself at Joseph and he rebuked her. Then, in a fit of jealous rage, she claimed Joseph attacked her. It was her word against Joseph's, and he lost that round big-time ending up in prison. In the end God redeemed Joseph, but the interim was brutal for him.

With the door locked, I continued inspecting the

apartment. The key to the deadbolt and the credit card were on the dining room table along with a manilla folder. Inside the folder were copies of random email threats to the senator from the past two months. Some looked to be typed by a ten-year-old with grammatical errors which made me think it was a drunken joke, while other threats seemed sinister, explaining how they would dismember the senator as slow as possible to maximize his suffering. All of them had been passed on to the authorities. The email addresses were gibberish one-time spam accounts.

After unpacking, I walked the exterior of the property. The brownstone overlooked the Potomac, with streets on three sides and one neighboring brownstone that was a law firm less than twenty feet beyond the Schilling's driveway. I expanded the walk around the neighborhood and stopped at a deli for an ice coffee and turkey sub which I devoured. The address for Senator Schilling's tailor was a half mile away allowing me to get an extended lay of the land. Small cute boutique stores dotted the pretty streets where most of the patrons were elderly. Pubs, restaurants, and gift shops made up the rest of the commerce. The absence of major chain stores and chain restaurants was a nice change from what I was used to seeing.

The tailor's brownstone address had a mounted wooden sign out front which read, *Walter's Tailoring Est. 1866*. Inside, it smelled of fancy men's cologne and looked like an elite golf country club with dark green carpet and cherry wood racks.

A skinny old man stood with the sleeves of his dress shirt rolled up and a worn tape measure draped over his neck the same way doctors carried stethoscopes. "Can I help you?" he said, with an accent that revealed an elite southern education.

"Are you Walter?"

"I am, but the original Walter was my great grandfather."

"Wow, this place has been in your family a long time?"

He nodded. "Great grandad Walter lost his leg in the war and couldn't go back to farming. Instead he turned to tailoring."

I whistled.

"I've got a year waiting list for hand-made suits, son."

I whistled again. "Why so long?" He wrinkled his nose as if I just insulted him. "Sorry, where I come from there's no waiting for anything as the economy's a bit more, shall we say, desperate."

"Where you from?"

"A small town south of here called Nathalie."

"Those is some nice God-fearing folk down there."

I made the mistake of looking at the massive price tag of a pair of cufflinks. "Your store is gorgeous."

"Washington politicians for the past century have come here for their suits."

"You make suits for any presidents?"

"My family made suits for most of them going back to Rutherford B Hayes." Before I could whistle again, he added, "It's more symbolic these days, though. Most of the president's suits are made elsewhere as many of them need to have a ballistic component to them which I don't do."

"Really?"

"We live in a different era. I still cater to almost everyone else in Congress, though."

"You have a preference which party of Congress you deal with?"

Walter smiled, but didn't answer. "How may I help you?"

"I was sent here by Senator Greg Schilling."

Walter nodded and looked at a scrap piece of paper on his desk. "Are you Mister Hall?"

"Yes, sir."

"Gregory told me you'd be calling. I can fit you for suits we carry off the rack, but nothing hand-tailored. Come here and step up on the stool."

Walter took a lot of measurements and wrote them in an old leather notebook. He spoke with the pencil between his teeth while he did this. "What kind of suits you need?"

"Something that will fit in with Senator Schilling's world."

Walter wrote some more information down. "Wool, single breasted two button."

As he took more measurements, I said, "My other

suits back home have a polyester blend which gives them a nice sheen."

Walter didn't find that funny. When he finished his notes, Walter picked out a conservative blue pinstripe, a grey pinstripe, and a lighter solid blue suit. I tried each on and he stuck pins in them where they needed to be fitted. Within a half hour I was done. I picked out five dress shirts. Four white and one blue and asked Walter to pick me out five simple ties with no more than two colors on each. I told him I got dizzy when I wore too many colors. Again, he didn't laugh.

As Walter wrapped up the shirts and ties, he said, "The order said to get you shoes. Go take a look and tell me what you'd like."

The wooden floor-to-ceiling shoe display looked like a piece of artwork. Shoes sat upon green velvet and cherry shelves with brass lamps casting a mirror finish on them. There were dozens of styles to choose from. From wingtips to slip-on loafers. I kept thinking of what would be most functional. I landed on a pair of Bostonian black ankle high Chukka's. Walter brought me out my size of ten and a half. My foot felt like it was cupped in a comfortable leather hand. At the register Walther had me sign off on the bill. My stomach tightened when I read three thousand six hundred and fifty dollars. Beneath the total were the words, *five complimentary handkerchiefs included*. Now that was funny.

Before I left, Walter handed me a navy-blue sport

coat. "Here's a loaner to get you by until I can get your suits ready."

The jacket fit perfectly. "Thanks, Walter."

"I'll have the suits delivered to Greg's address in the next couple of days."

EIGHT

O<small>N THE WAY BACK TO THE APARTMENT</small> I <small>STOPPED AT A</small> small bodega to get a few essentials. Coffee, two bottles of water, organic bread, almond butter, and a few power bars to fill in gaps when I couldn't get in a meal. Everyone in the store stared at the dark green paper bag with the cursive *W* I held. Shopping at Walter's was clearly a status symbol in the upscale neighborhood.

Back at the apartment I changed into shorts and a tank top and unpacked my only workout equipment. A jump-rope. After stretches, several sets of pushups and sit-ups I did several intervals of jump roping sessions on the patio before stretching again and taking a shower. The bathroom still smelled of expensive fancy shampoo from Mrs. Schilling. She also left lingerie sprinkled about the space, which I threw in the trash.

After the shower, there were two texts on my cell.

Senator Schilling asked to meet him for dinner at an address in Alexandria at six p.m. The second was from the leasing company. A driver from DC Elite Dealership was on their way to pick me up. I changed into khakis, one of my new dress shirts and ties, along with the new shoes and loaner jacket. I felt like a complete fake, but knew it was necessary. It was essential that I not stick out in this foreign environment, in either a good or bad way.

Outside on the patio, I sat and listened to the water trickle from the wall fountain. The lower garden unit was below grade and offered protection from the wind, so the sun felt extra strong. Lounging around in my fancy jacket I could see how attractive this high-end lifestyle was. I still missed my farm and loathed any congested city, but if any place could lure a country boy towards city life, it was Alexandria.

Someone cleared their throat at the top of the steps. I opened my eyes to see a young, tall, brunette woman dressed in a dark pantsuit, wearing fancy sunglasses. "Mister Hall?"

"Yes, ma'am," I said, getting up.

"I'm Bridget, from DC Elite Dealership."

I locked the door to the apartment and walked up to greet her. "Lead the way, Bridget."

She pointed me towards a gorgeous black BMW 740i sedan. The leather seats and posh interior were nicer than anything I had ever driven in before. The moment I shut the door Bridgette took off like woman on a mission.

"This is a sweet ride," I said.

Bridget didn't respond. In between red lights Bridget drove aggressively. Not something needed in southern Virginia. It reminded me of tactical driving we were taught in the military.

After another five minutes of silence I said, "You don't talk much."

"I'm sorry," she said, stopping at another red light. "We're trained not to ask questions of clients we lease vehicles to."

"Due to the DC cloak-and-dagger industry?" I said in a whisper voice as if someone were listening to our conversation.

"That, and we get a lot of foreign dignitaries who wish to remain anonymous as well."

"Ah, Washington DC No place like it in the world."

"I also try to not get personal with male clients, so they don't get the wrong message." The light turned green and she took off. "Some dignitaries in the past have assumed that I'm included with the vehicle."

I held up my left hand to showcase my wedding ring. "No fear there, Bridget."

She gave me a sympathetic smile. "Sadly, Mister Hall, around here that piece of metal doesn't carry much weight."

I looked down at my simple white gold wedding band and wondered how a man could take the ring off to cheat? She was right. I was naive and shouldn't be too friendly. I fixed my jacket and lowered a wrinkled pant leg bunched up over my new shoes before putting on my own five-dollar sunglasses.

A minute later she said, "If I can break protocol for a minute."

"Go ahead," I said, gazing out the window at the expensive colonial and antebellum architecture.

"You're not like my normal clients."

"How so?" I said,

"You seem like—" she cut herself off as if to search for the right word.

"A redneck," I offered.

She chuckled. "That's not it. You don't seem to fit in here. You actually seem like a nice guy."

"Thank you," I said. "I'm a farmer from southern-Virginia doing some security work for a month to put food on my family's table."

"Really? What area are you from?"

"Small town you probably never heard of named, Nathalie."

"I know it well," she said. "I grew up in Scottsburg."

"Your family still there?"

"My parents have both passed, but I have some other family members still living there."

"What's the family name?"

"Stockman?"

"Doesn't ring a bell."

"My momma's family is Burnell?"

"You're not related to the overall-wearing Burnell

brothers, are you?" Bridget smiled. "How could you be related to those chubby, hairy hillbillies?"

"Momma was adopted."

I laughed. "Kidding aside, I know those guys very well. They're rock solid people."

"I'm glad you think so. That entire side of the family was so supportive, and even raised some money to help me move up here for law school."

"Doesn't surprise me," I said. "They'd give anyone the shirts off their back. If they ever wore shirts under their overalls that is."

"Not sure why they love those overalls." Bridget laughed. "But to each his own."

"Where do you go to school?"

"Georgetown, but it's part time at night."

"That's still impressive," I said. "So, the dealership job pays the bills while you go to school?"

"Yeah," Bridget said, braking as a car cut in front of her. "I graduate at the end of summer, and then I'm out of here."

"Automotive world not for you?"

"Let's just say the *Me Too* movement hasn't found its way into my dealership just yet."

"What do you want to do after graduation?"

"I'd like to work in the FBI, but it's so competitive I don't know if I'd get through the front door even though I have straight As."

"It's that competitive?"

"Yes," she said. "I know it sounds cliché and idealistic, but I want to make a difference."

"Doesn't sound idealistic at all."

We pulled up to a fancy metal and glass building with marble floors. Inside, shiny Maseratis, Mercedes and BMWs were displayed on elevated stands throughout the showroom. All the employees, male and female, looked like runway models dressed in expensive suits.

Bridget stopped me. "Hold on a moment, Mister Hall." She fixed the collar on my shirt.

She reminded me so much of a grown-up version of my Emily. Both her looks and personality. We walked through the sales room and I could see the male salesmen stares go from me to Bridget. Most of their looks floated between her chest and legs. Due to her likeness to Emily, my dad-radar went on high alert. One of them grunted a *hey*, but Bridget didn't respond.

Inside a small office I signed a few pieces of paper and handed over the credit card the senator had left me.

"I'm surprised you chose this car," Bridget said, swiping the credit card. "It sat for a long time and was about to go to auction."

"Not many people drive stick shifts anymore," I said.

"Not pragmatic in DC."

After I signed the receipt, Bridget led me out a back door into a parking lot surrounded by a chain link fence. Inside were at least five million dollars' worth of expensive vehicles. From Bugatti, to Range

Rovers. Even some Ferraris. The Audi A5 I had ordered seemed modest next to the other vehicles.

"It was nice to meet you," I said, feeling like a dad saying goodbye to his daughter.

"I forgot how much I missed home until I met you," she said, moving almost to give me a hug but stopping short.

I shook her hand and got into the shiny black car. The leather seat seemed to mold to my body. The car may have been considered *old* for this high-end leasing company, but it was fancier than anything I drove. I started it up and felt the tight clutch engage as I put it in reverse.

Before leaving I lowered the window to say goodbye to Bridget. "Watch your six, kiddo. There's a lot of land sharks circling you."

"I will."

Once on the street, I found a lull in traffic and gunned the car for a few hundred yards. It had more than enough horses under the hood for what I needed. A short while later I pulled back up in front of the senator's brownstone. There were two parking spaces in front with a sign reading, *Designated Resident Parking only. Violators will be towed.* Parking spots did not always come with homes in the city and were extra. For the cost to purchase these parking spots someone could probably own ten to twenty acres of land in Halifax County.

Back inside the apartment, Annie called me.

"Uhm, your new boss already deposited thirty-grand in our account."

"You're kidding?"

"He must really like you."

"I don't feel comfortable taking money up front," I said. "I'll mention it later when we meet for dinner."

"Why did he go over the agreed upon amount?"

"No idea," I said.

It seemed like Annie and the girls were a million miles away and that I'd never see them again. I could tell she felt the same way. After we hung up, I sat on the sofa with a bottle of water to review the folder of email threats again. Both the Metro Police and Capitol Police were investigating all of them, so I had nothing to do other than log the data. The only patterns I found were a few emails with the same grammatical mistakes, which I assumed the Capitol Police picked up on as well. Most messages came across as angry citizens who had too much time on their hands. As if to remind me there were a ton of unstable people in the world, I remembered the senator mentioning white powder being mailed to his office and the doxing incident. To add an exclamation point to the thought, my dad texted me a two word reminder.

Stay alert.

AN HOUR LATER, I pulled up to a fancy restaurant

with a valet out front. The young man gave me a ticket and got in the car. I watched him stall the Audi three times as he tried to drive it around the corner into an adjacent parking lot. Inside, I was greeted by two female maître d's dressed in matching black pant suits.

"Are you meeting someone here?" one of the ladies said.

"Gregory Schilling."

"The senator's right this way," the other lady said, starting to walk me to the back of the restaurant. We passed by booths of dark leather filled with mostly old white men. Some of the men sat across from women who looked young enough to be their daughters. By the way the women dressed I assumed they weren't progeny. An open kitchen showcased chefs in all white cooking steaks over flaming grills. Bottles of red wine lined the walls with some behind small fancy wire lockers with names attached to each compartment. I recognized the names of some famous politicians. Schilling had a locker filled with both red and white wines I assumed were worth a small fortune.

The woman leading me said, "Sir?"

"Oh, sorry." I said. "My idea of dining out is taking my wife to the cafe at the local nine-hole golf course." The woman didn't laugh. "They have a salad bar to die for." Still no response. It seemed the closer I got to DC the less of a sense of humor people had.

She led me around a corner into an alcove where

the senator sat with another young male who texted on his phone. The senator marked up a document with a fancy fountain pen.

Senator Schilling got up when he saw me and pointed to my clean-shaven face. "Well look at you."

"Just trying to fit in up here, sir."

"Can I bring you something to drink?" the woman said.

"I'll have water please," I said.

The senator said, "Bring him a glass of my Twenty fifteen Pinot Noir." He turned to the man next to him. "Jim you want a glass?"

The man named Jim finished texting and put his phone away. "I'm good, sir." He reached over the table. "Jim Danberry."

"Brandon Hall," I said. "Nice to meet you."

After we sat down Jim said, "How do you know the senator?"

Before I could answer, the senator said, "Brandon's a friend visiting me for a couple weeks."

"First time in the area?"

"Yes," the Senator answered for me.

By his squinted look I could tell Jim didn't seem to accept the cover story. A moment later he got up. "It was nice to meet you Brandon. If you'll excuse me, Senator?"

"You're not staying for dinner?"

"Sorry, my fiancée's waiting for me across town, sir."

"You'll learn someday that marriage is overrated," the senator joked.

After Jim left, the senator said, "I'm trying to think of a cover for you. I don't want people thinking they have me scared and I hired security."

"There's a benefit to flying under the radar," I said. "Just tell people that I'm your driver for the next few weeks."

The senator shook his head. "A driver wouldn't come into a restaurant with me. I'm gonna have to say you're an outside contractor helping with work of some sort."

"I don't know much about politics."

The senator thought for a moment before snapping his fingers. "You're a contract speechwriter."

I started to rebuke the idea and he shook his head like the decision was made. "Writers are weird quirky people. You'll fit in the role nicely."

I grinned. Annie will appreciate that someone else described me as weird and quirky. "A speechwriter it is. By the way, sir, I don't feel comfortable with being paid so much up front."

Senator Schilling gave me a charming grin. "Can I be frank?"

"Of course."

"I know you're a blue-collar family. A paycheck-to-paycheck family?"

"Like most farmers," I said, feeling a bit insecure.

He raised both hands. "I didn't mean to offend you. I

heard what happened to your cattle and assumed you're in a financial panic mode." I nodded, wanting to ask how news of my herd dying made it up to him. "My point is," the senator continued, "I need you focused a hundred percent when you're here, not two hundred plus miles away. By paying you up front you can square away bills and be all mine. It's both a strategic, and selfish, move."

"Only a politician could have pulled that one out of a deck of cards," I said with a chuckle. "Why the thirty-grand? I thought this was a four-week gig?"

He waved his hand back and forth. "Could go a bit over."

"Well I'm going to give back any overage at the end of the—"

"I trust you." He clapped his hands together. "Okay, you've got to try the filet here. I promise you this beef will rival anything you've raised."

He was right. The steak and scalloped potatoes were unbelievable. I took a sip or two of the wine but couldn't appreciate it as I knew very little about alcohol. The senator pushed me to finish the drink, but I reminded him that I was on the job. He seemed to appreciate the response. After dinner, he signed for the meal and led me into a back area of the restaurant. We faced an oak door with a brass plate on it which read, *VIP ROOM*. The senator punched a code into a keypad next to the door. The door clicked open and we were greeted by a waft of expensive tobacco smoke as we entered the inner chamber of the restaurant.

"You'd die if I told you what membership costs for this place," he said, "but the connections alone make it worthwhile."

All the men in the room wore dark suits with power ties. I felt underdressed in khakis, tie, and a jacket. There seemed to be no women allowed in this inner sanctum. The senator shook hands with people I recognized as both democrat and republican politicians. Famous men. A few asked who I was, and the senator mentioned the contract speechwriter cover before ushering us onward. We sat in a leather booth in the back of the room.

"Excuse me," I said, moving in front of him to take up the portion of seat that faced the entrance. "Sorry, I'm not trying to be rude, but I need to be able to see the lay of the land so to speak."

"Ah, already assessing threats," the senator said. "But the entrance is a coded door to get in. He pointed to a couple young male waiters walking around with small wooden humidors. "Even the employees enter and exit through the same coded door. It's locked down tight. No one looking to do us harm can get in."

"Another way to look at it," I said, "is anyone looking to do us harm can also keep us in."

The senator smiled. "I feel safer already."

I pointed to an emergency exit door near us. "From now on when we go out to restaurants, I'd like us to sit near the emergency exits."

"Smart thinking."

"But never use one unless it's a last option."

"Why's that?"

"Sometimes active shooters place people outside exit doors to pick people off as they exit a building."

"You learn that in the military?"

"No, a security training class for my church."

The senator shook his head. "What a sick world we live in that we have people doing security assessments for churches now."

A young male waiter came over wheeling a large wooden humidor. Senator Schilling took out a thick cigar and lifted it up. The waiter cut the end and produced a sterling silver lighter. He turned the humidor to me, but I waived it away.

Senator Schilling blew out a smoke ring. "So, what do you think of Alexandria and DC?"

"It's beautiful," I said.

He leaned over the dark wood table to whisper. "It's a veneer."

"How so?"

"Scratch the surface and it's anything but beautiful."

"What, like drugs and money laundering?"

He laughed and took another puff of the cigar. "I love your innocence, Brandon."

"Still," I said, "the monuments and architecture are incredible."

"It is pretty," the sSenator said, "however, this town isn't as glamorous as they portray in the movies, and it sure doesn't offer a happily ever after."

"I guess I've held a naive view of DC. All the history and great men and women who served."

"Those people are long gone."

"I'd like to think there are a few left and I'm working for one."

He stifled a laugh like a celebrity who faced a gushing fan. "Thank you for the compliment, but you think higher of me than I deserve." The senator motioned to the fancy restaurant around us. "As much as I want out of DC, this place will be one of the few things I'll miss."

"Speaking of restaurants and routines," I said. "We need to go over a few things." I produced a list from my jacket pocket. "We need to review places you frequent on a regular basis, and make sure to mix up the days and times you visit them."

"I never thought of that."

"If you're being threatened, or stalked, you want to change up your routines, times, environments, and increase or shorten routes to places like work, restaurants, etc."

The senator grinned with the cigar between perfect white teeth. "Impressive."

"Thought I was a dumb redneck didn't you, sir?"

"I knew you were a poser, Brandon."

"I'll need a printed copy of your schedule."

"No problem."

"I'd like to do a walkthrough of your apartment and get a list of your staff as well. I also think it's best if I'm with you throughout the day unless you're in a secure government building where Capitol Police are posted." The senator nodded his agreement. "Can we lock the gate to your house at night including your driveway if we need to?"

"I have some combination padlocks we can use."

"Anything else you think I should be aware of, sir?"

"Nothing I can think of." He exhaled as if some weight had been removed from his shoulders. "I'm glad you're here, son."

He had never called me by that title before, but I took it as a compliment. The trust this famous politician placed in me was a nice way to feel like I was making a small difference for the country. I wanted to keep, and maintain, that trust. The Biblical story of Joseph and Potiphar's wife came back to me, but I didn't say anything about Mrs. Schilling. I prayed the situation would go away on its own, and the results would be something different than what I read about in the Bible.

NINE

AFTER THE SENATOR FINISHED HIS CIGAR WE MADE OUR way out front. I gave the valet the ticket and watched the surroundings for anything peculiar. Open windows in buildings, cars driving by too slow and pedestrians on the sidewalk. More politicians exited the restaurant. An elderly woman stopped and took out her phone to snap pictures of them including Senator Schilling.

I stepped between the senator and the woman. "Sorry, ma'am."

The senator placed his hand on my shoulder. "Brandon, this is fine?"

"No, sir."

Senator Schilling waved me off and wrapped his arm around the elderly woman as another, younger woman, took a picture of them with her phone. Both women gave me angry stares before walking away. The valet came around with the car and got out with an outstretched hand. My stomach turned. I still had no cash on me and looked to the senator ashamed.

The senator laughed and dropped a twenty dollar bill in the young man's palm. "Thanks, Ricky."

The young man's eyes widened. "Thank you, Senator."

Once in the car the senator spoke from the back seat, "Interesting choice of vehicle, Brandon. Mind if I ask why you went for an older car? I told you to get anything you wanted. The sky was the limit, my boy."

"Funny what you call old, I call brand new," I said. "Second, I wanted a stick shift, and this was the only four door sedan I could find with one. I know it will be a bit of a pain in DC traffic, but it's what I'm used to, and gives me more control."

I could see in the rearview mirror a smile more Hollywood than Washington DC. "What about if we're in a car chase and there's a shootout. Won't that be hard for you to drive, shoot, and shift gears at the same time?"

"I'm praying, and planning, for one simple word. Boring."

The senator chuckled. "Boring is good."

"Thanks for tipping the valet back there, sir."

"Stop calling me sir, and senator. You're my friend, Brandon."

"I'm also your employee."

"If this is going to work then we need to be a bit more informal."

"Then while we're being informal," I said, "I have

to tell you what you did outside the restaurant has to stop."

"What? Taking a picture with an old woman?"

"You're paying me a lot of money to protect you, and I can't do that if you're working against me."

"You see an old woman as a threat?"

"Overseas, terrorists use the elderly, young children, even the mentally disabled and handicapped as suicide bombers, or distractions, to allow time to set off IEDs."

"This isn't Iraq. We generally don't have roadside bombs."

"Tell that to the people who were blown apart at the Boston Marathon by a homemade IED."

"That was an anomaly and—"

"Sir, I witnessed a suicide bomber rush my home with a vest packed full of explosives while working on your son's case." The senator went silent. I had pulled a selfish trump card bringing up his son, and that past altercation, but if it humbled the senator enough to let me do my job then it was worth it. "At least for the time being I'd prefer you get in and out of unsecured places like restaurants quickly. Once we're inside, it's a different story. I can control the situation a bit easier, which will allow you to mingle at your leisure."

"I do see your point." The senator went silent again. "Sorry for pushing back on you. I'm not used to taking orders."

I looked in the rearview mirror and smiled. "But you're married?"

Finally, someone laughed at one of my jokes.

Back at the brownstone I walked the senator up to his front door. I pointed to the empty driveway. "Don't you have a car?"

"I don't like to drive. Before I hired you, one of my employees would pick me up in the morning." He punched in a code next to the massive oak door and the lock clicked.

"Mind if I see the layout of the place?" I said.

"Of course."

We stepped inside a bright foyer with a marble floor. "How many people have that code you just used?"

"Just my family, housekeeper, and you if you want it," he said.

"I should have it. How long has your housekeeper been with you?"

"Twenty years," he said. "Estelle's like part of the family."

"You trust her?"

"Enough that I'm selling the brownstone contingent upon any new owners hiring her."

The senator took off his suit jacket and placed it on a wooden wardrobe valet. "Care for a drink?"

"No thanks. Do you mind if I wander?"

"Be my guest. I got some work to do."

"Okay, I'll let myself out."

The first floor consisted of a massive living room

with red oak floors, high end leather couches, a gas fireplace, and no television. Not a pinch of dust was to be found. Even the leaves of the two potted indoor Ficus trees were dust free. The wood flooring gave way to a library the size of my home's entire first floor. In the corner of the library the senator sat on another leather couch, drink in hand, and already on a phone call. While not as ornate as the senator's Clarksville estate, the brownstone was still impressive and charming. In the back was a large clean kitchen with a commercial stainless stove. In the hallway leading back to the foyer were two small bathrooms side-by-side with male and female emblems on them, which told me the first floor was used for entertaining.

A narrow oak stairwell led up to a second floor with tall ceilings. Two glass doors opposite each other led to offices I assumed were the senator's and his wife's. Each office had a half bath. I closed interior plantation shutters that offered a line of sight towards any other buildings. At the end of the hall were two bedrooms each with full bathrooms. One was decorated in NASCAR themes, I assumed used to be Kyle's, and the other decorated with flowers and framed posters of teen heartthrobs, I assumed was the daughter's.

Another stairwell led me to the third floor with a large master bedroom. The white carpet was immaculate and the king-sized bed was made with creases that looked like they were done at a dry cleaner.

Large windows overlooked the Potomac as did a small deck with a bistro table and two chairs. I lowered the shades on the windows, and French doors leading to the deck. The master bath had marble floors, a large jacuzzi tub as well as a glass shower. Beyond the double sink and toilet, a cedar door led into a small infra-red sauna.

Back outside the bedroom a spiral staircase led up to a roof deck. Most of the roof was covered with walking stones and manicured potted plants. Lounge chairs dotted the area with a jacuzzi tub surround by tall boxwood bushes for privacy. A portion of the roof was fenced off where three air conditioning units were located. The traffic was a whisper as it was so far below. The silence coupled with the night-time view over the Potomac was stunning. The city light pollution washed out most of the nighttime sky but offered another canvas I wasn't used to seeing. Cars and building lights looked like fireflies dancing in the night. Descending the stairs, I came face to face with Mrs. Schilling. She was dressed in a black cocktail dress and looked like a woman in her thirties.

"We meet again," I said, trying to find a way around the woman.

"What do you think of our home?"

"It's very nice," I said. "I'd like the shades in the bedroom to remain shut as well as the shutters on the second floor, please. Don't let the senator onto the roof, or side deck, for now."

She huffed. "Good luck with that."

There was an awkward pause. "Well, have a good night Missus Schilling."

As I walked by, she grabbed my forearm and handed me a piece of paper. "Greg asked me to give you this." I opened it and saw my permit to conceal carry in the District of Columbia. "He said it took an act of congress to get that little piece of paper, and to keep it on you at all times."

"I'll go thank him."

"You can't."

"Excuse me?"

"He's gone."

"What do you mean?"

She shrugged her shoulders and walked into her bedroom. "He's off to see his assistant, Jane." She held up air quotes when she said the word *assistant* as if it held another connotation.

"I told him not to go anywhere without me."

She laughed, stepping out of her high heel shoes. "Gregory does what Gregory wants."

"He's so frustrating."

"That he is," she said, starting to undo the buttons on her dress.

I turned around facing the hallway, speaking with my back towards her. "Where's his assistant live?"

Without pausing she said, "Five thirty-eight Thomas Jefferson Lane, apartment C. Why don't you help me with the zipper on my dress, Brandon?"

I rushed down the stairs without looking back. At

some point I'd need to get ahead of this problem known as Mrs. Schilling. I doubled checked the entire second and first floors confirming the senator was nowhere to be found. His jacket was gone from the wardrobe valet. Outside, I tried the senator's cell phone, but it went straight to voicemail. I got in the car and plugged in the address Mrs. Schilling gave me into the vehicle's navigation touchscreen. Five minutes later I was parked outside the address. It was a nice middle-class brownstone apartment. I had no idea where apartment C was, and walked the perimeter confirming the front door was the only access point other than an old rusted iron fire escape out back that hung far above a dumpster. Back in the car I parked a few spaces down from the building and waited.

I texted Annie to check in. She sent back pictures of the girls playing with Lincoln Logs together on the living room floor. Annie wrote that Dad had not heard anything from the insurance company yet. I contemplated texting about the interactions with Mrs. Schilling but was concerned it might upset her. Regardless, Annie had to know what happened and I decided to call instead.

When Annie picked up I blurted out, "I just want you to know that Missus Schilling made a move on me again, and keep thinking of Potiphar's wife and Joseph going to prison and…and I don't want you to divorce me."

Annie laughed. "Slow down and say it again?"

"Missus Schilling."

"Is making the moves on you?"

I nodded like Annie could see me before realizing I had to respond. "Yes."

"Are you sure?"

"Uhm, when I entered the apartment she was in my shower and propositioned me. Then she just did it again a few minutes ago."

"What did you do?"

"Kicked her out the first time and fled a few minutes ago."

"Where are you now?"

"Long story."

"I don't worry about you," Annie said. "You're like a child who tattles on themselves. Just be careful. Missus Schilling's a very pretty lady."

"Not compared to you."

"Uh huh."

Before we finished, Annie suggested that we keep Mrs. Schilling in our prayers and reminded me that the woman had lost her son and was suffering. Up until that moment I had thought of Margaret Schilling as a caricature. A quintessential wealthy bored elite who was looking to fill boredom in her life. Annie was right, she was suffering and needed prayers and sympathy. Although Mrs. Schilling was gorgeous by the world's standards, my wife was beautiful both inside and out.

Forty minutes later, the senator came out the front door of the apartment. His tie was missing, and

JOHN THEO JR.

he looked disheveled. I pulled the car up along the edge of the street shadowing him. Eventually, he turned and walked over to the rolled down passenger window.

"Is this where you scold me again?" he said.

"Get in," I said, feeling like an annoyed parent picking his drunk son up from a high school party.

The senator jumped in the backseat seemingly carefree. "Where to, Dad?"

"Home."

"You're upset."

"You're not paying me to be upset."

"Come on, Brandon. I know you're a Christian. You're at least disappointed."

"Disappointed would mean that I'm surprised," I said. "Man is a fallen creature. I've seen a lot of men fall prey to this same temptation."

"So, you're giving me a pass."

"Uh no. I can't force my morals onto you. You're a big boy and have to live with yourself but sneaking out on me hinders my ability to do this job."

"But you see my offsite meeting as wrong."

"Of course, I do."

"You're very black and white."

"There's objective truth in the world."

"Well, you're still young. You may one day learn that what works in one marriage might not work in another."

"If you say so, sir."

A few minutes later we pulled back up to the

128

brownstone. I walked the senator up to his door and turned and walked away.

He called after me as if nothing had happened. "I have an eight AM meeting at a local charity. Then I'm heading into my capitol office."

"I'll be out front at seven forty-five. Don't forget to print me out your week's itinerary."

I went to bed that night disappointed in a man I had placed up on a pedestal. Based on our past interaction I assumed the senator operated with some code of honor, but whatever moral compass he lived by was far from Biblical. If the senator didn't treat his marriage with respect, then what else did he compromise?

The next morning, I wore another dress shirt and tie along with the borrowed blazer, khakis, and new dress shoes. I looked up on YouTube how to tie a Windsor knot and was impressed with my first attempt. Normally, I wore my gun in an appendix holster that stuck just above the belt line of my pants. I never tucked my shirt in, which allowed the gun to remain concealed. However, with the new attire I had to utilize a belly band holster, which was type of girdle with a slip pocket for the gun. This allowed the person to wear the gun beneath a tucked-in dress shirt. I snapped a selfie and sent it off to Annie. She texted back how handsome I looked, which put a pep in my step. I made a cup of coffee and grabbed a power bar and went outside. The sky was cloudy, and it was already humid. Birds chirped in nearby trees which added to the romantic setting of the gorgeous architecture. The senator came out a few minutes later on his cell phone.

He placed his hand over the phone when he saw me. "Twelve forty-five Baltimore Boulevard."

I let him in the back seat and plugged the address into the dash touchscreen. A few minutes into the drive he ended the phone call. There was a long awkward silence.

He spoke first. "Sorry about last night."

"It's none of my business," I said.

"I feel like I should explain. My wife and I haven't had a good marriage in a long time."

"The loss of a child can sometimes rip marriages apart."

"I wish that were the case, Brandon." He looked out the window at the old brick buildings passing by. "This goes back further. We were a DC power couple back in the day. A couple of convenience. Right or wrong, it's always been convenience."

"I'm sorry for you. There's a better way."

"I know what you're gonna say." He exhaled. "I'm gonna get my life, and my marriage, in a better place once I get out of this town." He dropped a piece of paper into the front seat. "Here's my itinerary for the remainder of the week."

"I thought of something else we should talk about."

"Like?"

"Your daughter."

"Amber?"

"She's at UVA, right?"

"Yes, why?"

"Do you think we need to do anything for her regarding security?"

"That's one area you don't need to worry about," he said. "I've notified campus security and they have her in a dorm with an armed campus security guard posted in the foyer twenty-four-seven. Within that building I have her in a single dorm room with its own alarm. I've also made her register this semester under her mother's maiden name."

"I'm impressed," I said.

"When it comes to my last child, I'm not taking chances."

"What about your wife?"

"What about her?" he huffed.

"You concerned about her safety?"

"That witch could fall off a boat into a feeding frenzy of sharks, wearing nothing but a meat-covered life vest and be fine." I was sipping from my coffee when the senator said this and erupted into a coughing fit. As if to make me further choke, he added, "She'd eat the sharks."

We arrived at the address. It was a beautiful old brick church dating back to the mid-1800s. The senator entered into a basement hall full of elderly women. They all clapped when he walked in the room. He shook hands as we walked towards a podium at the front of the room. I walked the area checking out the bathrooms and back kitchen where two elderly women baked something that smelled delicious.

"Excuse me," I said, recusing myself back into the main room where I took up a seat off to the side.

The banner at the front of the room read, *Daughters of the War for Independence*. A nearby brochure read that the criteria for eligibility to join the group was, *any woman 18 years or older who could prove lineal, bloodline descent from an ancestor who aided in achieving American Independence. The interested woman must provide documentation for each statement of birth, marriage and death, as well as the Revolutionary War service of her Patriot ancestor.* The group had chapters all over the country. I pocketed a brochure for Annie. Her family, like mine, went back before the Revolutionary War. As a child I would listen to my dad tell stories about colonial America and the early frontiersmen. People like Daniel Boone and Simon Kenton. Stories about the discovery of Kentucky, and the small period of quiet before the inrush of people through the Cumberland Gap into the West.

The senator stood behind the old wooden podium and looked like a school boy in front of the elderly ladies. His speech started off with the role Virginia played throughout the country's history, and how it produced more presidents than any other state.

"You ladies have an important job in our politically-correct society today," he said. "It's your duty to never let us forget our past with both its scars and its beauty. History is being washed and re-written before our very eyes in school textbooks. Don't let the country forget how pivotal the Revolutionary War was and just how smart the founders were. The United States Constitution has been in place since 1788. It's the oldest constitution in the world. Other countries have gone through numerous constitutions while only ours had stood the test of time. The American experiment is unlike anything in history as liberty is tied to its success. Without liberty, the system will collapse."

Every word Senator Schilling spoke had its own cadence and role in his speech. The man was an artist with words. For the next ten minutes he continued on about the greatness of Virginia, the founders, the Constitution, and the role they played within the United States.

"I see some familiar faces," he concluded, "and some new ones in this crowd. Attrition is vital to this group. Never forget that you ladies are a cornerstone in this great state. God bless you all."

The crowd gave Senator Schilling a standing ovation including me. I stood next to him while he shook a few hands and posed for pictures. When it looked like he was ready to leave, I exited first and stood outside the door to walk him to the car. Back in the car, the senator texted on his phone, acting as if what just happened was no big deal.

"That was a great speech," I said.

"Thanks, Brandon," he said, placing his phone into the breast pocket of his coat. "The old women love me. It's the kids I can't connect with anymore." In the rearview mirror I could see him wave his hand back and forth like he didn't care. "Doesn't matter. I'm done with this place anyway."

"According to your schedule we're heading to your office in the capital, but the address is Constitution Ave? We aren't going to the capital?"

"The Capitol Building was constructed in Eighteen Hundred when there were only One hundred thirty-seven congress. Since then we've ballooned to five hundred thirty-five with each member of congress having dozens of staff. My office is in the Russell Building which is near the capital."

"Interesting," I said. "Where will I park and walk you in?"

"There's video surveillance everywhere and security inside and all around the place. You can just drop me off on the fly."

"What about if there are votes on the floor of the senate. How will we meet so I can walk you over?"

"There's an underground subway connecting the Russell, Dirksen, and Hart Senate office buildings to the Capitol Building."

"Really?"

"It makes it efficient for us to go back and forth when we have multiple votes in a day. Traffic isn't disrupted and security remains unaffected."

"I had no idea," I said.

"Not many people realize there's an entire world beneath DC."

We passed from Virginia into DC and I could see a clear shift in the landscape. Resident brownstones gave way to government buildings. Police were everywhere, and traffic was even worse than Alexandria. Soon my left leg was sore from having to depress the Audi's clutch so often, making me second guess my choice of vehicles. We made our way past the memorials to the Russell Building. It was an enormous granite building with a United States flag over the entrance. Its beauty was in its simple design. First story windows gave way to second story Greek columns and larger windows. A faux battlement ran along the top as if to add a medieval gothic touch.

"Enjoy the afternoon," the senator said, stepping out of the car. "I'll see you here at six." He rushed up the granite stairs where a security guard let him in.

It took me almost an hour to drive the short distance back to the Alexandria brownstone. Outside my door I met a college-aged boy. He was dressed in khakis, a button-down shirt and carried coat hangers with my new suits draped in plastic.

"Hi there?" I said.

"Hi," he said. "Are you Mister Hall?"

"Depends," I said. "Are you from the IRS?"

He smiled. "I'm dropping off your suits from my grandfather's shop."

"Let me guess," I said. "Your name's Walter too?"

He smiled. "Yes, sir."

"Well, I guess I should give you my loaner back," I said, taking off my blue blazer, folding it and swapping it for the suits. I realized I should tip him. "Ah, Walter, I have no cash on me."

"It's fine," he said, turning to walk away.

"No, wait. I'm heading to get a sandwich down the street, which is near your shop. I'll get change there." He raised his hands as if to say no, but I insisted. "I'm getting lunch anyway and it's on the way."

I placed the suits inside the brownstone and walked with the young man down the street. The clouds had given way to bright skies and a humid day. I rolled the sleeves up on my dress shirt and put on my sunglasses. The young man didn't talk, and kind of looked out of the ordinary because he wasn't face-down with a smart phone in hand.

"Your family business has some cool history to it," I said. "You born and raised in Alexandria?"

"Yes, sir."

"What can you tell me about this area?"

He shrugged. "What you see is what you get."

"It's gorgeous."

"If you like the city."

"What do you like, Walter?"

"I'm a mountain man. I fly fish."

"I've done a lot of fishing, but never fly fished. You go to the Blue Ridge a lot?"

"Whenever I can."

We made it to the deli, and I took out cash from

the ATM and gave Walter a tip and insisted I buy him lunch. We both ordered chicken kabobs and bottles of water. We sat outside at a small bistro table where I proceeded to use the opportunity to pump him for some intel.

"You deliver a lot of suits for your gramps to local politicians?"

"Yes, sir."

"I bet you've seen some weird stuff in your time around here?"

He raised his eyebrows. "A bit."

"Are most of your customers politicians?"

"Politicians, lobbyists, and bankers."

"You interact with Senator Schilling a lot?"

"Some."

"What's your take on him?"

"He's your boss. Don't you know?"

I bit my lip thinking of the previous night. "I don't know him as well as thought."

"He's a stand-up guy as far as politicians go, but the few times I've met him he struck me as..." Walter paused to take a bite of his sub. It was if he were trying to find the right word. Finally, he said. "Always on."

"How so?"

"Promise this is off the record?"

"I promise," I said. "Between you and me, I've been hired as the senator's bodyguard, and I just need as much info as I can get to do my job. What do you mean by always on?"

"When I fly fish, I have to use the right fly to represent what insect larvae are hatching, and living, during that time of year. Otherwise the fish won't buy into the fake bait."

"Ah, one can never go wrong with a fishing metaphor," I joked.

Walter smirked. "Senator Schilling always knows what fly to use. People like that I find to be—" Walter paused again. "Disturbed."

"Really?" I said, expecting an adjective like *vain* or *arrogant*. "What makes you say that?"

"Disturbed is probably the wrong term," Walter said, thinking for a moment. "Well, you know those people who are always upbeat and happy no matter what's happening? The world could be burning around them, and you ask if they are okay and they're like, yeah everything's awesome."

"I know the type, yes."

"Well, many times they end up having a lot of anger under the surface if you know what I mean."

I thought for a moment back to my time in the Marines. I knew a couple of manic guys that fit Walter's description, and both ended up dishonorably discharged for going off the deep end. "You're quite an insightful young man, Walter. How'd you get so observant?"

He shrugged. "Eight years of therapy after your parents' divorce will do that to you."

"I'm sorry."

"Take my opinions with a grain of salt, sir."

"On the contrary," I said. "I find that a lot of times the people in the background who have the opportunity to observe can sometimes hold the best information."

After lunch we shook hands. "It was a pleasure meeting you."

"Please don't repeat what I told you," Walter said. "My grandfather prides himself on not getting involved in politics and drama."

I pressed my thumb and index finger together and ran them across my mouth like I was closing a zipper.

TEN

I spent the rest of the afternoon relaxing, which felt awkward. Other than Sunday afternoons I could not remember the last time I had down time during a weekday. There was always something to be fixed on the farm, or in our house. I tried on my new blue pinstripe suit and video called with Annie and the girls. Annie started to list off nice restaurants back home that I could take her to wearing my new suits. Emily seemed a bit down, and I forced myself to remain upbeat.

"Emily, how about when I'm done with this job, we look at puppies?"

Annie turned to Emily who shook her head back and forth. "I don't know."

"It won't disrespect Fescue's memory, sweetie."

"I guess."

"Okay, we'll give it some more time."

"I do have some good news," Annie said. "The

insurance company agreed to payout on the poison, so long as the government officials corroborate the story."

"Praise God!" I shouted.

"He is faithful," Annie added.

After the video call I changed and went for a two-mile run. When I came back Mrs. Schilling was pulling out of the driveway in her SUV. She started to say something from the car, but I waved and rushed down the stairs to the garden apartment like I had something to do. Inside, I dead bolted the door and stood with my back to it as if to add another layer of protection.

I picked up the senator right at six. It was so busy that I couldn't get out of the car to open the door for him. He had to jump in on the fly.

"How was your day at school?" I said.

He laughed. "You have no idea of the cannibalism that goes on inside the capital. Now that I'm leaving even my remora fish are treating me like a second-class citizen."

"Your what?"

"I call most of my staff remora behind their backs. Remora are the sucker fish that attach to sharks. They clean up bacteria on its body and, in turn, get a free ride. Watching the remora scurry to try to find another politician to latch on to is comical from my point of view."

"Doesn't sound like a fun place to work."

"It's a great job if you like street fighting in

designer suits." He exhaled. "I've lost the fire in my belly and they know it."

"Your schedule says we're going to another restaurant?"

"Yeah, Italian tonight with my chief of staff."

"You frequent it often?"

"Periodically. It's not on my regular rotation if that's what you mean?"

"How busy will it be?"

"Very. Why?"

"Normally, I'd be fine sitting nearby at the bar while you have your meeting but—"

"No, I insist you join us."

"Thank you. I'd feel better if I were close."

A half hour later we pulled into a fancy glass front restaurant. I waved off a valet and parked out back. I walked the senator in through the rear door. The aroma of fresh garlic and bread was a one-two punch that made my stomach growl. We were greeted by a handsome man with dark wavy hair with at least a gallon of hair gel holding it in place.

"Senator, so good to see you."

"Jack, good to be seen."

"We have you in the private room in the back."

Jack led us through a crowded restaurant decorated with water fountains, frescos, and dark wood. It took five minutes to get through the room as the senator shook hands with old white men in expensive suits. He asked one of two questions of the men. Where their children were clerking for the summer, or what ivy league school their grandkids got into. Eventually, we reached a private back room where a young man sat at a table, typing on his smart phone. He was a good-looking guy, late twenties with blond floppy hair. He was dressed in a sharp black suit and stood up when we entered.

"Brandon, this is my Chief of Staff, Larry Gregory."

Larry had a firm handshake. All he said was, "Hi."

"Larry's the only one who knows your true role. Everyone else thinks you're a speech writer."

We sat down and a waiter dressed in black mock turtleneck and black pants came over with a fancy bottle of water. After filling our glasses, he handed us a wine menu as well as a dinner menu. Nothing on the wine menu was under a hundred dollars, including half carafes. The dinner menu started at seventy dollars for entrées.

While the senator asked the waiter about the best merlot, Larry leaned over to whisper. "I'm curious why the senator chose you for his security? He didn't tell me much. What's your credentials?"

While Larry's tone was neutral, there was something about his directness that struck me as rude. Maybe because I had just met him?

Instead of trying to prove who the alpha male was, I tried to disarm him with humility. "I'm a nobody from Virginia helping the senator out for a few weeks."

"You didn't answer my question?" Larry said,

quiet but stern. "I asked about your credentials? Your background?"

"Why?"

"It's my job. I need to know if anything in your past could harm the senator's current work."

"I don't think so."

"That's not for you to decide," Larry's voice was still low, but now aggressive. "I vet everyone the senator comes in contact with."

"I guess not everyone," I said, looking down at the dinner menu.

Larry reached over and touched my forearm. I looked at his hand as if it were a foreign object. I hated random people touching me and fought the rising urge to slug him.

"Let me tell you how this works," Larry said. "I'm a Yale undergrad and Harvard law school grad. I've clerked for a Supreme Court Justice and I managed Senator Schilling's last re- election campaign. Now, it's your turn."

As much as I loathed bragging, I was impressed with the young man's resume. I motioned for him to come closer and whispered. "I'm a cattle farmer."

"Don't insult me."

"I'm not joking."

"You're serious?" I nodded and gave a goofy smile. "I thought you were a PI, or a cop or something, but now you're telling me that's not even your full-time job?"

"Oh no. I'm a cattle farmer. I do some PI stuff on

the side. Insurance claims, stolen tractor parts, property damage involving animals." I mock laughed. "In fact, you'll like this one, Larry. I recently had a case where a guy filed an insurance claim on a new tractor that died on his farm but turns out he was using it in competition tractor pulls, which is how he blew the engine."

Larry turned to the senator who was still asking the waiter about wines. The senator must have heard us, but ignored the conversation for some reason. Larry turned back to me and whispered, "Then why'd he hire you?"

I took a sip of water. "I guess he doesn't trust anyone up here."

"There's plenty of people to trust in DC."

"If you say so, Larry," I said, trying not to be baited into arguing further.

The senator turned to Larry. "I can't decide. Merlot or Sauvignon Blanc?"

Larry continued to stare at me but spoke to the senator. "What year's the Sauvignon?"

"Two thousand and five and Merlot is ten."

"I'd go merlot, sir."

"We'll take the Sauvignon," the senator said, handing the menu back to the waiter. Larry winced when the senator pulled this passive aggressive decision. Once the waiter left, the senator turned to us. "You guys make the introductions okay?"

"Larry doesn't believe that I'm a farmer," I said.

"Don't let Brandon's humility fool you," the

senator huffed. "He's ex-military, and has seen more action as a private citizen than some soldiers encounter on deployment overseas."

Larry's jaw tightened as if he were annoyed that I withheld this information and hadn't gone toe-to-toe with him in the resume department. "This man's safety is my responsibility," he spouted.

"In so much as it benefits his career," the senator added with a smirk while reviewing the dinner menu. "I think I'm going to get the chicken and capers. What do you think, Brandon?"

"I'm going with the spaghetti. Everything else is overpriced."

The senator laughed. "Nonsense. Order what you want. Larry, what are you getting?"

"I'm getting the filet."

"Rubbish," the senator said. "We're in the nicest Italian restaurant in town. Why don't you try the gnocchi?"

"No thanks."

"Then try the fish of the day?"

"Why, is it eel?" I interrupted.

The senator burst out laughing, and Larry's pale skin grew bright red. He got up to leave. "I'll catch up with you later, Senator."

I got up and blocked Larry's exit. Larry was an inch or two taller than my five nine but seemed taken aback at me blocking him. Part of me wanted him to take a swing at me, but I knew my comment was out of line.

"I'm sorry," I said. "I'm just playing with you. We need to find a way to get along. I promise I'm no threat to you. I have no interest in DC. I'm a middle-class farmer who just lost his herd and needs this side job." I gestured to the bench. "Come on, Larry. Please sit down."

Larry sat back down and started to text someone on his phone. The senator seemed to have enjoyed the interaction. Throughout dinner the conversation between the senator and his chief of staff sounded like Latin. Between the legal terms and bills they mentioned I had no idea what they were talking about. At one point the senator pulled out his fancy fountain pen and started marking up a speech Larry had given him. Within a minute the entire sheet of paper was covered in red ink.

"Who wrote this?" the senator said, crossing out an entire line. "Doctor Seuss?"

"Trevor Smith. Why?"

"You need to remind Mister Smith to use spell check, and he writes in the passive voice too much. And boy does he like adverbs." The senator turned to me. "I'm a bit of a grammar nerd."

The two men finished the bottle of sauvignon, as well as half of another bottle. Both seemed unfazed by the amount of alcohol. Larry mentioned the upcoming hearing where Schultz would testify. The senator said he was prepared and changed the subject. After dinner, the senator got a cannoli for dessert. I ordered a cup of decaf coffee and Larry excused himself to go to the bathroom.

The senator turned to me. "You handled yourself very well with my chief of staff. Most people cave under his aggressiveness."

"Aggressiveness? More like abrasiveness," I said. The senator giggled like a schoolboy who just played a prank. "Why do I feel like I was just put through some initiation psych test?"

The senator gave me a confused look, like he had no idea what I was talking about. Finally, he smiled. "Just collecting data."

I realized he hadn't been testing me but using me to test his chief of staff for some reason. Larry returned, and the senator signed for the bill. I tried to shake Larry's hand before he left but he didn't reciprocate.

Back in the car the senator said. "It's only eight-thirty. The night is still young. Where should we go?"

"Your schedule says this was it, sir. If you want to go somewhere else, you'll have to give me directions"

"I should just head home and answer some emails."

"You politicians never stop working."

"Public service is a twenty-four-seven job spending all those tax dollars," he said this in a self-deprecating tone.

"What's the national debt up to now?"

"Don't get me started," he said. "When it comes to

the national debt crisis, I work with a bunch of ostriches burying their heads in the sand."

After I walked him to his door I said, "Have a good night, sir."

"You too, son."

When I turned back, I saw a smile on his face different from the fake plastered ones I'd seen him showcase. It was sympathetic, almost jealous. Maybe it was my age, or the stability of my marriage? I contemplated talking faith and God, but he disappeared inside.

Before bed, I video conferenced Annie and Emily again. "I'm still trying to get a handle on things up here," I said. "So, I'm not sure when we can meet up just yet."

"I miss you," Emily said, clearly upset.

"Miss you too, sweetie. Remember I'm only a few hours away."

"Can't you come home just for one night?"

"Soon," I promised. Her pleading was a gut-punch that kept me up late into the night.

The next few days mirrored my initial days with the senator. The mornings started early and involved some venue where he shook hands, and kissed babies, before going into his capitol office. During the day, I'd get a workout in, and sometimes even a nap. After hours was usually a late working dinner with Larry who all but ignored me. The senator would try to draw me into some of their conversations, but I did everything possible to stay out of it.

However, one time when he asked me about the president's idea of selling arms to a middle east government, I mentioned George Washington's farewell address to the nation. In the letter President Washington made a point not to get involved in foreign entanglements. Larry rebutted my argument by saying the modern world was different from colonial times. He claimed there were too many *moving pieces*. I just nodded and let Larry have his victory.

Another time the senator asked me about a budget question and I said that Larry's idea was the best I could think of. The young chief of staff looked at me as if I were trying to insult him in some weird way when I was trying to compliment him and build a bridge. Otherwise the legal jargon and lawyer speak all but put me to sleep. One takeaway from all the legalese was a sad realization there was a lot of inertia in DC. It took a tremendous amount of effort to make minuscule changes in government. Larry tried to bring up the hearings with Gaspar Schultz at each dinner, but the senator brushed it away like it was no big deal and moved on to what he called more important issues.

When Larry left to go to the bathroom I leaned over to the senator. "If you don't mind me asking, why won't you talk about Schultz testifying at the upcoming hearing? If you need me to sit somewhere else I—"

"No," he said. "It's not you. It's Larry. I found out

his brother works for a financial firm owned by Schultz. I want to keep things close to the chest."

"Understood."

Larry returned and their conversation moved on to something called tort reform. I picked up bits and pieces only.

A few minutes in Larry turned to me. "What do you think, farmer boy?" I didn't want to engage him and continued to keep my face in a dessert menu. Larry repeated, "John Boy Walton, I'm talking to you."

"I can't follow what you guys are talking about," I said, not looking up from the menu.

"So, you have no opinion?"

"Again, not my area of expertise."

"But protecting the senator is? Do you even know how to assess a threat, or are you here just to pick out a dessert?"

"If you're looking to make me look foolish, I usually don't need help. With that said, I may be just a humble redneck from the country, but I do take my job serious."

The senator was wide-eyed. It was as if he'd been waiting for this confrontation.

Larry leaned in closer to me. "Looks to me like you're being a cling-on for free meals and a paycheck. I've seen you do very little in the time we spent together."

I placed the menu down and leaned in so our faces were inches apart. "You just came back from the restroom. So, tell me, Larry, how many people are in the main area of the restaurant?" He didn't respond, but I could see his eyes look up as if he was trying to recall a number. "Twenty-five," I said without breaking eye contact. "Ten couples, in their thirties. All are dressed nice. There's also one party of three, more than likely a family, leaving two single males alone. One of the males is dressed in a blue pinstripe suit, sitting at a table set for two. He's clearly waiting for someone. Yet the other single guy bothers me, Larry. Now you're gonna ask why? I'm glad you asked, because this man's attire is casual, which is in stark contrast to how the rest of people are dressed in the restaurant."

Larry started to back away into the confines of his portion of the booth. "Furthermore," I added, "this single man is wearing cargo pants and an untucked long sleeve shirt. Not many men dress like that at a restaurant of this caliber. The baggy shirt and pants could be hiding multiple weapons. He's also wearing new black boots. Not combat boots, but they do look tactical. And finally, he's sipping a beer with his left hand."

"What does that mean?" the senator said.

"If he's a professional then he would drink using his non dominant hand leaving the dominant hand free to quickly act and grab a firearm."

Larry's eyes widened as if I had just dumped a bucket of water over his head. "What should we do? Call the cops?"

I chuckled and picked the dessert menu back up. "For what? A guy dressed in casual clothes having a beer in a high end restaurant?"

The senator nodded his approval. "See Larry, I told you I chose well."

I put the menu back down and reached my open palm over to Larry. "I'm no threat to you, or your career, and I'm not out to get you." Larry seemed taken aback. "Let's stop with this nonsense. I'll be out of your hair soon enough." Slowly, Larry reached out to receive my handshake. "See, we're BFFs now."

Larry gave what almost seemed like a smile, but I wasn't sure his lips were capable of turning up.

ELEVEN

Saturday was another working day but started later than usual. I went for a run and ended up at my new favorite deli for a bagel and ice coffee. At 9:30 I met the senator out front dressed in my new grey pinstripe suit. Unlike me, he was dressed in jeans, button down shirt, and a blazer. We drove into a wealthy section of DC where brownstones similar to the senator's lined old streets. The senator had a meeting with a donor in one of the units. I double parked and walked him up to the door.

"You need me inside?"

"Only threat inside is a donor looking to suck my soul into eternal damnation before I leave DC," he huffed. "Other than that, it should be fine. You won't find parking anywhere near here. Go get a cup of coffee and I'll text you in about an hour to come pick me up."

I rushed back to the car just as a police cruiser

pulled up and turned on his flashing lights. I waved and mouthed the words, *I'm sorry*. He gave me a stern look, shut the lights, and drove off. For fifteen minutes I drove around before randomly finding a parking spot near the Tidal Basin.

I got out and walked along the water. The cherry blossoms had already bloomed and died, but the view was still gorgeous. The breeze coming off the Potomac was a clean brackish smell. Young couples walked hand in hand and other people of various ages ran, biked, and walked. Some had dogs on leashes. Everyone seemed to be enjoying the beautiful warm spring day.

In the distance, I noticed a familiar elderly African American man on a bench. He was dressed in a sharp suit with a herringbone Irish cap on his head. I realized it was my government friend, Roger Drake. Before I could call out to him. Another elderly Caucasian man dressed in khakis and a dress shirt came up and sat down beside him. I stood off in the distance and watched what I thought was a clandestine government meeting. It was like a scene from a spy movie. The two men spoke for a few moments before the new guy handed Drake a manilla envelope. Drake opened it and smiled before handing the man what looked like a wad of cash. They shook hands and the Caucasian man left as quick as he had shown up. I waited a full two minutes before I approached Drake from behind.

When I was a few feet away he spoke without

turning around. "You think I don't know you're there, Brandon Hall?"

"Dang," I said, walking around into view. "How'd you know?"

"I'm all knowing," he said. "Come sit next to your old friend and tell me what you're doing in my city." I sat down and he looked me up and down. "Well, don't you clean up nice. That one of Walter's suits?"

"How'd you know."

He pursed his lips. "Told you. I'm all knowing."

I rubbed my hands together like an excited kid about to open a present. "So, what did I just witness?"

Drake grinned and waved a hand. "Oh that? Nothing."

"Come on," I laughed. "Tell me, did you just pay for secrets from some foreign spy?"

"You watch too many movies."

"Oh, I get it. You're being coy. Trying to downplay what I just saw." I tapped the side of my head. "Mind games."

"Here," he said, handing me the manilla envelope he'd taken from the other man. Inside was a thin clear plastic sheet with a single stamp in it.

"You purchased a one cent Benjamin Franklin stamp?" I said, turning it over. "Is there some microfilm hidden on it or something?"

Drake took the stamp and placed it back in the envelope. "You ninny. That's a very rare, and very expensive, one cent Benjamin Franklin stamp. You've discovered my secret."

"You're a...closet stamp collector?"

"Ironic isn't it." Drake puffed his chest out. "On the surface I may appear like Superman but hidden on the inside I'm a Clark Kent nerd who collects stamps." We both chuckled. "Let's take a walk."

"Lead the way."

"Strange to see you up here," Drake said. "And strange to see you without a beard and in a suit."

"I know," I said. "I'm out of my element."

"So, you're guarding the senator until after the hearings?"

"How'd you—"

He pursed his lips again. "Told you, brother. I'm all knowing."

"But—"

"Why didn't you tell me about your cattle issue?"

At this point, I knew better than to ask how he knew this additional information. Instead, I shrugged like a kid whose mother just scolded him for not telling the truth. "It's not your problem."

"You need money?"

I held up my hand. "I'll be okay but thank you."

"Don't be stubborn. I know you'd never abuse the charity of friends. What do you need?"

"I'll let you know if it gets to that point."

"So, what's the senator's deal?"

"He's been getting death threats," I said, "but you probably know that already."

"He was smart to hire you."

"Why do you say that?"

"There's no such thing as being paranoid in this town."

"How so?"

Drake waved his hand over the expanse of water, nature, and granite memorials surrounding us. "The manicured gardens, and historic buildings are a veneer. This place is dangerous."

"Man, you sound like the senator."

"There's a lot going on beneath the surface of DC."

"Man, you really sound like the senator."

"Imagine the worst-case scenario?" Drake paused, as if to add emphasis to what he was about to say next. "Whatever you imagine, then double it. No triple it."

"Now you sound like my dad."

"Stay alert and sleep with one eye open, Brandon. These death threats could be nothing or they could be very real. Assume they're legit."

"Understood."

I looked at my watch. "I need to head back to pick up the boss."

"I'll text you the address of my church if you want to join us tomorrow morning."

"I'd like that."

Drake left me with a hug rather than a handshake. I had grown to love this man like a second dad. He saved my life on more than one occasion. I wished that more honorable citizens like Roger Drake would be lifted up to serve in government. The senator texted me just as I pulled back up to the brownstone. He came out looking like he hadn't slept in days. Like he was stressed.

After he got in, I said, "You okay?"

"Can't get out of this town quick enough, Brandon. Heavy donors want more than a pound of my flesh before I leave town."

As much as I wanted to ask for details. I didn't press him. I wasn't sure what was my business, and what wasn't. We made a stop at the dry cleaner where the senator picked up a couple dress shirts, then got lunch at a small restaurant back in Alexandria. We were home by three-thirty.

After I walked him up to his door, I said, "What's the plan for tomorrow?"

"I'm going to head into work. I'll email you my schedule for next week once I firm it up."

"I'd like to go to church after I drop you off, if that's okay?"

"Of course. I'll be in the office most of the day anyway."

As I walked back down the stairs I turned and said, "You're more than welcome to come along?"

He waved the offer away with a smile. "Some other time but thank you."

Back inside my apartment the conversation with Drake seemed to have more of an impact than my father's warnings. Dad had a bit of tin foil hat to him, but Drake was never one for drama. I used my phone to log on to the military surplus site I had searched prior to coming to Alexandria. The order for the Kevlar vest and Kevlar blanket were still in my cart. I pressed the purchase button. The email confirmation said it would be at my new address within twenty-four hours. I deleted the email in case Annie logged on my email from home and saw the receipt and panicked.

The next morning, I dropped the senator off at his office. He would text me a time later in the day to be picked up. I plugged in the address Drake texted me for his church in Alexandria. It was a plain brick building without the ornate stained glass and architecture some of the older churches exhibited, but I knew that's not what a church was. Inside the building was bustling with parishioners. I found Drake in a double-breasted grey suit, talking with someone, but the moment he saw me he excused himself to come over to greet me with a hug.

"Brandon, how's my brother from another mother doing?"

"I'm glad we bumped into each other," I said. "I've been feeling kind of alone up here."

Drake motioned to a pretty mid-fifties African American woman dressed in a navy-blue skirt and matching hat. "I want you to meet Claire."

The woman approached and hugged me. "Roger's told me so much about you that I think I already know your entire family. "

"I don't know what he's told you, but it's a one-sided friendship. Roger has saved my bacon a few times."

"You were an answer to prayer for me."

"Really? How so?"

"I wanted Roger to find more Christian friends."

"Come on," Drake interrupted. "Church is starting."

Drake shook hands and introduced me to at least two dozen couples and children. It wasn't until after the music started and people were raising hands to praise Jesus that it occurred to me that I was the only white person there. I got into the worship and even felt the need to raise my hands a few times with this different form of praise we offered to the same Lord.

Soon, a young deacon in his early thirties stood up at the pulpit. He looked like a body builder with bulging arms tight under his navy-blue suit jacket. "Pastor Jeremiah is on a mission trip to the Dominican Republic this week," the man said, "and he asked yours truly to step in."

Drake leaned over to me. "That's Jae. He's family."

The man known as Jae continued from the pulpit, "We've all heard the term Black Lives matter, or BLM. I worked in law enforcement and in those circles, BLM stands for Blue Lives Matter. However, the Bible says that all lives matter. The Bible says God created all of us in our mother's wombs."

Drake shouted an *Amen* along with several other parishioners.

"The Bible says in Jeremiah that, He knows us

even before He formed us in our momma's wombs."
Jae picked up a Kevlar vest from behind the pulpit
and held it up for the congregation to see. There was
a red piece of tape over the upper left chest. "When I
worked narcotics, this vest saved my life. Back in my
day cops didn't always wear Kevlar as part of their
day-to-day work, but God spoke to me in a powerful
way during my morning time of prayer. I listened
and wore my vest. You see, I was about to testify
against a fellow cop who was dealing drugs the side.
This other cop was a black man who thought I would
look the other way because he assumed he was my
brother." Jae lowered the vest back down. "But you
see I don't care how dark this man's skin was. I told
him that he wasn't right with God, and he surely
wasn't my brother." Jae pounded on the pulpit and
pointed to me. "See that white boy right there. He's
my brother more than that cop ever was." The man
known as Jae moved out from behind the pulpit and
looked down at me. "Sir, are you washed in the blood
of Christ?"

Everyone in church turned to look at me and I felt
my face go flush. "Yes, I am," I said, with a nervous
tone.

Jae pointed. "There you go. That's my brother in
Christ."

Claire wrapped an arm around my shoulder like a
proud parent and Drake nodded his approval with a
handsome grin.

"The Bible says in Galatians that there is neither

Jew nor Greek," Jae continued, his voice rising. "There is neither bond nor free, there is neither male nor female: for ye are all one in Christ Jesus." Jae held the vest back up. "So, this other cop hired a white gangbanger to take a shot at me later that day. He hoped a black cop getting shot by a white kid would cause a race riot and distract from what was going on. This racial divisiveness is a lie from the devil. He's a master at slight-of-hand. We need to walk out of here today unified in Christ regardless of the color of our skin."

Many in the crowd were nodding their heads with many *Amens* shouted. After Jae's sermon, two more songs were sung with clapping and raised hands. By the end I felt like I had participated in both a spiritual, and aerobic, workout.

After church, Drake introduced me to Jae. His handshake felt like he could crush a golf ball. "Sorry to put you on the spot up there," he said, "but it fit perfectly with my sermon."

"No problem," I said, rubbing my hand. "It was a great sermon and testimony."

"My wife wishes I'd gone into ministry instead of law enforcement."

Two young boys came up and hugged Jae's legs. Without a word Jae flexed his biceps and each child latched onto an arm. Jae proceeded to lift each child up as he did mock curling exercises. The children shouted with glee. While Jae did this, Claire passed her arm through mine and escorted me outside. We walked like we had been lifelong friends. Outside the sky was clear and the sun was brutal.

"I love your church," I said.

"You're welcome here for however long you're in the city. By the way, how do you like DC?"

"It's pretty but…"

"Not your cup of tea."

"No, ma'am. I miss my family and my farm."

"Shame what happened to your cattle. Did you find out who did it yet?"

"Not yet."

"If anyone will, it will be Roger."

"You mean he's looking into it?"

She placed a finger up to her lips. "Don't tell him I said, but he's snooping around in a little."

Drake joined us outside and insisted I come over to their place for lunch. I had no texts from the senator and nothing else to do. Their brownstone was about a mile from the senator's but in a modest section of town. While not as fancy as the Schilling brownstone, the Drake home looked lived in. The living room had an old leather sectional facing a television mounted over a fireplace with ashes in it. A smell of spices and hot sauce emanated from the back of the house.

"Hello?" Claire said.

"Back here, Momma."

Drake and his wife both rushed through the living room into the kitchen. They looked like two grammar school kids in a foot race. Shouts of joy greeted me as I wandered into the kitchen. A pretty, late-twenties African American woman stood in front of a stove with multiple pots cooking. She rubbed her lower back with her left arm while stirring a pot with her right.

Drake had an arm curled around her shoulder. "Brandon, this is Vanessa. My only child."

"Very nice to meet you, ma'am."

"Nice to meet you too, Brandon. I hope you're staying for lunch as I have a lot of food cooking."

"He is," Drake said on my behalf. "When did you get back into town?"

"A half hour ago. I was going to surprise you at church, but it was too late. I'm making your favorite."

"Cajun catfish?"

"Why don't you go and sit in the living room and let me take over," Claire said.

"I got this, Momma. You three go relax." The front door opened and closed. "I'm in here babe," Vanessa shouted.

A moment later Jae came in the kitchen. He had changed into a tight black tee-shirt and jeans, his enormous arms threatening to tear the small sleeves open.

"Hi again, Mister Hall," he said.

"Good to see you again, Jae."

Jae kissed Vanessa on the cheek. "How's my bride?"

"Missing you every minute I was away."

I turned to Drake. "So, this is what you meant by saying Jae was family?"

"Roger wouldn't let us date for a long time until I proved myself," Jae said.

"Daddy was a bit overprotective," Vanessa added.

"You'll understand someday," Drake said, "if, and when, you decide to give me a grandchild."

For lunch, we sat in the dining room adjacent to the kitchen. The table was piled with food. Catfish, steak, rice, steamed broccoli, and home-made bread. I ate more than I should have and had to loosen my belt.

I asked Jae and Vanessa what they did for work. Jae had left law enforcement and was in contract security and Vanessa worked for the department of education.

"How do you and my dad know one another?" Vanessa said. "Is it through his community work?"

"Brandon knows what I do," Drake said. "The community work Vanessa mentioned is real, but it's just a cover." Drake turned back to his daughter. "Brandon's the farmer I told you about. The one in southern Virginia who does private investigating work on the side. Twice his cases crossed my path—"

"And twice your dad saved my skin," I added.

Drake ignored my compliment and pointed to me with his fork. "This here man was the one I told you about who rescued that girl from that sicko in the Dismal Swamp."

Jae stopped eating. "That was you?"

"And your father-in-law," I added.

"No sir," Drake said. "That was all Brandon."

"You some freak savant or something?" Jae said. Vanessa smacked his muscular arm. "What? I'm serious. The media said that only a genius could have figured that case out."

I shook my head. "I'm as average IQ as the day is long. That discovery was a God thing."

"Amazing," Jae said.

I leaned back in my chair and wiped my mouth with a napkin. "So, Roger never told me what government department he worked for?"

Jae looked to Vanessa who looked to Claire.

Drake waved his hand in front of his face. "I told you I float a little here and there."

I shook my head and laughed. "You're so frustrating."

Claire put her hand on her husband's shoulder. "Don't I know that."

After lunch, we sat in the living room watching the Baltimore Orioles play the Red Sox for an hour until the senator texted me. Before leaving, I was given a Tupperware full of leftovers, and hugged by everyone including Jae who all but knocked the wind out of me. Driving away from my friend's house, the homesickness I'd felt was lessened ever so slightly.

When the senator got into the car I could tell something was wrong. He was flush and looked frail, like he'd aged.

I started driving. He mumbled something under his breath. I wasn't sure if it was meant for me or not.

"You say something, sir?"

"I'm done."

"What do you mean?"

He took out a handkerchief and wiped his eyes. "Someone emailed me an mpfour of my daughter walking from class back to her dorm today."

"Any other threats attached to it?"

"The video was the threat."

"That's not good," I said.

"Cuts me off at the knees, Brandon. I've got a thick skin and could handle almost anything that comes my way. My career could die, my wife could leave me, my houses burn down, my wealth disappear, but if anything happened to my baby girl, I'd die. Literally, I'd die."

"I understand. Are Capitol Police on this?"

"They say they are, as is FBI, but who knows? With the way the country is right now they're doing everything they can just to stay on top of the daily threats to congress. What do you think I should do?"

Without hesitation I said, "Pull Amber out of school."

"I can't. She'd never leave as she's got a week left before the summer break. But then what? Send her to some distant relative's house?"

My dad and Drake's warnings rang in my head. "No, we got to think worst-case scenario. If this is

Gaspar Schultz trying to tweak you, he has resources and a long reach and could find her in those places."

"Then what?"

"Send her to my house."

"I couldn't do that. Your home was already shot up once because of my son's case."

"Then let's bring her to your Clarksville estate. In the interim, I'll hire a security detail to walk her to and from class until she finishes."

"Who? You're the only one I trust right now."

"My friend's a Halifax County Sheriff. He's a stand-up guy if you don't mind me expensing his time."

"Spend whatever you see is fit to keep her safe." He exhaled as if my idea all but guaranteed his daughter's safety. "I'd like to go home and shower before dinner."

"No problem."

TWELVE

Two packages waited for me outside the door to the garden unit. Inside, I unwrapped the thin Kevlar vest I would ask the senator to wear along with a ballistic blanket I'd keep in the car. I felt a tinge of guilt purchasing this stuff, but the past few years flashed in my mind like a movie reel on fast forward. Shootouts, explosions, child abductions and crossing paths with a deadly globalist drove the point home.

Next, I called Tollers to ask his interest on side work.

"Always," he said. "What do you got? Something to do with the senator gig?"

"Yeah. It's a babysitting job. Senator's college daughter needs to be watched for the next few days as she finishes up finals. Someone sent the senator a video of her walking from class, so the threat is real. Once she finishes finals I need her escorted to the senator's Clarksville estate."

"I have tons of vacation and personal time accrued," Tollers said. "What does the job pay?"

"What do you need it to pay?"

"Am I watching her around the clock?"

"No. Just to-and-from classrooms for a few days, but you'll need to be close by. She lives in a secured dorm. I'd put you up in a hotel just off campus. However, once we get her to Clarksville it will be twenty-four/seven for a few more days at least."

Tollers exhaled. "I don't know. Is it going to cut into your job? I know you need the money."

"This is a separate job with separate pay."

"How about three fifty a day?"

I knew Tollers was low balling the number as he associated the job with me. "Five hundred it is," I said. "I'm sending an address and pic of the daughter along to you. She'll know you're coming. Can you get to UVA tomorrow?"

"Sure. I'll put in for the time off when we get off the phone. I can give you at least a week if not a few days more."

"I'll text you Amber's information shortly."

Dinner was at a fancy steak house. This particular night it was just the senator and me. The place was crowded, and I wasn't allowed to park my own car out back. The twenty-somethings around us were just starting out the night. I noticed the senator was not treated like royalty here like he was at other places. Dinner was Caesar salad followed by steak and potatoes. The senator's phone kept ringing and pinging from texts throughout the meal. He only took calls from Larry. Everything else he didn't answer. He mentioned nothing to Larry about the latest threat to his daughter.

EARLY THE NEXT morning I called Annie. She gave me a run down on farm stuff, as well as an update on the insurance claim. "First check should be here within a week," she said.

"Praise God," I said. "How's everything else?"

"Our backup freezer in the basement is acting up, so I put the meat in your parents' spare freezer."

"Girls?"

"They're good but we all miss you."

"That's why I'm calling. Why don't the three of you come up next Saturday and stay over? The apartment's small but Emily could sleep on the couch and you could bring the pack-n-play for Addison. We could spend an afternoon together and go out to lunch, but I'm at dinner with the senator. In the morning we could go to Drake's church and have lunch before you leave?"

"Sounds good to me."

I met the senator out front at the usual time, but we had no meetings or stops this morning so I dropped him off at the capitol office. After, I drove by the brownstone he'd had a meeting at the other day. I snapped a photo of the building and address and texted to Drake asking if he could give me a rundown on the owner. Within five minutes Drake texted back that it was a politically agnostic billionaire banker who donated to both parties. He said the banker was a scumbag but was no physical threat. Tollers texted me that he was already in place at Amber's school and all was good.

The senator got out of work early and I took him to a doctor's appointment for an annual checkup. Dinner was at another fancy steak house. Larry joined us with a couple speeches which the senator red-lined with his fountain pen. The steaks arrived and Larry excused himself for another appointment.

The senator placed a fancy embroidered napkin in his lap. "The doc made me promise to cut down on my red meat intake."

"I see you're not listening."

He took a sip of red wine and smiled. "Brandon, you're gonna learn that some things in life are worth dying for."

"Oh, your poor wife," I joked.

"Ha, poor me is more like it."

"If you don't mind my asking, why doesn't Missus Schilling ever join us?"

The senator finished chewing the first bite of his blood rare steak and wiped his mouth with the napkin. "She has her life and I have my life. It works for now."

My stomach turned as I was about to have a very

difficult conversation. "You know how much I appreciate this job."

"And I appreciate your loyalty."

"Yeah, it's about that loyalty thing. I gotta confess something regarding Missus Schilling and it's gonna sting."

He took another bite of steak and said, "My wife made a move on you, didn't she?"

My jaw almost fell onto the table. "Either she did, or I'm really stupid with how people in DC greet each other."

"What was the end result?"

"I said *no,* of course, and she got mad at me, but I feel like I needed to tell you." I let my head hang low like I had done something wrong.

The senator pondered the confession and wiped his mouth again. My mind raced as I had no idea if he believed me or not. I tried to learn from the Biblical story of Joseph but was terrified it was going to turn out with similar punishment.

The senator placed the napkin back down. "My wife and I have a somewhat unorthodox marriage. Like I said, she has her side hobbies as do I."

"So, you're aware of this stuff?"

"Sure," he said, seeming unfazed by my revelation and confession.

"And you believe me?"

"Of course, I do."

"So, you're not gonna fire me?"

"For what?" he laughed. "Turning down a good

looking hot-and-bothered rich elitist woman. It only proves your loyalty to me that much more. Heck, I should give you a raise."

I exhaled. "Thank you, Senator. I've never been put in a situation like this before."

"Did my marital revelation scar your image of us?"

"Well, that's not the way God intended marriage."

"Today's marriages have about fifty different shades of grey to them. At least that's what I'm told."

"We aren't gonna see eye to eye on this."

"I hope you don't look down your nose on us, Brandon?"

"When I look at your wife, I see a woman suffering at the loss of her son, not someone craving attention."

"Ah, I appreciate your sympathy," he said, pointing a fork-full of bloody steak at me, "but I give her less credit than you do. She's been like this since day one."

I had nothing else to say. It was a sad situation. I knew it, and the senator knew it.

Outside, the sidewalk was filled with young, sharp dressed, men and women. I placed a hand on the senator's shoulder so we wouldn't get separated. He reached up and patted my hand as if to say, *I'm good*. I took out the car slip to hand to the valet. Suddenly, several dull explosions silenced the crowd. I couldn't place the location, or if they were gunshots or not. People crouched down and a few shouted out of fear. I grabbed a tuft of the senator's suit jacket and half-dragged him back into the restaurant foyer.

Once inside I said, "You okay?"

He looked wide-eyed but nodded an affirmative. "What was that?"

"I think it was some punks setting off fireworks, but I'm not sure." I turned to the maître d' and gave him the slip for my car. "I'll get my own car."

"But sir, we don't allow people to pick up their own cars due to—"

"I'll get my own car thank you," I repeated, this time with a tone that clarified it was a statement, and not a question.

Outside, the pedestrians already walked back and forth like nothing had happened.

The maître d' handed me the key. "What's going on out there?"

"I think someone set off firecrackers," I said.

With key in hand, I ushered the senator through the restaurant towards the back door. I stepped out into the dimly-lit parking lot which was full of expensive cars and SUVs. A couple cooks on break smoked cigarettes by a dumpster. No cars seemed to be running, but I couldn't be sure as many of the new cars were whisper quiet. I motioned for the senator to come out, and walked him by the crook of his arm to the car. Once inside I realized there was only one way in and out of the parking lot. Had I rented an SUV, or had my truck, I could have driven over the curbing and mulched flower beds onto a back road.

Instead, I would be forced to drive out the bottle-neck driveway entrance.

"I think you're right," the senator said. "Those were firecrackers."

"The question is, were they set off deliberately?"

"What do you mean? To distract people?"

"Or to size up your security detail."

The senate grew sober. "Boy, I hope you're wrong."

"Me too."

I drove out the narrow alley towards the front of the restaurant. No pedestrians were near, so I tore off onto the street in front of a Ranger Rover whose driver proceeded to flash their high beams at me.

"I'd feel better if we went straight home," I said, shifting into third gear and slowing down. "I'll come in for a cup of coffee and hang out for a bit."

"You know what, Brandon. I'd like that."

I came to a stop at a red light but kept revving the engine. A dark minivan with tinted windows pulled up alongside us. The light turned green and the Audi's wheels chirped when I popped the clutch. The van stayed behind us for a mile or so. I stopped at another red light and the minivan pulled up behind. The front windshield of the minivan seemed to have a tint to it as well, but I could still make out two figures moving in the front seats.

The senator cleared his throat. "You know this reminds me—"

"Quiet, sir," I said.

I gunned it through the red light just as it turned green. The traffic was heavy, and I was forced to stop at another red light. The senator saw me looking in the rearview mirror and turned around.

"Eyes foreword, sir."

He whispered, "I'm starting to get nervous."

"Might be nothing," I said.

The minivan pulled up behind us again. The side door slid open quick as if someone had disabled the auto door mechanism. I popped the clutch and tore off through the red light narrowly missing another car t-boning us. I didn't know if the minivan was a threat but had to assume it when the door opened.

"What's happening?" the senator almost shouted.

"Sorry, that minivan was making me nervous."

In the rearview mirror the minivan also blew through the red light. I down shifted into third gear and ran a yellow light. "Hold on."

There was no way that van could keep up with the Audi on a straightaway, but the congestion of traffic slowed us down to a dangerous speed. I couldn't find a turn-off, or a lull in traffic in the opposite lane which would allow me to pass cars in front of me. The minivan was gaining on us. I checked my appendix holster. I had seven in the mag and one in the chamber with a spare magazine in my breast pocket. Sixteen shots total if needed. I turned down a side street and onto a larger two-lane road. The minivan turned down the road as well.

"This ain't good," I said.

"What are we going to do?"

"Now's a good time as any to start praying, sir." In the rearview mirror I saw the barrel of a rifle stick out from the side door to the van. "Get down," I shouted. "And pull that blanket up over you."

"What?"

"The blanket on the floor. It's ballistic." The senator did as he was told as I turned onto another main road, this street was less congested and a two lane. We were getting closer to the highway. I approached a yellow light and sped through, taking the Audi into the red.

The senator's muffled voice came from under the blanket. "What's happening?"

"We're being chased and, unless I'm losing my mind, I saw what looked like the barrel of a rifle sticking out from that van."

Up ahead there was a traffic jam. I slowed down looking for an alternative route. That's when the loud crack of the rifle exploded through the car. No glass shattered but I heard the senator shout. The cabin filled with the smell of gunpowder and something burning.

"Are you okay?" I said, unable to turn around.

"I think so," came the senator's voice. "Get us out of here, Brandon."

"Doing my best, sir."

I turned down a narrow side street with the minivan close behind. Up ahead was the ramp leading to the highway.

"Thank you, Lord."

I pulled onto the highway and weaved in and out of traffic doing ninety plus miles per hour. High beams were flashed as well as middle fingers. Within minutes the van was nowhere in sight behind us. Still, I didn't slow down.

"You can get up now," I said.

The senator sat up stretching. His perfect hair was a mess. Through the rearview mirror I could see him feeling his side.

"What's wrong?"

He turned around and looked at the back seat-rest. "The bullet came through the trunk, back seat, and nicked off my fanny and lodged in the passenger seat. I'm sore, but fine thanks to your smart blanket. What is it?"

"Kevlar," I said.

"I'm gonna start calling you Linus," I said. "A boy and his blankie."

"Call me whatever you want," he said. "That was some fast thinking, Brandon. Well done."

"There's a vest on the floor as well that I'd like you to put on. It's thin enough to wear under your dress shirts too. You do realize that we ran a bunch of red lights and are gonna get a lot of tickets from street cameras."

The senator waved his hand. "I'll take care of everything."

"I'm mad at myself that I got distracted. They shouldn't have been able to get as close as they did."

"You did fine," the senator said. "What's the plan?"

"I'm getting you out of the city."

"Where do you want to go?"

"I gotta get you someplace where I can control the situation. I think we fall back to your estate in Clarksville and regroup."

"Will we be safe?"

"I'm gonna hire my own security. People I trust."

"Make sure you pay them well."

I dialed Colt who picked up on the first ring. "You still looking for side gigs?"

"Always."

"You got a PayPal account?"

After I got off the phone with Colt, I said, "I want you to call Missus Schilling and tell her not to leave the house until she can be escorted out to Clarksville."

The senator huffed. "That woman would make a hit man shoot himself in the head."

I shifted lanes and slowed down further. "You two need some couple's therapy, sir."

"Nothing a bottle of Jack and a twelve gauge can't fix," he mumbled.

"Senator!"

"Sorry." He laughed. "I'm a bit jacked up from what just happened."

I called Tollers on speakerphone, who picked up on the first ring. "We just had an attempt on the senator's life," I said. "I need you to pull the girl now."

"Roger that. Where to?"

"Take her back to your place and wait to hear from me okay? Make sure you're not followed."

"She's a stubborn nut," Tollers said.

The senator chuckled from the back seat. "Just like her mother. I'll text her. She'll listen to me."

I got off and on the highway about a dozen times. Once in Richmond I stopped to top off the gas tank, get a cup of coffee, and the senator a bottle of water. I popped the trunk and sure enough the bullet passed through the tailgate, through the back seat just nicking the senator, who was under the ballistic blanket, before lodging in the front passenger seat. Next, I crawled under the car with my penlight and found small magnetic black cube near the rear bumper. Clearly a GPS device. Instead of breaking it, I re-mounted it under a police cruiser two cars down from us.

Back in the car the senator said, "I wonder if I should call anyone? Capitol Police, or FBI, or—"

"Not yet," I said. "Call Larry and have him cancel all your appointments. You're going to miss work until the hearing."

"But the hearing's still a week away," he said.

"You can telecommute for a few days."

"You're the boss."

I called the number on the card that Bridget had given me for the dealership. She picked up on the first ring. "Sorry, to bother you this late, but I need a favor."

"Something wrong with the leased vehicle, Mister Hall?"

"I need to ditch this car in Southern Virginia. Can I text you an address for it to be picked up?"

"No problem. We've accommodated far stranger requests than that."

"Okay, but just know it has some damage to it."

"You paid for insurance so it will be covered."

"I hope it includes bullet holes." She gasped, but showed tremendous restraint not asking for details. "I'll text you the address to pick up the car."

Two and a half hours later I pulled into our farm. Annie came out to greet me with a huge smile. "What a nice surprise," she said, giving me a long kiss. I had almost forgotten how good her lips tasted. She looked impressed with my suit, which turned to confusion when she saw the senator standing behind me in a Kevlar vest. "What are you guys doing here?"

The senator came over and gave Annie a hug. "Ask your husband."

I pointed to the senator. "Someone tried to uhm chase us down in Alexandria. We're swapping cars and going to his Clarksville estate. We'll be out there for a while."

"Wait," Annie said. "What do you mean chase you down?"

"Someone tried to assassinate me, and your husband saved my butt," the senator added. He touched his left hip and winced. "Literally, he saved my butt."

I gave Annie a watered-down version of what happened including the chase and mentioned a bullet being fired, but didn't tell her it came in the car. She pressed me for more details. I told her not to worry, which only irritated her further. I went inside and checked on Emily and Addison who were both asleep. I kissed each of them and fixed their blankets. Things were getting serious and I prayed for God's continued protection over my family.

THIRTEEN

Downstairs in my bedroom I stripped off the suit and put on my worn jeans, a soft button-down shirt, and my cowboy boots. It felt good to be wearing something familiar and comfortable. Like Batman wearing on an old cape and cowl, this was my go-to outfit for both farming and PI work. Inside the closet I took out my AR-15 along with four spare mags. Before I closed the lid, I took Annie's Smith and Wesson .380. When I walked back outside both the senator and Annie's eyes widened.

"How serious is this?" Annie said.

"No idea," I said, handing her the .380. "Carry this with you for now."

I loaded the AR into the back seat of Hazel and handed the Audi keys to Annie. "The leasing company is sending down drivers to pick up this car in the morning."

"I'm glad you'll be close by," Annie said. "I'll be praying for you both."

I kissed her more than once. "I love you forever," I said, motioning the senator into the truck

As we left the driveway, I said a selfish prayer that God would allow me to see my wife and children again. With the glass packed muffler, my truck was louder than the Audi. It rode heavier, but I felt more at home. With the Audi, I had gone the route of speed and it served me well, but I now wanted protection, and strength.

The senator sat next to me and seemed to enjoy the rough ride of the old truck. "I'm jealous of what you have," he said.

"My truck?" I said, knowing he meant Annie. "She's a Nineteen seventy-six F two-fifty."

"No, your marriage, dummy."

"Money may be tight, but I feel like the richest man in the world."

"I hope to find that one day."

Maybe it was the near-death experience or the adrenaline, but I felt no hesitation to share the truth with him. "God can fix what's broken in your marriage. I've seen it done before."

The senator nodded and went quiet at the mention of God. For the next twenty minutes the senator was on his phone with Larry talking business. He avoided questions about his whereabouts and told Larry he was offsite for a couple days taking care of personal business. Larry tried to pressure him into coming back into the city to address certain critical meetings, but the senator stood his ground.

After he got off the phone, I called Drake and explained what had happened while on speakerphone. "Once we're at his estate in Clarkesville, should I notify the Metro Police, FBI, or Capitol Police?"

"I have a handful of patriots in the Bureau I can reach out to who will handle this and keep it quiet."

"Thanks."

"It's becoming a full-time job to watch your six."

"Love you, my brother."

"Love you too," Drake said. "Be safe."

When I got off the phone the senator said, "Who were you talking to?"

"Buddy of mine in government?"

"Bureau?"

"No?"

"CIA?"

I winced. "He uhm never told me what department he works for."

"And you trust him?"

"With my life on several occasions. He's on top of this and will contact the right people and try to keep it out of the news."

"Ironic," the senator said. "Were I running for re-election I'd want this all over the news. Talk about great PR."

"How your brain works is amazing," I said.

"Thank you."

"I didn't mean it as a compliment, sir."

Fifteen minutes later we pulled up to the senator's Clarksville estate. Blocking the main entrance was a dirty fifth-wheel RV. Wes Burnell was outside directing the driver who was in an old F350 dually. Wes had on jean overalls with no shirt. His hairy shoulders poked through the shoulder straps like a heavy woolen sweater.

"Hold up, Colt, or you're gonna rip the iron gate off its hinges," Wes shouted to the driver of the truck.

The senator spoke into his phone. "Larry, let me call you back." He hung up and leaned over. "What's this circus?"

"This circus would be your security detail," I said, slouching down in the driver's seat a bit.

"I hope you know what you're doing," he said stepping out of the truck.

"Me too," I said, shutting off my truck.

I walked by Wes. "Thanks for coming right over."

"No problem, Brandon."

I approached the driver's side window of the truck to find Colt. Unlike his bare-chested brother he had the decency to wear a tee-shirt under his jean overalls. "Evening, Colt."

"What's going on, Brandon?"

"Uhm, this your mobile headquarters, I take it?"

"Huh? Yeah. If we're gonna be here for any length of time I want us stationed by the gate." He inched the truck forward.

Wes shouted from the back. "Cut the engine. You're tearing up the lawn."

The senator stood next to me and dropped his head. "I'm gonna head inside. It's been a long day."

"I'll take care of this, Senator."

"Senator?" Colt said, shutting the truck off and stepping out. "Do you remember me, sir?"

"It's been a crazy week son, so if you—" the senator paused and squinted like he had just recognized a long lost relative. "Your name's Magnum right?"

"Colt."

"Sorry," he chuckled. "I knew it was a firearm of some sort. You, and your brothers were my son's pit crew, weren't you?"

"Yes, sir. Horrific what happened to your son. Drew was like family."

The senator shook Colt's hand. "Well, any friend of Drew's is welcome here." The senator seemed reinvigorated with the presence of his late son's friends. "What's the plan?"

"We're going to stay here until the last minute of the hearings," I said. "Colt and his brothers are your pit crew now and will guard this place like Fort Knox. Twenty-four hours before the hearing we'll head back into DC with the Burnell brothers as our entourage."

The senator belly laughed. "I can't wait to see those elites in DC when I pull up with this motley crew."

"We ain't pretty," Colt said, "but we'll keep you safe."

"I'm sure you will, son."

"Colt, I want twenty-four-seven eyes on the gate." I pointed to the tall brick fence line. "Any other entrances, Senator?"

"One more gate down below near the garage, but I'll secure it."

The senator left, and I helped direct Colt as he drove the RV onto a portion of the meticulous lawn. We unhitched the truck from the trailer and Wes parked it around behind the house.

A short while later, Mrs. Schilling pulled up in her Mercedes SUV and lowered the window. "I'm here per your orders, Brandon."

"I told the senator to have you wait until we could get you escorted out here?"

She waved her hand like I was being dramatic. "No need. I'm here and I'm safe?"

"That's not the only reason I wanted you escorted," I said. "Do you know if you were followed?"

Mrs. Schilling looked away like I had caught her doing something wrong. "What's going on here?" she said, pointing to the tiny home.

"Security?"

"Looks more like a barnyard hoedown."

I waved her inside the gate, but she didn't move the vehicle. "How long do I need to be here, Brandon? This is really disruptive."

"For a few days to start," I said.

"I was perfectly safe at our place in Alexandria?"

"I have a bullet hole in my rental car that says otherwise."

Her eyes widened. "Where's Greg?"

"Inside," I said, motioning her towards the house. "Please just park your car and get inside the house, Missus Schilling."

After she drove onto the property, I shut the wrought iron gate. Colt chained and locked it shut. Colt went into the RV, brought out a long rope running through about a dozen six-inch pieces of garden hose. Nails had been driven through the small hose sections.

"Caltrops," he said, laying the tire puncturing line of nails across the driveway just inside the gate. "In case someone tries to break through the gate."

"Colt, you're genius," I said.

When Wess returned, I said, "You guys need anything else from me?"

"No sir," Wes said. "Moss an' Wyn are on their way and we'll set up a rotation."

"Run everyone by me who wants access to the property. Including anyone claiming to be employees or law enforcement." Before heading up to the house I made the mistake of asking what they brought for protection.

"Two Mossberg twelve gauges along with a Remington," Colt said. After a pause he added. "A thirty-thirty lever action, two Glock seventeens, and a Smith and Wesson AR-fifteen." He paused counting his fingers as if to make sure he tallied everything correctly. He turned to his younger brother. "I miss anything?"

Wess added, "Don't forget the Mosin-Nagant."

Colt snapped his fingers. "And did you bring the Smith and Wesson Governor?"

"Yup. That reminds me, I think we also have the Ruger single action somewhere too."

"The forty-five colt or three fifty-seven?"

"Three fifty-seven," he said.

Colt turned to face me with a concerned look on his face. "What do you think?"

"I think you're good."

I left the Burnell brothers at the gate and drove Hazel around back and did a quick perimeter walk of the home. External lights lit up the property like a summer midday. The perimeter fence was a thick brick wall at least ten feet high which was ideal. I emailed my tech friend JT for some additional advice.

He called less than a minute later. "How you holding up, brotha," he spoke in his northern Massachusetts accent.

"I'm good. You didn't have to call me right back. You could have just waited until morning.

"Nonsense. What's going on with the farm?"

"The farm loss is gonna be covered by insurance."

"Praise God."

"In the interim, I've taken a contract job and could use some of your help."

"Name it."

"I just escaped a potential hit on my client and I'm at his Clarksville estate. I got it physically locked down, but I'd like to get it locked down virtually as well. Anyway you can do this with the internet and cell signals coming out of this place?"

"I can put some firewalls on the place to make email hard to trace back there, but cell stuff is government level and above. Call me tomorrow as I'll need passwords and such to set it up."

"Thanks, JT."

It was around midnight by the time I went inside the home. I wandered up to the second floor to claim a guest bedroom with a full bath and crawled into the shower. I sat in the base of a clawfoot tub as hot water poured over me from the shower head. Slowly, the muscles in my shoulders eased moving down my back. After fifteen minutes in the shower I entered back into the bedroom in a towel to find Mrs. Schilling on my bed looking at her cell phone in one hand and holding a glass of white wine with the other.

She saw me and put the phone down. "You take long showers."

"I'm exhausted," I said, holding onto the towel tight around my waist like it was a shield against this spiritual attack.

"The question is, are you completely out of energy?" she said, getting up to walk towards me. "You look like a scared animal, but don't worry, I don't bite unless asked."

I reached back into the bathroom and grabbed my phone from the sink, hit the video button, and began video-taping her. "I'm gonna keep this rolling until you leave me alone, Missus Schilling."

She didn't seem intimidated by the camera, but emboldened. "We're not on the same page, Brandon."

"No, we're not," I said.

"You don't want me as an enemy, Mister Hall."

I repeated back to her. "I don't want you as an enemy, Missus Schilling. However, I want my wife to know that I take fidelity seriously." She upended her glass of wine and walked towards the door. Before she left, I said, "When my job's done, I'll delete this. Until then let me protect your husband."

"Good luck with that," she said.

Maybe it was the alcohol talking, but I thought her response was an odd thing to say? I emailed the video to Annie just to cover my marriage bases and went back into the bathroom to get changed. A few minutes later I went downstairs to confirm all the doors and windows were locked before going to bed. Mrs. Schilling was in the library with the lights off facing a lit fire. In her hand was another glass of wine. I ignored her as I checked the latches on the room's windows.

Before I left the room, she said, "By the way, Greg's not here?"

"What do you mean he's not here?"

In the flickering firelight I could see her bright white smile. "If you walk down the clamshell path it leads to a garage where we keep an antique car. He took it and snuck out the back gate."

"To go where?" I nearly shouted.

"Where do you think? His assistant followed him down here like a puppy in heat. They're probably heading to some offsite rendezvous."

"I'm gonna kill him," I said.

I could hear her cackle as I rushed out of the room. She literally ended up with the last laugh. Sleep was going to have to wait.

I jumped in my truck and drove down the back clamshell pathway mad at myself for not checking the entire property before going inside. I had let my exhaustion get the better of me. Sure enough, the old brick garage had a wooden door raised. Inside was an antique BMW motorcycle and a space where a car had been parked. Next to the garage was a wide-open wrought iron gate. I drove out of the property and called Colt on his cell asking him to secure the back gate. The senator's cell phone went straight to voicemail.

I drove into downtown Clarkesville. The entire road was empty. Even some of the streetlights were out. It was strange to think that in just a few hours the stores would be open and busy with customers, but at this moment it felt like the setting for a post-apocalyptic movie where the population had been wiped out. In the distance I picked up a 1930s model

A Ford putting down the hill towards the Tisdale Bridge.

"Where does he think he's going?" I said to myself.

A fog covered the surface of Bugg's Island Lake and the lights along the mile-long Tisdale bridge. It looked like I left one world and entered another just like George Bailey on his bridge in It's a Wonderful Life. It seemed like we were the only two vehicles on the planet. One from the 1930s, and one from the 1970s. Both out of place in the modern world with its high-tech smart cars.

A quarter of the way over the bridge I pulled up in front of the old Ford and slowed down until Senator Schilling pulled over and stopped. I shut the truck down and rushed to the driver's window of the vehicle. Inside, a young thirty-something blonde with a jacked up skirt sat in the driver's seat. Senator Schilling texted on his phone in the passenger's seat.

"What are you doing?"

The senator pointed to the woman. "Jane, this is Brandon."

"Hi, Brandon," she said, sticking a hand out the window as if to shake. "Nice to finally meet you."

I raised both my hands to the sky. "Am I the only sane person here, or am I missing something?"

"My assistant and I are going offsite."

"Seriously? After what we just went through?"

"I'm shaken up a bit," the senator said, "and need to get away from everything for the night."

"You're being ridiculous," I said, trying to control

my frustration. "I can't protect you when you're acting like a horny little teenage boy."

The senator hung his head. "Am I gonna be punished, Dad?"

Jane giggled at her boyfriend's joke.

"This isn't funny," I said. "Now turn this car around and head back to your estate."

As I walked back towards my truck the breeze picked up. Over the sound of the wind and lake water splashing against the bridge I heard another humming noise that seemed out of place. It reminded me of the sound of a drone. With the fog, I couldn't see more than a few feet around me. As much as I loved the open air and nature, this was the first time in my life I couldn't wait to get back indoors.

Jane drove the antique car back into downtown Clarkesville and stopped in front of a darkened coffee shop. She got out and walked around to the passenger's side to kiss the senator goodbye before getting into a black SUV and driving off.

The senator drove the old Ford back up to the main entrance of the home where Wes let him in. I trailed the senator around the house and back to the lower garage where he returned the antique vehicle to its proper place. The senator got in my truck without a word and we drove back up to the estate. After I shut the truck off he slammed the truck door and stormed off into the house like a teenage boy who just had his car taken away.

Colt approached. "What happened?"

"High school drama is what happened," I said, walking towards the house. I could barely keep my eyes open. "I gotta get some sleep. Call me if there's an emergency, okay." Just as I reached the front door something told me to turn around. Colt had not moved from the side of the truck.

"What's wrong?"

"Uhm, she's gone," Colt said.

"Who?"

"Senator's wife."

"What? Where'd she go?"

"I don't know. A car pulled up out front of the gate. We didn't let them in, but she walked past me and got into it. Said something about someone picking her car up tomorrow."

"Did you try to stop her?"

"Yeah, but she's, uhm, intimidating."

"That she is." I took a deep breath.

"What do you want to do, boss?"

"Don't sweat it," I said. "Our job is to protect the senator."

Inside, I checked the first floor again and knocked on the bedroom door of the master suite upstairs. "I'm just down the hall, Senator." I heard a toilet flush and movement and didn't wait for an answer. I went into the guest room and crawled into my bed. The last thoughts I had before sleep took me were joyful images of pastures, cattle, green tractors.

FOURTEEN

IT WAS EIGHT A.M. WHEN I WOKE THE NEXT MORNING. I couldn't remember the last time I'd slept in this late. I had no voicemails, a few spam emails, and an email response from Annie about the video I had sent. She replied, *are you okay?* I emailed back that all was fine, and I wanted her to know how important transparency was with this sort of thing, and to keep praying for Mrs. Schilling. Colt emailed me a run down from the night. He and Wyn had pulled the dead man's shift and reported nothing out of the ordinary before trading places with their brothers and going to bed.

Downstairs in the caterer's kitchen I found a jar of instant coffee and a box of cereal. I sat on the front porch in a wicker rocking chair, reading from the Bible app on my cell phone. I wondered what the King James translators from the 1600s would have thought about their version of the Bible showing up on a cell phone in the twenty-first century. I continued my reading from The Book of Exodus. At this point the Israelites had been supernaturally delivered from Pharaoh. They had witnessed numerous miracles yet were already worshipping a golden calf while Moses received the Ten Commandments on Mount Sinai. It amazed me how short memories we humans had.

Ten minutes later a blacked-out SUV pulled up in front of the front gate. Moss and Wes each pulled out a different firearm.

I sprinted off the porch running down the driveway. "Hold up guys," I shouted.

I reached the end of the driveway, panting. Wes unlocked the gate so I could walk out to the vehicle. I approached the vehicle with my hand under my shirt resting on my gun. I couldn't see who was inside as the windshield was tinted just like the minivan who shot at us. The SUV shut off and the door opened. I held up my hand for the person to stay in their car, my gun now out. They ignored me and a moment later Jae stepped out. He was dressed in cargo pants and a tight black tee-shirt. He wore sunglasses and looked like an action movie star.

"What are you doing here?" I said, putting the gun away under my shirt.

"I work with Drake," he said, taking out a large duffle bag.

"I should have guessed," I said.

"He wants me to help you out a bit."

"Help?"

"Survey the layout and make sure his friend stays safe."

"Drake's okay with nepotism in government?" I joked.

"My father-in-law holds fidelity above anything. In his current role he has carte blanc to use whoever he wants for his group."

"And his group reports to which department?"

Jae smiled and walked past me into the driveway. The Burnell brothers lowered their firearms.

As Jae walked past them, he said to Wess, "Your safety's on, son." He continued and pointed to Moss. "You should clean that Glock before you end up with a misfire."

The Burnells both looked at their guns. "Dang it, Wess, you weenie, he's right."

I trotted to catch up with Jae. "Why's Drake always looking out for me?"

"He likes you for some reason."

"Come on. No one's that nice."

Jae stopped. "Off the record?"

"Of course."

"I suspect he's trying to recruit you."

"For what?"

"Our group."

"Why?"

"Like I said, loyalty doesn't exist in DC. He doesn't trust anyone."

"And your group's name is?"

Jae smiled. "So, where's the center of the property located?"

"You're not gonna answer me, are you?" Jae didn't answer but continued to scan the property. I said, "Over there near the front entrance to the house."

Jae walked over to the spot I pointed to and lowered the duffle bag to the ground. He removed what appeared to be a small metal rocket ship about three feet high. I recognized the multiple battery packs but was curious why they had antennae on them. He unfolded two 100-watt solar panels. For the next few minutes, I watched him assembled the items.

"Go ahead," Jae said.

"What?"

"Ask what the heck I'm doing."

"Uhm, what the heck are you doing?"

"Drone UAV jammer."

"Seriously, the government has that technology?"

"Oh yeah," Jae said, attaching wires to the solar panel. He angled the panel towards the rising sun. "Don't let those hillbillies at the front gate mess with this gear, okay?"

"Okay."

"Gaspar Schultz uses cutting edge technology, including drone technology. If he's the one after the senator, then he could try to snoop around here."

"You know my dad thinks our farm was poisoned by drone. My old man has kind of a tin foil hat to him but—"

"Roger does too."

"Really. He never said anything to me. Why?"

"No idea, but if anyone will find out he will." Jae stood up wiping dirt off his pants. "Okay, care to give me the tour of the property?"

We walked around the interior of the brick-walled perimeter. Jae seemed to take in every detail of the grounds.

"Drake's almost too good to be true," I said. "I fear the day I find a chink in his armor."

Jae continued to scan the property. "Roger's not Christ. Perfection's not attainable this side of Heaven, but he is the real deal. I grew up without a dad, and Roger took me under his wing when I was a teenager at the community center. He encouraged me to enter into the police academy and guided me in my career." Jae stopped to inspect a portion of the brick wall that had crumpled. He looked a few fragments of brick on the ground as if to make sure the disturbance wasn't recent, or man-made. We continued walking and Jae continued. "Roger has been a role model for me. After my shootout—"

"The one you talked about in your sermon at church?"

"Yeah. After that, Roger help get me into government work, eventually recruiting me for his team." Jae smiled, "And he eventually let me date his daughter, but only after he saw me put my life on the line. I think he saw something in me that I didn't see. Some potential and was recruiting me from way back in my teen years."

"Or maybe he was recruiting you to be his son-in-law and the job was an added bonus."

Jae chuckled. "Maybe so. Bottom line is, I'd follow that man to storm the gates of hell."

Down at the lower garage I unlocked the wrought iron gate so we could walk the outside perimeter of the property.

Jae pointed to a magnolia tree that extended over the brick wall. "That's an easy access point there."

"I'll make sure it's pruned back."

We made our way around to the front entrance of the property passing by the Burnell brothers again. Both looked impressed when Jae walked by this second time.

"Mind if I walk the interior of the first floor of the home?" Jae said.

"Of course not."

For the next ten minutes Jae checked windows and doors along the first floor. He tightened a few latches, and closed shades.

Back outside, he said, "Make sure you keep an eye on housekeepers and grounds crew. If anyone calls out sick, then you flag them. Any substitutes show up, you don't let them on the property."

"Roger that."

Moss Burnell called my cell. "What's up, Moss?"

"Got a guy at the gate claiming he works for the senator."

"He got a name?"

"Larry something."

"Floppy blond hair? Angry?"

"That's the guy."

"I'll be there in a minute."

I walked Jae out to his parked SUV. Behind the SUV I could see Larry in a silver BMW on his phone.

I shook Jae's hand. "Thank you, and please pass my thanks along to our mutual friend."

"Will do," Jae said. Larry beeped his horn and both Jae and I ignored him.

Jae got in the SUV and started to back up. I could see Larry throw his phone aside and back up before being hit. Once Larry was out of the way, Jae tore past him in reverse. Once clear, he pulled a one-eighty spin dropping the SUV into drive and pulling away without so much as a moment of the vehicle stopping.

Larry pulled up, his window now down. "Who was that guy, Hall?"

"Wrong address."

With phone in hand he pointed towards Wes and Moss Burnell in their jean overalls. "Who are these jokers?"

"Security."

"You're an idiot," he said, placing the phone back to his ear and driving onto the property spraying dirt and gravel at both Wes and Wyn. Part of me wanted to jog up to the front entrance and pound Larry the moment he stepped out of his fancy car. Both Burnell brothers seemed upset. I didn't mind being treated like a second-class citizen, but the Burnells did nothing to deserve this.

I took a breath and said a prayer out loud as I walked past my bearded friends. "Lord, please give me patience with Larry because if you give me strength, I'm gonna need bail money to go with it."

The Burnell brother's frustration turned to laughter and, in turn, my eagerness to inflict harm on the senator's chief of staff abated.

A moment later my phone rang. "Brandon Hall speaking."

"Mister Hall, this is Jane, the senator's assistant."

"What can I do for you, Jane?"

"I can't get a hold of Senator Schilling."

"He's still asleep. We all had a late night last night if you don't remember."

"Yes, I remember, but he always calls me every morning."

"So, how's that my problem," I said, with the frustration of a parent being drawn into a high school breakup.

"Mister Hall, I know you don't approve of our unorthodox relationship, but I know him a little better than you do."

"I'm confident both you, and his wife, know him better than I do."

She huffed on the other end of the phone at the mention of her boyfriend's spouse. "Greg told me about you being a Christian. You Bible thumpers think you're all high and mighty, but some of us less enlightened people are struggling to get through this thing called life."

I took a breath and realized this was an opportunity to witness to a non-believer that was slipping away from me. "I'm sorry, Jane. I've seen these scenarios play out before, even in a church setting. It's never a good ending. Again, I apologize." There was a pause on the other end of the phone. "Are you there?"

"Sorry, I've just had a tough past with Christians acting all holier than though with me."

"Someone recently once told me perfection won't be attained this side of Heaven. We Christians also fall short on a daily basis and need Jesus."

She started to cry. "I don't know if you knew, but Drew and I had a relationship at one point, and the senator and I found each other in our mutual mourning after his death. It's just so hard and—"

"I'm walking up to the house now, Jane. Why don't I go check on him?"

Larry came out of the house looking frustrated. I placed my hand over the phone. "What's wrong?"

"You know where the senator is?" he said.

"He should be sleeping upstairs?"

"Door's locked and I pounded on it for five minutes."

I could hear Jane saying something on the phone. "Jane, let me call you back," I said, placing the phone in my back pocket.

A boom exploded throughout the property. Both Larry and I crouched down. It was clearly a gunshot, but unlike anything I had ever heard before. Down the end of the driveway Wes and Moss Burnell produced guns. I motioned for them to stay put. Larry was the first to place the sound within the house and took off.

"Larry, wait—" I said, taking out my gun and running after him.

Larry burst through the front door and ran up the stairs three at a time. I struggled to catch up and continued to call after him to wait. On the second floor, Larry sprinted down the hallway and kicked open the master bedroom door. The wood door splintered and swung open. Larry entered the room and screamed like he was on fire. I rushed inside sweeping the room with my gun only to find the senator slumped over a small antique desk near his bed. Larry stood next to him screaming obscenities. The room reeked of gunpowder and was full of smoke. I checked the closet and master bath to confirm they were clear before approaching the senator. Blood ran out from a wound in the side of his head, spilling over the desk onto the bright white carpet below.

Larry fell to his knees beneath the senator, wailing, "Oh no, no, no." He tried to cup the dripping blood off the table as if he could save it and replace it back into the senator's body.

In the senator's hand was an old civil war cap and ball black-powder pistol.

Larry stood up hyperventilating now with cupped hands full of blood. He nudged the senator's body with his elbow. "Get up, sir. We have work to do. You gotta get up."

I put my gun away and checked the senator's pulse to confirm he'd expired. I was in full crisis mode but knew the image of my dead friend would come back to disturb me at a later date.

Larry jumped up and down, blood splashing out from his hands. "Brandon, call nine-one-one. We gotta get him to a hospital."

"He's gone, Larry."

The senator's chief of staff opened his palms letting the blood splash onto the white carpet. He wiped his hands through his blond hair and all over his suit. Larry fell onto the senator's bed, continuing to cry. Colt burst into the bedroom with an AR-15, dressed in pajama bottoms. He lowered the gun when he saw the scene.

He pointed to the dead senator. "What's the call, boss?"

"Call your brothers and tell them everything's secure and to stay at the gate for now."

After he got off the phone, Colt said, "Who do we call about this? Nine-one-one or Capitol Police?"

"Let me think for a second," I said, trying not to look at the senator's head wound. "Take Larry out and get him cleaned up in one of the guest bathrooms."

Colt shouldered the AR and helped Larry up who hung onto Colt as if he could not stand on his own. I could hear Larry's wailing continue as they walked down the hallway.

I dialed the one person who could guide me through this mess. Drake picked up on the second ring. "Brandon let me call you back in a minute-"

"Schilling's dead," I blurted, starting to break down myself.

"What?"

"Shot himself in the head moments ago."

"Are you okay?"

"I'm fine," I said. "I'm just shaken up a bit."

"I'm just glad you're safe," he said. "Are you sure it was suicide and not foul play?"

"Door was locked from the inside," I said, walking over to the windows. "Windows are locked, and he's got a pistol in his hand."

"It's okay, Brandon. We'll get through this. Send me a picture of the scene."

I snapped a photo of the gruesome scene. Under the senator's right hand was the cap and ball revolver. Under that was a closed laptop with a piece of paper on top of it splattered with blood and chunks of brain matter. The senator's fountain pen rested next to it with red ink bubbling around the tip. I read the paper without touching it, "he sacrificed my only son to Gehenna."

"What did you just say?" Drake shouted.

"There's a note that reads, he sacrificed my only son to Gehenna."

"Anything else?"

"No. There's a closed laptop under the note."

"Okay this is what I want you to do. I'm sending Jae back there, and will quarterback getting the proper authorities onsite. Jae told me you have friends guarding the entrance. Make sure they don't let anyone in unless Jae okays it?"

"Understood."

"Now I need you to do one more thing. It's gonna be tough but I need you to remove the note and the laptop." I didn't respond. "Are you okay, Brandon?"

"Okay just give me a second."

"Take your time. I know this is traumatic."

I went to move the senator's hand that held the pistol but stopped. "This a crime scene," I said, trying to keep from vomiting at the grotesque site. "Don't we leave it for the proper authorities?"

Drake spoke slow, like he was trying to rationalize with a person about to jump off a bridge. "Brandon, there's only a couple of us in my new group. We call ourselves SOL."

"SOL?"

"Sons of Liberty," Drake said. "It's in homage to the Founding Fathers. I liaise with DHS, FBI, NSA, CIA, and ATF but report directly to Vice President Prince. Whenever I'm onsite, I'm in charge." Drake said this with zero arrogance. "The senator's note is a federal issue that could involve Homeland Security. I have the authority to allow you to take the note and his laptop, son."

"But what does Gehenna—"

"I'll explain everything when I see you. For now, I need you to gather those items. Find his cell phone and take it as well. Then I want you to gather your things and inform your friends that when Jae gets back there he's gonna take point on this and to do what he says."

"Yes, sir," I said.

"It's gonna be okay, son. Take the laptop, power cord, the senator's note, and try to find his cell phone then go straight home."

"Then what?"

"I'll meet you there."

FIFTEEN

I KNELT IN THE POOL OF BLOOD AND MOVED THE senator's revolver aside with a piece of toilet paper from the bathroom so I could access the note and laptop. Next to the bed on a nightstand was his cell phone and charger which I also took. Before exiting the room, I said a silent prayer for the senator's soul, a prayer for his wife, and one for his daughter. Colt was in the bathroom of the guest room I had slept in the night before. The burly man crouched down with his AR slung over his back, rubbing Larry's back as he vomited into the toilet. He seemed sympathetic for the young ivy league lawyer. I collected my things and motioned for Colt to step from the bathroom into the bedroom.

"I'm leaving," I whispered.

"You're what?"

"The muscular guy your brothers met earlier is on his way back. He's from the government and is gonna quarterback this and need your help to control traffic once word gets out to the media." My phone rang. It was Moss. I motioned for Colt to go back into the bathroom to deal with Larry. I answered the phone. "Moss, is the guy in the SUV back?"

"Yeah?"

"Let him in."

"Okay, Brandon. What's going on?"

"I'll explain in a minute."

Jae was already breaking down the UAV equipment when I went outside. "Drake called and brought me up to speed. I'm staying here until he tells me otherwise. Were there any witnesses?"

"No. The senator's chief of staff was first in the room. He's shaken up pretty bad."

"Where's he at?"

"Inside."

Jae finished loading the duffle bag and motioned for me to follow him over to the SUV. He popped the trunk and placed the bag in the back. Inside the trunk, where a third row of seats would have been, was what looked like a modified lab. On the left, in a locked cage, was an M27 rifle as well as H&K semi auto handgun with multiple spare mags. Next to the duffle bag were several laptops, and to the right were small black MOLLE bags I assumed were first aid kits and communications gear. Jae closed the trunk with a heavy thud, which told me the vehicle was armor plated as well.

"Roger's on his way to meet you at your place," Jae said. "You should hurry."

"Hurry? It's gonna take him at least four or five hours to get there from DC?"

Jae removed black latex gloves a coroner would use. "Roger's coming in by chopper to your farm. He'll be there in an hour."

"Why the urgency?"

"He'll explain when he gets to your place."

I loaded all my bags back into my truck and walked Jae inside. Colt was in the kitchen, making Larry a cup of tea. I motioned with my hands that I would call him. Jae and I shook hands and he went upstairs to the senator's bedroom. I didn't envy him and was happy to leave the property, and never wanted to return. At the gate I debriefed Wes, Wyn, and Moss on what transpired. They didn't seem to want me to leave and I felt bad doing so. I told them Jae would handle everything and to do what he said. I drove off feeling like I had abandoned my four bearded sons.

Fifteen minutes into the drive the permanence of the situation hit me. I wept for the loss of my friend and was furious I hadn't been a stronger witness to him for Christ. Throughout the drive Jane kept trying to call, but I let it go to voicemail. I'd let someone else tell her the news. I stopped for gas in South Boston. It was only then I noticed blood on my hands and jeans. A guy in a F250 filling up next to me nodded. He must have thought I had just gutted a fish or slaughtered a chicken or something.

When I pulled up to the house Emily came rushing out to greet me. I made sure to stay in the truck so she didn't freak out at the site of blood on my clothes. "What's going on, baby girl?"

"Mom said you were back in the area. Want to go shoot with gramps and me?"

"Oh, I can't. Be safe though, and make sure to wear ear and eye protection."

"Yes, sir," she said, rushing off towards the path that led to my parents' log cabin.

Annie came outside dressed in her workout clothes, holding the baby. "What are you doing here?"

I got out and her eyes widened seeing the blood on my clothes. "Senator Schilling's dead," I said.

Annie grabbed my hand and brought me over to the rocking chairs on the porch. She sat next to me, holding Addison, who was trying to stuff her entire fist into her mouth. "What happened?"

"Suicide."

Annie shook her head and fought back tears. "He seemed like such a nice man."

"He had a lot of problems."

"How's his wife taking it?"

"She's missing."

"We need to pray for her—"

"And pray for their daughter, Amber," I added.

Annie shook her head. "This poor girl lost her brother and now her dad—"

"And her mother's a flake," I said.

"Brandon."

"Sorry, but Missus Schilling doesn't seem to be into the idea of family very much."

"Based on her hitting on you?"

I nodded. "I have a laptop and cell phone in the truck I'm handing off to Drake when he gets here."

"What? Why's Roger coming here?"

I shrugged my shoulders. "Not sure. Something with the senator triggered a red flag with him."

"When is he coming?"

As if to answer her question I could hear helicopter rotors thumping in the distance. I pointed skyward. "I think he's here."

I hopped the fence into the main pasture. The blue and white Jet Ranger helicopter came into view and lowered nearby. I motioned with my right hand outstretched straight and my left bent under it to direct the pilot to move left. There were gopher holes and unstable muck in this part of the pasture I didn't want him to land on. I motioned with my arms crossed in front of my groin to signal him to land. He landed, and a moment later a high-pitched whirring sound signaled the chopper was powering down. Drake exited the passenger seat while the blades were still spinning. He was dressed casually in jeans and an untucked dress shirt. He rushed over to me with his head ducked down. I shook his hand and motioned for him towards the house.

Inside, Annie held a piece of ice for Addison to suck on. "You make quite the entrance," Annie said.

"Sorry, Annie," Drake said, giving her a hug and a kiss on the cheek. He gave Addison a kiss on her head as well.

"I'm going upstairs to try put the baby down and leave you two alone," Annie said.

I went out to my truck and got the laptop, cell phone, and piece of paper and brought them inside. Drake looked everything over wearing latex gloves.

"What is going on?"

"I'll tell you in a minute." Drake looked at the blood-spattered note before trying the cell phone. It was locked out. He placed it aside and opened the laptop. The large screen blinked as if waiting for a screensaver password to be inserted. Drake took out a small flash drive an inserted it in the side USB port which allowed him to bypass the screensaver.

"Big brother has a lot of tech the rest of us don't," I said.

"You have no idea."

He typed away for a few minutes before grunting. "Everything's been wiped. Whatever he opened had a virus on it that cleared the hard drive. There's no documents, or pictures, mp4s, or even apps on this laptop." He turned the note around. "he sacrificed my only son to Gehenna."

"I don't understand," I said. "The senator's son, Drew, died in a race car explosion?"

"An explosion which turned out to be murder," Drake said.

"I know. It was my case."

Drake pointed to the computer like he could explain everything if only he could pull information from it. "The girl, and group, tied to Drew Schilling's murder were a radical organization funded by Gaspar Schultz."

"I'm with you," I said.

"Schultz is the current high priest of Gehenna."

"Now I'm lost," I said. "Correct me if I'm wrong, but Gehenna is a biblical term, right?"

"It is," Drake said. "Gehenna, translated from the Hebrew ge-hinnom is also known as the valley of Hinnom, or the valley of the son of Hinnom. It was an area south of Jerusalem, where pagans sacrificed children by fire to Moloch . The area became a place of refuse where waste, animals, and even human criminals were dumped. They kept a constant fire burning to consume everything. Because of its history, and imagery, the area became another term for hell." Drake leaned back in the kitchen chair. He looked skyward as if to think.

"I'm totally confused."

"Gehenna is also the name of a real place today, where some of the most wicked vile elite meet once every ten years. The name Gehenna is also the name of the actual group that meets there with Schultze being the ringleader."

"When you say elite? Do you mean like the "Illuminati"?" I said, holding air quotes. Drake nodded. "You got it."

"I wasn't being serious."

"Brandon, if you're a believer you know there's evil in the world, right?"

"Of course. I've seen it first-hand."

"Then don't be naive," Drake said, as if to scold me. "Groups like the, Illuminati, secret societies, globalists, one world government types, and the deep state are very real. The enemy has soldiers all over the world working against the children of light, but Gehenna is the apex predator of those groups. It may seem like what I'm fighting against in my little corner of the world are arms dealers, and drug traffickers, but in reality, my small group was created to fight a spiritual proxy war against satanic groups like Gehenna."

"So, did Schilling just realize Gaspar Schultz's ties to this Gehenna?"

"I don't know," Drake said. "The senator was all over Schultz, and already connected the dots between Kyle's murder and Schultz's radicalized political groups like AFA, and the North American Poverty Law Group. From the note the senator knew Gehenna existed, but I doubt he knew Schultz was affiliated with it." He paused and placed his hands together with the tips of his index fingers under his chin. "Which may be what sent him over the edge."

Drake looked at me and I shrugged my shoulders. "He never mentioned anything about Gehenna to me.

He implied there was a lot more going on beneath the surface of DC than what I saw, and that it was evil, but that's it."

Drake leaned forward and closed the laptop. "When was the last time you flew in a helicopter?"

"A long time ago. Why?"

"I need you."

"For?"

He gave me a handsome grin showing a near perfect smile. "To defeat evil."

"You're serious?"

"I'll fill you in on the way back to DC."

Annie came back downstairs just as Drake said this. "You're going where?"

Drake turned to Annie like a teen caught trying to sneak out in the middle of the night. "I need to borrow your husband for a couple more days."

"For what purpose?"

He gave her the same handsome smile but added in a theatric bow. "To help save the republic, madam."

"Aren't there like thousands of government agents out there who can help you save the world, Roger?"

"Not from my point of view. There are very few people I trust."

"What's the problem?"

"All I can tell you is there's a globalist group we've been tracking for quite some time, and, when the senator shot himself, your husband's path crossed mine." Drake grew serious. "I could use his help."

"Is it dangerous?"

"No one will be safe if we don't get to the bottom of this."

Annie's eyes widened. "Roger, you're not telling me what I want to hear."

"Don't worry," Drake said, his smile returning. "What does Matthew six twenty-five say?"

Annie said, "Not to worry."

"About?"

"Anything," Annie said, her beautiful smile returning.

Drake turned to me. "So come along, Joseph, it's time to go save Egypt."

I turned to Annie, looking for permission. She waved her hands. "Go. Your government needs you."

Drake stopped at the screen door to the porch. "Annie, there's a higher authority at work here that needs Brandon."

"Just keep him safe."

"I always have," Drake said, exiting onto the side porch.

I called after my friend. "Do I need anything?"

"If you mean gear," Drake spoke through the screen door. "Nothing. However, if you have a suit bring it."

"I have one suit from the other night, but the rest of my suits are in the senator's apartment in Alexandria."

"We'll need to clear that space anyway."

"Give me ten," I said, looking at my blood splattered jeans. "I need to clean up."

I jumped in the shower and scrubbed my scalp, arms, and fingernails until they were raw. During the shower I said multiple prayers to help calm my nerves. I was still going on adrenaline and hadn't fully processed what had happened. It felt like I was back in the garden apartment shower in Alexandria and that when I stepped out, I'd find Senator Schilling outside waiting for me, but that world was gone. Obliterated with a gunshot. I got dressed in another pair of jeans a button-down shirt and my cowboy boots. On the way out I grabbed my new fancy shoes and walked with them under my arm like a child with his lunchbox going to the first day of school.

Annie stopped me at the door and kissed me deeply. "You okay?"

I nodded. "I will be."

"Don't be a hero."

I kissed her back. "I love you always."

Outside, Drake texted on his cell phone by the oak tree I had once buried Fescue under. The dog was no longer there. Taken by some government agent for an autopsy before being incinerated. It seemed like a lifetime ago that Fescue, and my cattle, died. A tragedy which kicked me onto the path I was now on.

"You ready?" Drake said.

"Let's go."

Out in the field, Dad and Emily talked with the helicopter pilot.

Dad had met Drake only once and shook his hand. "How are you, Mister Drake?"

"Fine, Mister Hall. Good to see you and this beautiful granddaughter of yours again."

"Are you gonna fly in the helicopter, Dad?"

"I think so," I said.

"Can I come?" Emily pleaded. "Please?"

"Not this time, honey. This is a work thing."

Dad put his hand on my shoulder. "Everything okay?"

I winced and shook my head as if to tell him that it wasn't okay, and that I couldn't talk in front of Emily. "Annie will fill you in."

Dad took Emily's hand. "Let's go up to the porch and watch them take off."

Before they walked away, I gave Emily a hug and a kiss. I followed Drake into the backseat of the Jet Ranger. Once I was inside and buckled, Drake motioned for me to put on a headset and lower the microphone on the side. Drake reached into the front seat and tapped the shoulder of a young pilot dressed in jeans, sneakers, and a tee-shirt. The pilot nodded and fired up the helicopter. With the sound-deadening headset on, the whirring of the copter blades was felt more than heard.

Drake spoke into the microphone and sounded like he was far away rather than right next to me. "Rick, what's our ETA?"

The pilot chirped over the headset and seemed as

distant as Drake. "Give me a second and I'll let you know."

My stomach did a somersault as the copter rose into the sky. Emily and my dad waved from the porch and soon morphed into two dots as did the farmhouse. Soon, the 500-acre farm itself was just a small patch of grass below us.

"ETA is about an hour and fifteen," the pilot said.

"Thanks, Rick," Drake said. "I'm going offline for a few."

"Roger that."

SIXTEEN

Drake unplugged our headsets and plugged them into different ports. There was a long beep in my ears. When it finished Drake started talking. "We're secure. You ready for the info dump?"

"I think so."

"Gehenna is one of those places like bohemian grove or pizza gate. Places, and events, that people chalk up more to urban legend than reality. The problem is, the group, and the location, are very real. They meet once every ten years with this year a meeting year. Unlike the globalist group that meets at Bilderberg out in the open, the place of Gehenna, and the group itself, are hidden. From the little chatter we've gleaned from the dark web and intel we've acquired, we believe this year's meeting is to plan a false flag of some sort on US soil. So, it's paramount we discover their location."

"So, Gehenna is what, a satanic group?"

Drake nodded. "And like the original Gehenna, they're into every form of child sacrifice imaginable. From trafficking, to pedophilia, to funding abortion clinics, to actual child and infant sacrifices. Including me, there were only four of us in SOL. Myself, two agents, and one analyst. One of my agents, a close friend, was killed by one of Gehenna's assassins while in Israel." Drake went quiet for a moment. The pain was written across his face.

"Leaving you, Jae, and your daughter," I said.

For the first time in the history of our friendship I saw Drake look dumbfounded. "How'd you figure my baby girl into this?"

"Hunch," I said.

"Seriously. How'd you guess?"

"The fact she knew your real work when you talked at dinner, and her cover was the department of education." Drake smiled and I added, "I also know fidelity is important with you, and with Jae being involved I knew nepotism concerns went out the window."

"See, there's a reason I chose you."

"I thought you just wanted to be my friend?"

"Who doesn't like to work with their friends?" he said.

"I'll help you out for a couple of days, but this cloak and dagger stuff is above my pay grade."

"That's one of the things I love about you, my brother."

"What?"

"Your fake humility."

"Fake," I laughed.

Drake tapped his index finger against the side of his nose. "You pose as a humble country bumpkin, but I got your number."

What seemed like minutes later the helicopter started to descend. I looked out the window and could only see pastures and woods. Two horses sprinted across a pasture away from the lowering helicopter. We touched down, but the copter continued running. Drake reached into the front seat to give the pilot a thumbs up *thank you* before motioning me outside. We took off our headsets and both stepped out and walked away hunched over until we were beyond the helicopter's rotors. Drake held the laptop over his head, and I held my shoes. We walked through a gate and watched as the helicopter took off.

"This property is gorgeous," I said, pointing to the pastures. "Where we at?"

"A friend's farm in Upperville, Virginia. Not far from DC."

A blacked-out SUV waited for us. I wasn't surprised when Vanessa got out of the driver's seat rubbing her lower back like she had been driving for hours.

Drake handed her the senator's laptop and cell phone. "The suicide note is in a plastic baggy between the laptop. Be careful."

Vanessa got into the back seat and opened the

laptop like a child excited to try a new video game. After I got in the passenger's seat, Vanessa said, "Welcome to the team, Mister Hall."

"I'm just helping your dad out for a couple days." I said, buckling the seat belt. I turned to Drake who was in the driver's seat. "By the way, just what am I helping with?"

"Everything," Drake said, tearing out like a NASCAR driver. When we got on to the main road Drake didn't slow down.

"Why the rush?"

"Gotta get your stuff out of the senator's Alexandria home before media catches wind of his death and camps out there." Drake looked in the rearview mirror to see Vanessa. "What's your hubby saying?"

"Jae says we're on borrowed time. Nobody's been onsite yet, or heard of anything, but he's nervous that Missus Schilling is unaccounted for and the chief of staff wants to start calling people."

"Thanks. Any thoughts on the laptop?"

"The thing's been scrubbed. Whatever the last item was that the senator opened was a trojan horse that wiped the hard drive."

"That's my assessment too. See what you can do with his cell phone."

A little over an hour later we entered Alexandria and blew through a red light, two stop signs, and the speed limit. Police cars passed by but seemed uninterested in pulling us over. I assumed they scanned our license plate and confirmed it belonged to someone working in high level government. Drake pulled up a block away from the senator's brownstone.

"I'll just be a minute," I said.

"Take the time to wipe the place of your prints. We're not going to hide the fact you were there, but I don't want to leave breadcrumbs either. I want to manage how this intel gets out."

"Got it."

Drake called after me. "You got access to the primary residence?"

"Yeah."

"I suggest you do a sweep of the place to confirm the wife isn't there."

"And if she is?"

"Then bring her out and we'll take her someplace safe for the time being."

I collected all my clothes and items from the guest apartment and brought them out to the SUV. Drake popped the back, which was a mirror image of the SUV Jae drove. Back inside the garden apartment I emptied the food from the pantry and refrigerator and wiped every surface down with a paper towel and bleach spray from under the sink. I brought the rest of the items out to the SUV before going into the primary residence. No one was there. This would be the last time I would step foot in the senator's home. My contract job had been a failure. While I had kept my client safe from enemies without, I had failed to see the enemy within that killed him. I wiped the door handles down and left.

Back in the car Drake said. "You know where the senator's daughter is?"

"My buddy brought her back to his house."

"Good. Leave it as is for now."

Back in DC we pulled up to a sub shop a few blocks over from the Mall. "Come on," Drake said. "We gotta fuel up. Brandon, bring one of your suits in with you."

Drake pulled a small bag out of the trunk as well. Inside we ordered subs and got changed into our suits in a dirty bathroom. It was a far cry from the restaurants I frequented with the senator.

"What am I getting dressed for?"

"We have a debrief at seventeen hundred hours."

"Where?"

"Fill you in shortly."

The three of us sat in an orange laminate 1970s booth eating turkey subs. I hadn't realized how famished I was until the food was in front of me. Once I tried to bring up work, but Drake nodded back and forth as if to say, *keep it quiet* in public. Back in the SUV he continued to drive with reckless abandon. We passed near the White House. A group of protesters were outside with signs stating it was the right of mothers to kill their unborn children. On one sign was a cartoon image of a woman on her back with four coat hangers above her signifying how many abortions she'd gone through. Everyone wore pink hats as a form of solidarity.

Drake soon pulled up to a guarded gate at Number One Observatory Circle. Two armed Navy guards stepped out. Drake showed an ID. They nodded, walked the car and scanned beneath with a wand before allowing us through. The massive iron gate rolled back to reveal a long driveway. We drove up the meandering road coming to a stop in front of a large Queen Ann style white- and green-trimmed home.

"Who lives here?" I whistled. Drake looked in the rearview mirror at his daughter and smiled as if it were an inside joke. "What?"

"Come on, Brandon. Time to go to work."

Drake led us up to a large front door with a window in the middle. A secret service agent with sunglasses, and an earpiece, stood on a gorgeous wraparound porch. He produced a wand and scanned each of us. Once clear, the agent motioned us onward. The front door was unlocked, and Drake walked inside as if he lived there. We entered a foyer with a dark wood polished hardwood floor. To our right was a formal sitting area. To the left was an alcove with a grand piano. Beyond that was a living room with dark colonial blue walls. In front of us a staircase ascended several floors with an exposed center.

A middle-aged man dressed in a shiny black suit

appeared out of nowhere. "Mister Drew, come right this way."

I looked at Drake who shook his head as if to say, *just go with the new name.* We walked down a hallway, passing by a kitchen and stopped in front of an elevator. It was odd to see something so modern in such an old home. The four of us waited for the doors to open. We entered, but the man in the shiny suit stayed behind. The doors shut and the elevator descended for almost ten seconds before opening into a dim concrete hallway. A secret service agent stood nearby. We walked to an unmarked door with another secret service agent outside. He opened the door for us. We entered a modest bright room with leather couches, wallpapered walls, and a fancy electric fireplace. There were no desks, and no windows. Suddenly, a portion of a bookcase opened like a door revealing a hidden bathroom. Who stepped out next shocked me more than the secret door. His white hair and tanned face were recognizable anywhere.

The man looked at Drake and Amanda and shook both their hands. "Good to see you again." He turned to me and smiled. "And this must be Mister Brandon Hall?"

He held out his hand and I shook it. "Vice President Prince," I said, trying not to reveal how intimidated I was. "My wife's never gonna believe I met you."

The vice president smiled. "Please have a seat."

The three of us sat down on one couch facing the vice president on the other.

"Sorry with the cloak-and-dagger routine, but Roger and I like it this way," the vice president said.

"As you observed," Drake said to me, "even the staff don't know my real name, or that we exist."

The vice president turned to me. "Do you follow alternative media at all, Brandon?"

"A bit."

"As you might know there was a soft coup over the past few years between the mainstream media, Hollywood, and many in DC trying to bring down this administration. Only alternative media and citizen journalists reported on it."

"I've seen quite a bit of fake news skewing your work here," I said. "They've been relentless nitpicking your administration and making up stories."

He nodded. "That's just the surface level attacks. You should see what goes on behind the scenes. There are members of our own party trying to take us down as well, which is why I hand-picked Roger to lead this team. He's one of the few people I trust in DC. He's loyal to this country and the Constitution and has proven this fidelity countless times." The vice president sat back in his leather couch and crossed his legs. "I bet you're wondering why you're here, Brandon?"

"Because of Senator Schilling?"

"Horrific what happened to him. We didn't agree on some things, but I respected him professionally."

The vice president turned to Drake. "What's the status on the news breaking of Schilling's death?"

"We've got it locked down for now, but his wife's MIA, and his chief of staff is about to blab, and it's only a matter of time before his mistress finds out. If I had to guess, it will make the news before the end of day."

"How much have you told your new employee about what you're working on?"

I was about to correct the vice president regarding my employment status when Drake said, "A quick background on Gehenna, and what we think they're up to."

The vice president nodded before turning back to me. "Brandon, we believe this terrorist group Gehenna is going to execute some sort of attack on US soil over the next month."

"Sir, with all due respect, I'm a nobody blue-collar cattle farmer from Virginia. There must be thousands people in the greater DC area who can help better than I can."

"And out of those people there are many I'd trust with my life," the vice president said. He leaned forward and jacked a thumb towards Drake. "But Roger's the only one I'd trust with the life of my children." He paused before adding, "You understand how tight this circle has to be, son?"

"I do, sir."

"You're a child of God with an impeccable character who's been tasked with standing in the gap during a time when this country is under a massive spiritual attack. If Roger says he needs you, then he needs you. Besides, your past interactions with Schultz's groups have made you more than qualified." The vice president turned to Vanessa. "What's the latest on Gehenna's meeting?"

"There's very little chatter on the dark web," Vanessa said, "but much of it is coded. And I'd need a cypher to decode it."

"Based on the suicide note," Drake added, "Senator Schilling was tied to Gehenna somehow, whether he was innocent or guilty, only time with tell, but he clearly found something out so horrific it triggered the suicide."

"Anything on his laptop?"

"No, sir," Vanessa said. "We believe whatever triggered his suicide was viewed on the laptop, but it contained a worm which wiped everything upon its viewing."

"What about the cell?"

"Working on it," Vanessa said.

The vice president turned to me, arms resting on his knees. "This is the greatest collection of evil in our lifetime. What you see playing out in our culture is just the ripples from the tsunami that is forming. We know Gehenna is planning something big, and we must find the location and stop them at all costs."

"Where do we think this Gehenna headquarters is located?"

"Israel," Drake said. "That's where my agent was

killed chasing down a lead. The problem is, there's no evidence of any modern group meeting anywhere near there. Mossad would have found it by now."

"Do we know who's in the group?" I said.

"Very little," Vanessa said.

"We know Schultz, some European royals, and a few old blue blood families in this country," Drake said, "but that's why we need to get eyes on it. We're monitoring hundreds of people we suspect could be affiliated, but it's like finding a needle in a haystack, but at night."

Vice President Prince turned to me. "What geographic places come to mind when you hear words like old world, Illuminati, or secret societies?"

I thought for a moment. "Europe."

He looked to Drake. "You say the Holy Land."

Drake nodded.

"I tend to think the same thing," the VP said. "The US has only been around a few hundred years. Gehenna goes back to Biblical times. It must be seated in someplace with ancient roots. Even older than England, France, or Germany."

The vice president turned to Vanessa. "Your guess?"

"Maybe Greece?" she said. "But if Schultz is in town for the hearings, then it could have been moved stateside at some point. The globalist Bilderberg Group is named after a hotel in the Netherlands where the very first meeting took place. To this day,

Bilderberg is still named after that original hotel, but the location changes yearly."

"This is a different animal," Drake said. "Bilderberg is amateur compared to Gehenna. Bilderberg goes back to Nineteen fifty-four but like the vice president said, Gehenna goes back thousands of years."

The vice president slapped his knee. "If only I could unleash the full power of the intelligence community on this."

"Why can't we?"

"Gehenna has tendrils everywhere," Drake said. "They'd find out and go dark."

"There's that much swamp to drain in this city?"

The vice president nodded. "Parts of the CIA have been compromised as well as the Bureau, and Homeland Security. We even had to fire the head of FBI when we took over the executive branch, for trying to influence the election."

"So it's up to us to save the republic," Drake said. "No pressure."

"If we miss this opportunity," the vice president said, "then we have to wait another decade before they meet again. We have no idea who will be in the White House by then, and for all we know it could be one of Gehenna's Manchurian candidates, or—" he stopped himself. "We just need to find them and stop them at all costs."

Back in the SUV, Drake drove without as much

urgency. "What did you think of the vice president?" He said.

"Seems like the real deal. Is the president in on this?"

"He's briefed," Drake said. "He's got his hands full dealing with dictators around the world, budgets, as well as fighting fake news the media throws at him on a daily basis. In the end, he leaves the spiritual battles up to Vice President Prince."

Vanessa said, "Where to next, Dad?"

"Back to HQ."

We parked in a small driveway behind Drake's brownstone next to an old white unmarked van.

Drake opened the trunk to get his bags. "Grab your stuff, Brandon."

Instead of walking up to his home's back door, Drake went up to the next-door neighbor's attached brownstone. He typed on an alarm pad and the door clicked open. He held the door open for both Vanessa and me.

"Welcome to my vacation condo," Drake said.

We entered through a modest kitchen and walked past a full bathroom into a living room with a leather couch. I followed them upstairs. Two large bedrooms were on either side of the hallway each with a full-sized bed and three quarter bath. A third bedroom was set up as a modest gym with a full bathroom.

Drake brought me back to the larger of the two guest bedrooms. "This is you. I'll be sleeping next door and Vanessa lives down the street."

"Get settled and we'll meet you downstairs," Vanessa said.

I dropped my stuff on the bed and went into the bathroom to wash my face and get changed out of my suit and back into my jeans, worn button-down shirt, and cowboy boots. In the mirror, my scruff was starting to grow back, but it would be months before my beard was at the length I liked it.

Downstairs, I found Drake and Vanessa in the kitchen, drinking bottles of water. Drake handed me one. "Follow me."

"Where we going?"

"Time to earn your paycheck," Drake said approaching a door I assumed led to the basement.

"Uhm, we never discussed pay?" I said, walking to catch up.

Rickety stairs descended into a dusty basement. A large water heater, a boiler, and a breaker panel took up most of the space along with a small work bench with dusty tools scattered about. Behind the water tank was a bricked alcove with shelves and old paint cans. Drake flipped a switch and a bright LED light shined onto a metal door that looked like it was from a Jules Verne novel, complete with welding marks and bolts. Next to the door was a keypad. Drake pressed his thumb on a flat black surface next to the keypad and the door clicked open. He pulled back on the thick heavy door. LED lights came on to reveal a large room at least twenty by thirty feet. A desk ran the length of one side of the room and was covered with computers and flat screen monitors. Opposite the wall of the computers were two couches facing a flat screen television. Beyond the couches was a small kitchenette complete with a microwave, sink, and stove top. It looked like a space station habitat from a sci-fi movie.

"Welcome to SOL's command center," Drake said.

SEVENTEEN

WHEN I STEPPED FROM THE DUSTY BASEMENT INTO THE high-tech spy universe, Senator Schilling's comments about the tunnel under the senate building came back to me. *Not many people realize there's an entire world beneath DC.* The visit to the vice president's bunker was another example of both a literal, and figurative, world existing beneath DC.

"Is this your fortress of solitude, Superman?"

Drake chuckled. "This bunker is bomb proof, hurricane, tornado, and earthquake proof, along with being a temporary nuclear fallout shelter if needed." He pointed to the air vents in the ceiling. "Air's filtered so no bacteriological contaminants can enter. There's a full bathroom down here as well as stocked provisions and medical supplies. Couches fold out into beds."

Drake plugged his cell into a strange thick charging cord. "The command center is EMP proof, so cell phones have to be boosted to get a signal outside."

He started texting while Vanessa sat down at a computer station that looked like it was from NASA. She plugged her cell phone into a similar cord, and the senator's cell phone into a laptop.

"What should I do?"

"Make yourself comfortable," Drake said. "Kitchen's only stocked with freeze dried food and MREs down here, but we have normal food in the upstairs kitchen."

Vanessa's cell phone pinged. She read a text. "Jae says Schilling's chief of staff got the word out about the suicide and the media's starting to congregate around the Clarksville property."

"Are my guys still there?" I said.

"Yes. Jae says they're doing a good job keeping people at bay for now."

Drake looked up from his phone. "I'm glad we got your stuff out of the senator's primary residence. It's gonna be a madhouse over there."

"I can't lie if the authorities ask if I worked for him."

"I know," he said, "however, by removing your items we're ahead of the game."

"Game?" I said.

Vanessa added, "We don't know who the enemy is, Brandon. Someone could try to pin this on you by planting some of your personal items somewhere suspicious. The senator is tied to

Gehenna somehow and they operate at a very high level."

"Gehenna plays chess while the rest of the world plays checkers," Drake said.

"More like Chutes and Ladders," Vanessa corrected.

"This is all so above my pay grade," I said. "Are you sure I'm gonna be of any help?"

They both said, "Yes."

Drake got on a phone call while Vanessa continued to work at a computer station. I was impressed, but not surprised, when I heard Drake start speaking fluent Hebrew. I walked over to see what Vanessa was doing.

Without turning around, she said, "Congress, Supreme Court Justices, and White House staff all get encrypted cell phones. It's gonna take me a while to hack his cell, but I'll get in."

"Final word on the laptop?"

"It's fried," she exhaled. "I just hope his cell phone gives us a clue as to what it was."

While they worked at their tasks I wandered over to the couch and found an old King James Bible and started to look up passages for Gehenna.

After a few minutes I said, "Why can't I find Gehenna in this Bible?"

"S'leexa," Drake said in Hebrew, before placing his hand over the phone. "There's an Interlinear on the table."

Vanessa turned from the computer. "Gehenna

translates as hades, hell, etc."

"Thanks."

"We've analyzed that word a hundred different ways and came up with very little," she said, "but have a go at it."

Drake finished his phone call and came over to sit next to me on the couch. He pointed to the Bible in my hand. "In the old Testament you will see it appear as the valley of Hinnom or the Valley of the son, or children, of Hinnom. In the New Testament it's translated as hell. At times hell is translated from the word *sheol* which means the grave. At other times it's from the word h*ades,* which also means the grave. One time from the greek word t*artarus* which means a place of darkness, and from the word g*ehenna, or ge-hinnom,* which means a place of burning."

I sat back in the couch. "Boy, you've really studied up on this."

"Don't give up," Drake said. "You might find something we missed. In the meantime, I have an important job for you, being the newbie on the team."

"What is it?" I said, excited I had a job to do.

"I texted in an order at a pizza place around the corner. It's already paid for."

All three of us laughed. Drake placed a hand on my shoulder. "Don't worry, Brandon, you're here for a reason."

"Dad's right," Vanessa added. "I've been praying about it as well."

"And that reason is?"

"We don't know," Drake said, "but are anxious for God to show us."

"Okay," I said. "But how will I get back inside the fortress once I get the food?"

Drake waved his hand back and forth like it was no big deal. "I've already inserted your thumb print into the front door pad as well as the safe room door pad. I have a numeric code to give you as well for backup."

"How'd you get my thumb—"

"Don't worry about it," Drake said, barely able to contain a grin. "Pizza's getting cold."

It was surreal walking down the brick sidewalk. The last time I had been for a walk in Alexandria I was employed by Senator Schilling who was alive. Time was quickening, and recent events already seemed like years ago. Above, the setting sun fell behind cloud cover and a cool breeze picked up. It was a nice break from the humidity, but I knew the heat would return with a vengeance. When I returned to the basement with the pizzas, Vanessa had laid out paper plates and bottles of water. I took up my same spot on one of the couches while Drake and Vanessa continued to work at computer stations.

"How goes the battle?" I said, taking a bite of pizza.

"Vanessa's continuing to monitor the dark web for any chatter about Gehenna as well as work on the cell phone. While she does that, I'm dealing with fallout from the senator's death."

"Is Jae still onsite at the Clarksville estate with the Burnell brothers?"

"He left about an hour ago. FBI are there with local sheriff's office. Burnells have been sent home. FBI knows you worked for the senator and want a sit-down to make sure your story corroborates with the chief of staff who found the senator."

"When?"

"As soon as possible. Don't worry, I'll manage that meeting."

"Missus Schilling still missing?"

"No, she's back at the brownstone and has received the news," Vanessa said.

"I wonder how she's taking it?"

"No idea. Media's already camped outside her place."

"Why don't you go get some shut eye upstairs," Drake said. "I'm heading back home in a few."

Vanessa looked at her watch. "I'm going to take the senator's cell phone home with me and try to work on it some more." Vanessa packed up half a pizza to bring home for Jae. "I'll see you two in the morning."

"I'm gonna take your advice and head upstairs," I said. "Mind if I take the Bible and Interlinear?"

"Be my guest."

In the guest bedroom I found a notepad in a nightstand. I did a search on Hinnom in the Old Testament as well as hell, hades, tartarus, and sheol. Myriads of passages popped up. I started with verses from the old testament. The first passage to jump out at me was from Second Chronicles thirty-three: *Manneseh was a wicked ruler. And he caused his children to pass through the fire in the valley of the son of Hinnom: also he observed times, and used enchantments, and used witchcraft, and dealt with a familiar spirit, and with wizards: he wrought much evil in the sight of the Lord, to provoke him to anger.*

Another passage from Jeremiah read: *And they built the high places of Baal, which are in the valley of the son of Hinnom, to cause their sons and their daughters to pass through the fire unto Molech; which I commanded them not, neither came it into my mind, that they should do this abomination, to cause Judah to sin.* Drake's description of this modern Gehenna was in lock-step with their ancient counterparts when it came to the way they tortured children.

Before going to bed I used the credit card the Senator Schilling had given me to pay Tollers in advance for his work, and to pay the Burnell brothers for their work, along with a bonus for their short duration and frustration. After those two transactions were complete, I took out my pocket knife and carved the card up. My job for the senator was done and I had no reason to use the card further. Annie and I texted, and I reminded her to keep the conversation light as our cell phones were not secure. She said the girls were fine and we each ended with an, *I love you.*

I tossed around in the foreign bed for hours

unable to get to sleep. During my time in the Marines I could sleep on the hard ground using my pack as a pillow. Old age had softened me to the point where I had trouble sleeping if my pillow wasn't firm enough and I didn't have my fluffy comforter. My dreams that night were plagued with images of blood and the sound of Larry's screams. Images of the senator's posh bright bedroom changed into a stone cavern with a darkness that felt like a heavy cloak.

The next morning, I awoke to someone tickling my feet and the smell of coffee. I opened one eye to see Drake and Vanessa at the foot of the bed. Jae towered over the two of them from behind. "What time is it?" was all I could get out.

Drake looked at his watch. "Seven AM. I thought you farmers were up at the crack of dawn?"

"Didn't sleep well," I grumbled. "I needed my blankie."

"Looks like you need to borrow some jammies," Jae said, pointing to my jeans and wrinkled shirt.

"I usually sleep in my undies," I said, "but didn't want to scare you guys." I opened and closed my hand like a baby motioning for a bottle. Someone handed me a cup of warm aromatic coffee.

Drake pointed to the open Bible, Interlinear, and notepad on the bed. "What were you working on?"

"Doing word searches last night."

"Anything jump out at you?"

"Not really."

Drake picked up the yellow pad of paper. He

flipped the pages as if he were speed reading. "Interesting."

Vanessa walked over "What?"

Drake read from Proverbs five in a stoic voice, "For the lips of a strange woman drop as an honeycomb, and her mouth is smoother than oil: But her end is bitter as wormwood, sharp as a two-edged sword. Her feet go down to death; her steps take hold on hell." He closed the pad of paper. "Sounds like a lot of women in DC."

"Or my wife," Jae laughed.

Vanessa turned and slapped Jae's muscular shoulder. "Not funny."

I whispered. "What did you just say?"

Drake turned to me, confusion on his face. "I said that this description sounded like a lot of women in DC?"

"A lot of women in DC," I repeated. After a long awkward pause, I said, "Senator Schilling must have been insane to have shot himself, right?" Everyone nodded. "Or disturbed beyond measure."

"Go ahead Brandon," Drake said. "What are you thinking, son?"

"I copied that passage you just read in a hurry as I was just trying to get everything on paper, and didn't think too much about it, but that description is Missus Schilling to a T."

Everyone looked at me like I was guilty of something. Vanessa said, "And you know this how?"

"Please don't say you knocked boots with her?"

Jae said, only to be slapped in the shoulder by his wife again.

"Nothing happened between us," I said, "but boy was she trying. The sad thing is, Senator Schilling knew of her extra-curricular proclivities."

"They had an open marriage?" Vanessa said. "Disgusting."

"Whenever I interacted with her, I kept thinking of the story of Joseph and Potiphar's wife, as both of us worked for the women's husband, but this proverb describes Missus Schilling better. And you know what I—"

After a long pause Drake said, "What are you thinking?"

"Where's the senator's note?"

"Down in the safe room. Why?"

I put the coffee down, pushed through everyone, and sprinted downstairs in my socks. I could hear the footsteps of everyone close behind me.

"The senator was a stickler for grammar," I yelled back to them. "That's why he always carried that red fountain pen."

"I'm confused, but trusting you," Drake said, trying to keep up with me.

I reached the basement and tried to remember what to do to open the thick metal door. Jae came up behind me and placed his thumb on a nondescript black silicon pad. The metal door clicked open. I rushed inside, looking over the computer work stations. Everyone came in behind me.

"Where's the senator's note?"

"Here," Vanessa said opening a small metal container on a shelf. She handed me a sealed plastic sheet that contained the note.

I held it up to a halogen lamp but saw nothing new. It still read *he sacrificed my only son to Gehenna.*

Jae exhaled. "Is the savant doing his thing again?"

There was another smack as Vanessa cuffed her husband again.

"The senator was a stickler for grammar," I said, looking at the backside of the note.

"You said that already," Jae said.

"Yet he starts the sentence off with a lowercase *h*."

"So?"

"Quiet, Jae," Drake said. "Let Brandon figure this out."

I pulled out my pocketknife and went to cut the top off the hermetically sealed plastic sheeting. "Okay if I open this?"

Vanessa nodded. "I fingerprinted and found nothing." She handed me a pair of latex gloves. "Take these anyway."

I put the gloves on before slicing open the top off the plastic sheet. The piece of paper was flimsy like my theory, but I held it up to the lightbulb overhead just the same. In the light, the sentence still read, *he sacrificed my only son to Gehenna.* I moved the letter up and back against the light and found what I was looking for.

"Well team," I said. "I believe *he* is a *she* with a capital S?"

Drake, Jae, and Vanessa crowded around me. I pointed to a splotch of blood just before the sentence started. Look close. There's an S buried under a drop of blood. The fountain pen's ink color is almost a perfect match to the color of blood, which is why we missed it.

"I don't see—"

"I see it," Drake said, pointing. "There."

"Unbelievable," Vanessa said. "Good job, Brandon."

I read the corrected note out loud, "She sacrificed my only son to Gehenna."

"We were looking for a motive that sent the senator over the edge, right?" No one answered. "What if the *she* in this note turned out to be someone close to Senator Schilling?

"Like his girlfriend?" Vanessa said.

"Maybe," I said, "but would a girlfriend have the ability, power, or influence to send him over the edge?"

"You think the *she* in the sentence is Missus Schilling, don't you?" Drake said.

I nodded. "That's what I'm thinking."

"The senator knew his wife slept around," Jae said. "If that didn't make you crazy, then I don't know what would."

"You're right," I said, walking around the room. "So, what did Senator Schilling mean by saying that, she sacrificed his only son to Gehenna?" I placed the letter back in the plastic bag and hand it to Vanessa. "What do you guys know about Margaret Schilling?"

"Not much," Vanessa said. "Why?"

"I know her family goes back to the founders," Drake said.

"Could she be one of the elites involved in Gehenna?"

"We can check her out," Vanessa said.

"So, connect the dots for us," Drake said.

I thought for a moment. "What if you found out your wife was affiliated with a group whose leader was responsible for murdering your son, and yet she continued to stay with the group even after she found this out?"

"That could put someone over the edge," Drake said.

Everyone went quiet. I was shocked we were talking about a scenario where a mother could do this. "Gehenna is that evil, huh?"

"You have no idea how wicked this group is, Brandon."

"We need to get eyes on the senator's wife," I said, heading out of the room.

"Where you going?"

"To take a shower," I said. "Why don't you go grab breakfast down the street, Drake, being the newbie and all. I'll take an ice coffee."

Jae and Vanessa burst out laughing at the turn of tables. Even Drake belly laughed.

EIGHTEEN

When I came back downstairs sure enough there were bagels and an ice coffee in the room.

"I was kidding about the breakfast," I said, taking a sip of the coffee.

"You've earned your stripes," Drake said.

Vanessa handed each of us a sheet of paper. "Here's Margaret Schilling's full bio." I read along as Vanessa highlighted the sheet. "Margaret's family name is Collen. They came over in the late sixteen hundred's. Established plantations in Southern Virginia. Made a fortune off of tobacco in the seventeen hundred's, and then railroad investing in the eighteen hundred's. In the early twentieth century they had inside information about the stock market crash which allowed them to pull all their assets out of the market by August Nineteen twenty-nine. This move allowed them to buy up land and businesses at an alarming rate during The Great Depression, doubling their fortune."

"How'd her family know about the crash?" I said.

"Many believe the crash was manufactured to accelerate a one world government," Drake said.

"Seriously?"

"Think about it," Vanessa said. "What were the results of The Great Depression. A massive growth in government in the US with things like the New Deal and the expansion of the Federal Reserve. On a global level the United Nations were created, to replace the League of Nations."

"The swamp's origin," Jae said.

"I never thought of that," I said. "I always just believed what was written in school history books. Next you're gonna tell me Gehenna was behind the Nineteen twenty-nine crash." No one responded. "Seriously guys?"

"I wouldn't say they caused it," Drake said. "However, let's just say a lot of elites were prepared for the crash."

"I was once a skeptic like you," Jae said, "but the things I've seen have opened my eyes to what goes on in the world."

Vanessa read off more bullet points. "Margaret Collen Schilling born December Twenty-first, Nineteen sixty-three. The Collen family does, in fact, have loose ties to old Europe and the Illuminati."

I held up my hand like a grade schooler asking to

go to the potty. "Uhm when you say old Europe, you mean England?"

"Older. We in the States think old families are dynasties who can trace their lineage back to the Mayflower, but we have no idea what old means. Yes, the Collen family does go back to England, but it keeps traveling farther east to older places like Romania, Bulgaria, Walachia, Bucharest, and even Transylvania."

"Like Count Dracula?" I said in a Bela Lugosi voice.

"Don't laugh. Drinking the blood of children has long been seen as a way of life extension for the elite."

I placed the piece of paper down on a table. "There are really people like that?"

Drake rested his hand on my forearm. "This life-style is as real to them as Christianity is to us. They're more devoted to their beliefs than many Christians I know." He saw the disgusted look on my face and added, "Did you forget the underwater tank we found in the Dismal Swamp?"

"I've tried to purge that memory from my mind," I huffed.

"I understand, but this is a real spiritual war we're fighting, Brandon. Any frame of reference you have for evil, including the Dismal Swamp incident, will be dwarfed. There's unspeakable horrors in this world that you cannot even imagine."

"Part of me wishes I could go back in my farm bubble and forget this stuff exists."

"Greater is He who is in me—" Drake stopped, waiting for me to finish the line from First John.

"Than he who is in the world," I finished.

Vanessa cleared her throat. "Can I finish?"

"Sorry," I said. "This is just upsetting, and to think it's real is—" I trailed off surprised at how emotional I was. The memory of Senator Schilling's death came back to me, as if for the first time. I pushed my fingers against my closed eyes like I could force the memory back down into the abyss of my psyche. I walked over to the kitchenette's sink and splashed water in my face like I had dirt stuck in my eye. I kept repeating the action, hoping the tears I couldn't hold back would disappear into the water I threw on my face.

"You okay?"

After a minute I said, "Sorry, guys. The past couple of days just hit me."

A heavy muscular arm rested on my shoulder, which I knew belonged to Jae. "It's all right, brother."

Drake and Vanessa both came over and put an arm around me. For some reason it didn't help. It made me more upset. I turned and splashed more water on my face.

"Brandon?"

"I'm okay," I announced. "Sorry."

Jae said, "Never apologize for getting upset by what you've seen and experienced. The day these things don't bother us is the day we need to hang it up."

"Amen," Drake added.

Vanessa continued like nothing had happened. "I'm upset that I never connected Margaret Collen to the European Collin family, with an I. Ironically, it's one of the Gehenna clans that we know the least about. A couple financiers came from the family then it goes dark."

"What else do we have?" Drake said.

Vanessa continued, "Margaret met Greg Schilling when they were both at Yale undergrad. She helped him get into the Red Skull secret society. They married after graduating, and used her family's wealth to support Greg while he went back to Yale Law school. Greg's family had some money from a construction company, but nothing close to what the Collen family had.

I raised my hand again. "So, there's a difference between wealth and old money?"

"Correct," Vanessa said. "Even though the Schilling family goes back to the eighteen hundred's they weren't considered part of the elite. The Collin family lineage, and wealth, goes back centuries, maybe even a thousand years. That's what you call elite."

"Bring us up to present day," Drake said.

"After grad school Greg and Margaret Schilling moved back to northern Virginia where Greg worked in DC as a banker, a lobbyist, and became a senator. I'm printing a dossier which will list everything the senator voted on during his tenure in the senate which we can break down."

Drake kissed Vanessa's head. "Good job, sweetie."

"We're getting close," Jae said. "I can feel it."

"Where's Gaspar Schultz now?" I said.

Vanessa turned to a computer. "He's holed up in his company's building in DC. He was scheduled to testify before the senate in two days, but since the announcement of the committee chairman's death, the hearing was postponed."

"Stay on it," Drake said.

Jae went upstairs to the guest room that had been converted into a gym, to work out while Drake and I stood before a whiteboard in the safe room. We wrote every bit of information down about Mrs. Schilling from the paper Vanessa gave us to see if we could connect some dots seeing it in large print. We added a separate list of bills Senator Schilling voted on and bios of staff. Around lunchtime Jae and Vanessa went home while Drake and I walked down the street to an Italian restaurant. Sitting in the back of the busy place I watched as patrons came in for takeout as well as sit-down food. Most were dressed in business suits. I wondered what they'd each seen during their time in the swamp of DC.

"Brandon?"

"Huh?"

"I asked what you thought you were going to get?"

"Oh sorry. I'm still in bodyguard mode. I'm gonna get the chicken, pasta, and capers."

Drake closed his menu. "Sounds good. Me too."

Drake didn't let me bring the dossier on Margaret Schilling with us, but I brought a couple folded pieces of yellow legal paper and a pen which I took out.

"Can we talk here?"

Drake took out what appeared to be a thin mylar bag. "Put your phone in this just to be safe." He saw my confusion and added. "My cell's encrypted but yours isn't. Hold onto that bag. From now on whenever we're not in the safe room you should bag your phone if we're talking about anything to do with work."

After I bagged the phone I said. "You think I'm grasping at straws bringing the senator's wife into this?"

Drake shook his head. "No. I think you uncovered something I should have found months ago. I saw Senator Schilling as someone to be observed from afar while he chased after Schultz in his own way."

"You do realize this all hinges on a pronoun in a suicide note."

"Who else could the *she* in the note be?" Before I could give other options, Drake added, "Jae's looking into the senator's girlfriend, and Vanessa already said his daughter's squeaky clean. Margaret Schilling's the key. There's no other woman in Schilling's life."

After lunch, I video called Annie and the girls on the walk back to the brownstone. Dad had received the first insurance check and would receive a supplemental within thirty days. I said a prayer of thanks. We weren't going to lose the farm in the foreseeable future.

After I hung up, Drake said, "Got a little pep in your step now?"

"Nice to have some good news," I said.

Back at the command bunker Jae and Vanessa worked at two separate computers.

Vanessa had on a headset and turned to us. "We got some activity from the three Gehenna families we know of.

"Like what?" Drake said.

"Private jets coming into the US, but it's impossible for me to find out who's actually on board."

Jae added. "None of them are under family names but corporate fronts they own."

"Where they landing?"

"Coming into Dulles Airport."

Drake sat down. "This is amazing."

I shook my head back and forth to show my confusion. "Can someone fill me in?"

"We know of only a few of the families associated with Gehenna, but not the actual family members."

Jae added, "Some of these families have hundreds of people in them. Most of which are not involved in Gehenna so tracking every one of them is impossible."

"And the fact that several of the families are showing up at Dulles at the same time is huge."

"What does it mean?"

"It means you were right, Vanessa. Gehenna must have been relocated here."

"I told you knuckleheads," she said.

"So, what do we do now?" I said. "Just follow them to Gehenna?"

"Easier said than done," Vanessa said, getting up to walk around.

Jae sat at a computer, watching live video streams from the airport. He had either tapped into Dulles' cameras, or had access to a satellite.

"Look at this," he said. "The people exiting this first Gulfstream are using dark umbrellas to cover their identities from surveillance cameras and getting picked up by no less than four blacked-out SUVs. I bet they will leave the airport in four different directions."

Sure enough, once loaded, the four SUVs took off in four separate directions.

"We're gonna have a hard time tracking these people," Jae said.

"We need more resources on this," Vanessa said.

"Can't risk it," Drake said.

Vanessa rubbed the lower part of her back as she paced around the room.

"Sciatic nerve?" I said. She nodded. "How far along are you?"

Jae and Vanessa's mouths dropped open and Drake nearly fell to the floor. Drake collected himself. "What did I just hear?"

I tapped the side of my head like I knew all their

secrets. "I'm all knowing," I said, mimicking Drake's phrase he used on me at the park bench. I didn't let on that Annie rubbed her back the same way Vanessa did when she was pregnant with Emily.

"Baby girl?" Drake said. "What did I just hear?"

"We were gonna wait a bit longer before telling you, Daddy."

Drake burst into tears and hugged his daughter and son-in-law. Then he hugged me.

"I had nothing to do with it," I joked.

Drake peppered them with questions about due dates, and concerns about Vanessa's workload affecting the pregnancy. He calmed down after more hugs and a video conference with his wife.

"Can we get back to work please?" I joked.

For the next twenty-four hours we watched as three more private jets landed at Dulles and drove off with multiple matching vehicles. Jae traced a few of the vehicles to estates in Alexandria owned by DC politicians while a few went to the the Four Seasons, the Jefferson, or Ritz Carlton hotels in DC. From there, everything went dark. Between meals, and sleep, my life now revolved around that modest brownstone, which was becoming claustrophonic.

The next night, Drake brought me to a nonde-script building in downtown DC where I met a pair of FBI agents in a basement room with no windows. They took my statement about Senator Schilling's death. Fortunately, my story lined up with Larry's. I signed a couple documents and was released into Drake's custody. Early the next morning I went to the bakery and brought back coffee and bagels for everyone. Vanessa was at a computer and Drake was on his phone when I entered the safe room.

I placed the bagels down in front of Vanessa. "Where's Jae?"

"Chasing down a big lead. As you know, we were only able to track a couple of those limos that picked up the Gehenna families from Dulles, but daddy found a common thread. They all used the same car service." Vanessa grinned. "I couldn't hack into the car service's mainframe, so I did the next best thing and hacked into their building's computer utility system and took down their HVAC. Jae's going in undercover as an HVAC tech and gonna try to get some intel."

"Anything else new?"

"I got into Senator Schilling's phone."

"And?"

"There are calls to and from staff, and his girl-friend. The websites he visited were all government and legal stuff. Most of the texts were from staff with work related questions. He has a younger brother who runs the family construction business, who left him a work-related voicemail. There is one text from his wife with an attachment, which I haven't opened. I'm assuming it could be the smoking gun he opened on his laptop. If it is, then whatever worm is embedded in the file will wipe the phone like it did the laptop once we watch it. I've bypassed my hard drive and have it connected directly to the monitor. I'll record what we see with my cell phone's video function so we can play it back. Are you two ready?"

Drake nodded and Vanessa activated the link button on the text. The phone screen opened an mp4 video file which also appeared on the flat screen monitor. It was a bedroom where Margaret Schilling lay in bed with another man I couldn't see. She looked at the camera and smiled before giving the camera the middle finger. Slowly the man on top of her turned around and smiled at the camera. It was Gaspar Schultz. Both of them laughed. The screen went dark and the phone shut off.

No one said anything for long moments.

"Having sex with the leader of a satanic group who killed your son," Vanessa said, "and then sending a video of it off to your husband who's obsessed with bringing this same man to justice."

"It's straight from hell," Drake said.

"I can't begin to imagine how evil this organization is," I said.

Drake rested a hand on my shoulder. "Brace yourself. It's worse than you think." He turned to Vanessa. "Where is Margaret Schilling now?"

"She's left her home in Alexandria about a half hour ago heading into DC."

Drake started to dial a number on his phone. "Track her."

"Already on it, Daddy."

"How'd Missus Schilling get past all the media camped outside her home?" I said.

"The media frenzy surrounding the senator's death died down now that the president is in a new social media battle with some actress I've never heard of."

"It's amazing how ADHD our culture is," I said.

Drake got off the phone. "Jae's on his way back with a thumb drive. He said to tell you to take the governor off the car company's HVAC system, so they think he fixed it."

Vanessa typed away at the terminal. "Done." There was a beep and Vanessa rolled her chair over to another terminal. "You guys aren't going to believe where Margaret Schilling just drove her car to?"

"Where?"

"Six sixty-six Tartarus Lane," Vanessa said.

"That's Gaspar Schultz's building."

I laughed. "You're serious? Gaspar Schultz's address is six six six Tartarus Lane?"

"Oh yeah. He's got a penthouse apartment there for when he's in town, with underground parking, so we have no idea when he comes and goes. His building's technology is hardened to the point of some small countries. The only way I can get intel in a situation like this is if I have an inside person, or if I send drones by with thermal scans to see if there are people in the penthouse. I don't have the former in place, and the latter is impossible due to the building's proximity to the white house."

"You'd think with all the technology we have available we could figure this out."

"If we had the full resources of the FBI we could," Drake said.

"But it's been compromised," Vanessa reminded us.

"So, what should I be doing?"

"Wait and pray."

"I can pray, but I'm bad at waiting."

An hour and a half later, Vanessa tracked Mrs. Schilling's car back to her Alexandria brownstone. Jae returned dressed in blue overalls. It reminded me of the first time I had met Drake on a college campus. He was also undercover dressed as a janitor investigating a radicalized college group.

Jae left to go upstairs to shower while Vanessa worked on the thumb drive.

Roger said, "Go put on a suit, and make sure you shave. We're going to lunch." Drake turned to his daughter. "Vanessa you want me to bring you anything back?"

"I'm fine. My husband the health-nut now has me on sprouts, salad, and a piece of organic chicken."

After a quick shower and shave I had on one of my pinstripe suits. I forgot how good Walter was at his craft. The suit hung off my frame like every stitch was meant for me. It wasn't even a hand-made suit, but one off the rack that he altered. I met Drake out by the SUV. He was dressed in a double-breasted black suit and fedora.

"Where are we going, boss man?"

"Surprise."

NINETEEN

Drake drove us in the SUV past the White House. We turned onto Mass Ave toward Dupont Circle but had to take a detour onto 19th Street due to construction. We found our way to the address 666 Tartarus Lane. It was a tall, non-descript, plain stucco building with very few windows. In between the windows were bulbous sections of stucco that made the building look like it had cancerous tumors growing out of it. No doubt some architect thought it looked artsy. We drove into the underground parking garage and took a ticket at a kiosk.

"What are we doing here?"

"Getting lunch."

"Seriously?"

"Come on."

We took a glass elevator up to the first floor. This street level was commercial space with a steak house, a boutique store selling fancy pocketbooks, a hair salon, and coffee shop. I followed my friend through frosted glass doors into the restaurant also named Tartarus. It was a dark room with fancy booths filled with candlelight. Along the walls and ceiling were frescoes of ancient nude figures. It wasn't yet noon, so the place only had a few customers. A maître d' led us to a booth in the middle of the restaurant.

Bread and a fancy bottle of water were placed before us by a young woman. "Our specials today are lobster bisque and Maryland stuffed crabs rubbed with Old Bay spice. I'll give you gentlemen a few minutes."

After she left, I said, "I feel weird eating here."

Without looking up from the menu Drake said, "Greater is He who is in me than he who is in the world."

"Keep telling me that," I said.

Drake ordered steak and scalloped potatoes and a ginger ale. I ordered a chicken Caesar salad with sparkling water. After the waitress left with our menus, I took out my phone and the mylar bag and slipped it inside. Drake winked like a coach who was proud of his star athlete.

"Can we talk?" I whispered.

"A little," he said, "but don't go into too much detail."

"What are we doing here?"

"I've been in here before scoping it out, but I wanted to look at the parking garage."

"What are you thinking?"

"Not sure yet, but our tenant rarely leaves this building when he's in the country. He has another high-rise in New York, and a palace in Bucharest where he lives most of the time."

The food came, but I was hesitant to eat it. I felt like it was some sort of food offered to idols. Drake reminded me this food was prepared by normal people who were innocent.

"I've run background checks on everyone in this restaurant," he said. "They're not involved in the family business. Even the vendors who supply the menus, napkins, and food are clean."

After lunch, we got coffee at the super posh, and super expensive, shop next door. We next walked the perimeter of the building. There were cameras mounted at ten-foot intervals, which was not uncommon in a post 9/11 world, but I was surprised at the frequency of them. Drake pulled his hat low and I kept my head down as we walked.

"Building seems kind of bland for a billionaire," I said.

"I know. His New York high-rise is just as ugly, but his overseas property is extravagant. Kind of strange if you ask me."

We ended up back in the parking garage and walked around with our coffee. The parking garage went down three levels. The rows of fancy cars looked like they were straight off the lot of Bridget's car dealership. At the lowest level Drake found a manhole cover which he sniffed around. He moved over to a nearby fresh air grate built into the wall. I gave him my pen light and he looked around inside. The only thing visible was some sticks, trash, and dirt.

"What are you looking for?" I whispered.

"A gateway to hell," he said. I chuckled but my friend didn't. Drake coughed and moved away rubbing his eyes. "Smell that?"

I took a whiff and my eyes started watering. "It smells like something burning."

He shut the flashlight off and handed it back to me. "Brimstone."

A voice cleared its throat from behind us. I turned around to see a muscular young Caucasian man who had to be at least six foot six. "What are you guys doing?"

In one motion Drake dropped to his knees. "I knew it's around here somewhere, mate." His accent was now Australian.

I picked up on Drake's faux act. "My friend lost his contact lens."

"My fault for deciding to chuck-a-sickie," Drake said, still on his knees.

"You guys have business in this building?"

I held up my ice coffee with the coffee shop's logo on it. "We just had lunch at Tartarus and got coffee."

"Ah, I found it." Drake said, still in his Australian accent. He pretended to blow on a contact lens before looking up and placing the make-believe contact back in his eye. He walked past me right up to the security guard and patting the man's broad shoulder. "Whatever they're feeding you mate, tell them to stop."

The security guard followed us over to the SUV. In the rearview mirror I could see the guard take a picture of our license plate with his cell phone as we drove away.

"What's he gonna pull if he looks up our plate?"

"Just a nondescript untraceable government plate," Drake said.

"Won't that be a red flag?"

"Crikey, we're in DC. These plates are everywhere."

"Will you stop with the Australian accent."

We drove around Dupont Circle and found a tree-lined side street to park.

"What are we doing now?"

"Taking a stroll," he said.

We walked through the park, passing dozens of men and women dressed in fancy business suits in a rush to get somewhere. A few people jogged, and some walked with purebred tiny dogs. Drake kept wandering around the massive central granite fountain like he was lost.

"I'm here, whenever you feel the need to let me in on your secrets," I said.

"Did you remember seeing where that construction work was when we were re-routed on the way to the restaurant?"

"I didn't. Why?"

"Just a theory," he said.

We walked across the street from the park where Drake proceeded to step onto a fire hydrant balancing on the left and right water caps with surprising dexterity. He took out a small monocular from his coat pocket and looked back at Gaspar Schultz's building in the distance. He held up his hand as if to draw a make-believe line from the building to us. He put the monocular away and jumped down from the fire hydrant.

"Meridians."

"Huh?"

"There's a direct line between that building and us. I've driven by it a thousand times but never made the connection. Gehenna was under my nose the entire time."

"We're in a park?"

"Do you know what's under us?"

"No."

"Come on," he said, walking towards the parked SUV. Back in the vehicle Drake said, "There's almost a hundred thousand square feet of underground space below Dupont Circle. And that's just what we know of. It was supposedly a trolley station between nineteen forty-nine and nineteen sixty-two." Drake held up air quotes when he said, *supposedly*, as if to say he didn't believe it. "During the cold war it became a fallout shelter but was shut down in the mid-seventies." Again, he used air quotes when he said *shut down*. "In the nineties, part of the tunnel system was opened up as a food court called *Dupont Down Under*, but it shut down within a year."

"You're not buying it?"

"Maybe. Maybe not. When I was with the CIA, we'd sometimes spend years opening up an overseas fake businesses to use as a front. The business had to be viable with real employees and it had to make a profit. We'd go through a tremendous amount of work to make sure this fake business was bullet-proofed in case anyone became suspicious, or the government chose to audit it, but at the end of the day it was still a front."

"So, you think the underground ventures were all a front?"

"Not all of them," he said. "Maybe just one of them was a cover so Schultz could construct Gehenna. How else could you get away with major work in the middle of DC without drawing attention to yourself? You'd have to have a legit reason that was verifiable from anyone looking in. From DC building inspectors, to the CIA looking for Cold War Russian satellite locations."

"So, you think Gehenna is beneath DC?"

Drake nodded. "Somewhere between Dupont Circle and six sixty-six Tartarus Lane."

Back at the safe room Jae and Vanessa were at a white board, writing down notes on the Gehenna families they knew of.

"Jae's thumb drive allowed me to track all the

vehicles attached to pickups at Dulles. We've found every location."

"And we have movement," Jae said. "Guess where they're all going?"

"Six sixty-six Tartarus," Drake said, getting a bottle of water from the refrigerator.

Both Vanessa and Jae gave a disgusted look like a skunk just sprayed them, "How'd you—"

"Gehenna's beneath Schultz's building," Drake said. "I think it's tied into the Dupont Circle Tunnels." Vanessa knew some of the history of the tunnels, but Drake had to explain the full history to Jae. After the update Drake said, "If we miss this window, Gehenna isn't meeting for another decade. Vanessa, I need you to pull every map you can find of the tunnel system and get it programmed into my GPS as well as printed on paper. Jae, you, me and Brandon are going into the tunnel system tonight."

"What's the mission? Recon?"

Roger looked at me like I had ten heads. "More than scouting, son. This group must be stopped, as Vice President Prince said, at all costs." He turned to Jae and nodded.

Jae walked to the end of the safe room and took down a mirror. He placed his thumb on another black pad and the entire section of wall opened to reveal a small pantry-sized room that looked like an armory.

"What size body armor you take Brandon?"

* * *

THAT NIGHT, Claire brought dinner over to us. The first-floor dining area of our headquarters brownstone had an unloved antiseptic feel to it compared to the Drake's home next door. Dinner was rice and grilled chicken, but no one seemed to have an appetite. Vanessa reviewed maps of the DC sewer systems as well as the tunnel systems with us. The maps were bits and pieces she could gather from the different projects over the decades, which left many gaps to be filled in. Claire was stoic, clearly upset that her husband and son-in-law were about to go into harm's way. I could sympathize with her. I'd much rather be the one facing danger than the one left behind in safety.

After dinner, Jae made me go into the bathroom and try on all my gear. He outfitted me like we were going to war. I was given boots and black unmarked fatigues made of some man-made lightweight material. Jae even gave me underwear, socks, and a tank top made of the same material.

"Clothes are waterproof and have Kevlar woven into them," he said. "Won't stop a bullet or knife thrust but will prevent scrapes and wick water away."

When I came out, he continued to load me out with the gear. I was given a headset and throat mike, a helmet with night vision, an M27 rifle along with spare mags. We weren't bringing rucksacks, so most of the gear had to fit in a body armor MOLLE chest rig. On my hip was a Glock 17 with three spare mags, a canteen, and an IFAK. Jae tightened straps and inserted lightweight plates into the vest front and back, along with flexible pieces for the sides.

I pointed to the plates. "Stuff is much lighter than what I used back in the day. New technology?"

Jae nodded. "Nothing but cutting-edge stuff for us."

He continued to fit me with elbow and knee pads as well as fingerless gloves. The more gear he put on, the more claustrophobic I felt. Jae was meticulous and made sure I was aware of how everything worked, including simple things like adjustable straps. He made me field strip the rifle and Glock to make sure I was familiar with those particular weapons.

Upstairs, in the guest room I took off the gear and loaded it into a large OD green duffle bag. Everything in that bag was meant for one focus, to go to war and kill. Part of me wanted to leave the bag where it was and rush out the front door back to the farm. That same cowardly part of me started to believe this was not my problem. I had a family and a farm to run. New cattle would be delivered soon, and my family needed me. I wasn't meant to fight evil on this level. This was for people like Vice President Prince, special forces, and Drake's team. I had done my part in the past for the senator's family, and against this global cabal. I said a prayer to help calm my out-of-control nerves.

In the mirror, the clean-shaven late thirties male I barely recognized repeated back to me part of an oath he had taken a long time ago. "I will support and defend the Constitution of the United States against all enemies, foreign and domestic. So help me God." The Marine oath reminded me that I still had a duty to my country, but Drake had reminded me there was a higher power at work here. This went beyond fighting bad guys. Drake was fighting a spiritual war. When I looked down at the large bag again a gentle reminder came to me. The gear in that bag was not just meant to kill, but also meant to protect. The Bible said to defend the poor and fatherless.

I recited Tennyson's famous line from the *Charge of the Light Brigade*. "Ours is not to reason why; Ours is but to do or die."

As if in answer that morbid line, a passage from John 15 came to mind. *Greater love has no one than this, than to lay down one's life for his friends.*

Reinvigorated, I texted Annie to say I loved them and would be offline for a few hours. If I mentioned anything more, she'd panic. Annie tried to video call me, but I didn't answer. The last thing she needed was to see me decked out in black fatigues. I plugged the phone in to charge on a side table where it would stay until the mission was over.

Drake found me around ten p.m. I had packed all my personal items from Senator Schilling's apartment into bags and laid them out on the bed along with a folded note.

Drake picked up the note but didn't open it. "Is this what I think it is?"

I nodded. "My stuff's packed. If anything happens to me just give everything to Annie and the note will explain—"

Drake tossed the note back onto the bed. "I'm not gonna let anything happen to you, Brandon."

I rested a hand on my friend's shoulder. "You can't promise something that only God can deliver."

He nodded. "If you want to back out, I'd understand—"

"I'm in this with you to the end," I said, now completely focused on the mission. "My job is to watch your six, and let God beat the bad guys."

Drake started to say something but got choked up. "I love you, son."

"Love you too, old man."

"It's time to go."

TWENTY

Downstairs, Vanessa and Claire hugged us like we were Boy Scouts about to head off on a camping trip. Each man puffed up a bit from the affection from his spouse. I was jealous of the kisses each wife gave their husband and wished Annie could be here for my send-off kiss.

Out back, we loaded everything into the white nondescript van that was parked next to Roger's SUV. Vanessa got in the driver's seat while we piled in the back with no gear on, just fatigues and duffle bags. Claire waved from the back steps, her opposite hand to her mouth.

"I'm dropping you guys off on the fly," Vanessa said, starting to drive off. "Then I'll go back and monitor everything from the command center."

Jae handed me a fluorescent reflective vest a city DPW employee would wear. "Put this on so we don't look odd when we step out of the van." He put on his own vest and handed one to Drake. "You tell the big boss what we're doing?"

"I called Vice President Prince earlier to debrief him," Drake said. "He's got three personal secret service agents ready to come and help if needed."

"What did you tell him?"

"I asked for them to stay in a holding pattern unless I call for them."

Vanessa drove towards Dupont Circle. Buildings and apartment complexes were alive with lights in windows, but due to it being late at night there was minimal traffic, and no one seemed to be in Dupont Park. Instead of going towards the park, Vanessa entered a short traffic tunnel that went under the park. About halfway through the tunnel Vanessa stopped the van next to an old metal pass door with a padlock on it.

Drake got out with Jae and me following. Each of us carried our gear bag and wore the city worker vests over our black fatigues. The moment the van door shut, Vanessa tore off chirping the wheels. We dropped our bags and stood around the door like city workers going to check on utilities. Jae produced a palm sized bolt cutter and snapped the lock off. He opened the door and the three of us stepped inside. Jae shut the door behind us with a clang. The air was musty like a wet basement, but with a slight breeze.

"Gear up," Drake said, producing a flashlight which gave us just enough light to see by.

Within minutes we were fully loaded with three

empty green duffle bags and reflective vests lying on the floor. The periodic noise of traffic driving by outside the metal door had a rhythmic sound that seemed to call back from the world we had just left. Drake shut off his flashlight and lowered his night vision, motioning for us to do the same.

Using his throat mike, Drake checked in with Vanessa. "Eagle to Falcon. You copy?"

"Loud and clear. Will be at workstation within ten."

Drake turned to us. "Ready?"

Using a GPS mounted on the underside of his forearm Drake led us down a dusty plain cement pathway. Each of us walked with our rifles in the low ready position. Graffiti was everywhere, mostly swear words interspersed with phrases like, *can you smell what the Rock is cooking*, and *booyah*. Jargon from a pre 9/11 era when homeland security wasn't as much a priority, and homeless people could wander in, and out, of the tunnel space. The hum of traffic disappeared. In its place was the soft padding of our boots and a periodic squeak from a rat nearby. Behind me, Jae exhaled and shuffled closer as if he were afraid of the rodents. Drake pointed to an old video surveillance camera, mounted about eight feet up on a wall, with the wires cut. We continued walking and Drake pointed to a small modern wall-mounted camera with a single green light. From our mission brief I knew this was a motion detection device tied into Homeland Security. Drake held a zip-drive-sized piece of metal up to the device and the light turned off.

He motioned us onward. "Hurry, it will reset itself in ten seconds."

We rounded a bend and the setting went from a plain underground tunnel into something from a post-apocalyptic movie. In front of us was an abandoned coffee kiosk, sub shop, and other food court vendors. From the history Drake reviewed, I knew they were a holdover from the 90s. Stores that were part of a failed program to re-capture, and re-purpose, the underground space for public use. Standing before the broken-down storefronts it seemed like hundreds of years since humans had walked the space. The green light from the night vision goggles only added to the creepiness. I was ready for a zombie to walk out from behind a doorway, arms outstretched, ready to eat human flesh.

Overhead, I picked up the hum of traffic again. Drake looked at his GPS and led us just beyond the food court where it turned back into a plain cement tunnel. He stopped and pointed to a manhole. Jae produced a small pry bar. It took him a minute to clear the debris around the cover enough to get the pry bar in place. Once Jae popped the cover, he slid the heavy disk aside like it was a frisbee. Below us, a ladder descended into fuzzy darkness with the sound of water dripping.

"An underworld beneath the underworld," I whispered.

"Fitting," Drake added. Through his throat mike Drake checked in with Vanessa who responded back in a crackled voice. "Falcon," be advised, "We might lose coms."

Jae moved into position to climb down the ladder, but I stopped him. "I'm lighter," I whispered. "The ladder could be compromised."

Jae looked like he was about to argue with me but must have realized the logic behind my proposal and nodded. I secured my rifle and descended the ladder. It was wet and slippery. Twice my feet slipped off the rungs forcing my heart into my throat. I counted thirty rungs before splashing down into a shallow puddle on a cement pad. Surrounding me were pipes, wires, rusted metal, and wet rock. It reminded me of pictures I'd seen of Cheyenne Mountain, the massive underground military bunker in Colorado, built during the cold war. A deep nuclear bunker where ancient rock blended with modern technology in a dystopian sci-fi setting. The only difference was this underground space had been left rotting for decades. Drake and Jae dropped down next to me.

Drake looked at the electronic GPS strapped to his left forearm, but it was a scrambled mess from being too far underground. He raised his goggles and pulled out a backup waterproof map as well as a small red light to read it by. On his other wrist was a brass compass which he checked. We stood in a tunnel that went in a north south direction. Drake pointed north and motioned for us to follow him.

A crackle came over my headset. Jae and Drake both lifted their hands up to their ears. I assumed it was Vanessa trying to reach us, but we were too far underground. We were alone, without support. Drake continued to lead us with his rifle in the low ready position. I knew my friend was in his late fifties, but he moved with a dexterity of a pro athlete in his twenties. Jae took up the rear behind me. I hadn't been in a situation like this since my days in the Marines, and never would have imagined doing it again, let alone on US soil, or under it for that matter.

What few utilities were left in the tunnel veered upward towards the underground vendor space above. We soon came to the end of the tunnel and faced a solid rock wall with a long pool of dark water in front of it. The only noise came from the patter of water dripping from high above into the water in front of us. We each raised out night vision and took out flashlights.

"It should continue on," Drake said, looking back and forth from his map to the rock wall. "Maybe there was a cave in?"

"Can't be," I said. "That's solid rock in front of us. We'd see boulders and dirt. Let me see the map?" Drake handed it over. "How old is this?"

"This portion of the map was pulled from thirty-year-old archives, so who knows what's been done since then."

I pointed to a slight dip in the tunnel sketch. "The

grade descends before inclines. This would create a U shape like a trap under a sink, which would allow water to collect over the years."

Jae knelt at the water's edge. He shined a flashlight into the clear water. "He's right boss, the grade descends under the water."

I started to strip off my gear.

"Where you going?"

"I'm gonna go take a dip."

Drake pointed to the pool of dark water. "You think there's a throughway down there?"

"Only one way to find out," I said, taking my boots off.

"Boots are waterproof along with all your clothes," Jae said, continuing to peer into the water.

Still, I removed my boots and slid into the cold water with my pen light in my mouth. Although not skintight, the fatigues had a light neoprene feel to them and offered some protection from the chill. I gave my partners a thumbs up before taking a couple long breaths and ducking underwater. The penlight cut a small swath into the clear water which had been filtered through dozens of feet of rock before it ended up in this pool. I resurfaced and swam the remainder of the distance until I reached the rock wall. After another breath I dove under. Around three feet down I found the top of a tunnel. The opening extended down at least eight feet to the bottom. Were the water removed, it would have been easy to walk through.

I resurfaced for another breath and called back to the guys with an update. "There's an opening. I'll be back."

After taking a couple deep breaths I dove underwater again. I paused just before entering the underwater tunnel. The darkness played havoc with my psyche. Irrational thoughts entered my mind that maybe a giant eel or sea monster waited for me inside the passage. I reminded myself this was fresh water and there shouldn't even be a minnow in the water, let alone a Loch Ness monster. Inside, the tunnel was big enough to turn around in, and swim back if needed. I bumped my head on the stone ceiling above. In all my years of scuba diving I had never cave-dived before and the thought of not being able to break the surface above for a breath of air was unnerving. I continued on, watching the grade on the bottom start to turn upward. I was nearing an event horizon moment. Either I committed to finding the end and hoped it arrived with oxygen, or I turned around and went back. Something urged me onward.

Long moments passed before I swam almost straight up and broke the surface into darkness. I inhaled fresh air over and over and said a prayer of thanks. There was a rhythmic thumping I felt in my chest. Using the penlight, I did a three sixty scan. There were no utilities, or man-made materials, anywhere. Just rock and dirt. I realized the thumping wasn't my heart but a distant sound. A drum beat. I crawled out and scanned the immediate area to make sure it was safe. If any threats presented themselves, I would jump back into the safety of the water and swim back to my friends who were armed. Within seconds my entire outfit including my underwear, tank top and socks were dry. The gravel was sharp on my socks but I felt no discomfort. Jae wasn't kidding about the clothes. The tunnel continued as far as the flashlight would show. The slow rhythmic thumping of the drum continued.

I crawled back in the cool water and reversed my swim, this time more confident in my strokes. I broke the surface on the other side and received a flashlight beam in the face.

"You were gone too long," Drake said, moving the flashlight beam aside.

"Good news," I said, swimming back to them. "Water is contained in this decline, and the tunnel continues on like I suspected."

"Hot dog," Drake whispered. "I knew it. How far do you think it continues?"

"Don't know," I said, "but there's drums coming from somewhere deep in the tunnel."

"Gehenna," Drake said, smacking Jae in his muscular arm.

"It's a bit of a swim, so I suggest we leave anything we don't need here. Or I can come back and ferry it over. I'd also suggest taking our boots off as we'll need to swim hard."

Drake snapped a glow stick and dropped it to the

ground to give us light. He started to take off some of his gear, but Jae stood, hand on his rifle, stoic.

"What's the matter, you big baby?" Drake said.

"I don't do bathtubs," Jae said, "let alone swim into dark pools of water a hundred feet underground."

"I don't like the water either," Drake said, "but this is the obstacle in front of us." Jae didn't budge, and Drake shook his head, clearly trying not to laugh. "What my daughter saw in you I'll never know."

I wanted to prod Jae to help lighten the mood, but I could see real fear on his face. I'd seen grown men in the Marines who could face down a dozen men in a firefight, but who cowered at the sight of water. Jae had the same look.

"It's not that far," I said.

"How far is not that far?" Jae said.

I couldn't help myself and joked. "As long as you can hold your breath for a couple minutes, you'll be fine."

"Ain't gonna do it," Jae said, shaking his head back and forth. "No, sir. I ain't gonna do it."

Drake decided we would leave our helmets and night vision. "We can use the night vision scopes on our rifles, and I have monocular which switches back and forth."

Jae kept shaking his head back and forth. "No, sir."

Drake snapped his fingers. "Dangit, Brandon. I forgot a piece of gear."

"What?"

"A binky for my son-in-law."

"No, you don't," Jae said. "You're not gonna shame me into this. You know how I feel about water."

"Then stay here," Drake said, placing a hand on Jae's broad shoulder. "Just tell your wife that her daddy loves her, in case something happens to me."

"Sometimes I hate you," Jae said, starting to strip off his gear.

Jae and I followed Drake's lead and left our helmets, and night vision. Jae also left his IFAK, canteen, and two spare mags for his sidearm. He jumped up and down as if to test the new weight, but still didn't seem happy and left a multi tool and fixed blade knife as well.

With boots wrapped around our necks and rifles slung over our shoulders we dove down into the cold water. I led the way with my flashlight followed by Jae and then Drake who had snapped another glow stick. It was much harder to swim with all the gear, but I had confidence in knowing where the end was. Near the other side Jae started to struggle. I reached back and he grasped onto my arm with the same grip that almost broke my hand the first time we met. I ignored the pain and swam and pulled. We broke the surface with Jae praising God. Within minutes we had cleared our rifles and sidearms and put on our boots.

From the darkness the sound of rhythmic drumming increased as if whoever was there knew we were coming. It sounded like the heartbeat of an ancient dragon. Maybe we were in the belly of a beast and didn't know it? Drake took out his small monocular from a pocket and touched a button on it which I assumed turned it into night vision.

"Where you going?" Jae whispered.

"I'm gonna do a little recon. Be back in a minute." Within seconds he was enveloped in darkness.

I turned to Jay, handing him my canteen for a drink. "He always this bold?"

"Roger fears no man." A wide grin formed on his face. "Just Claire."

Five minutes later, Drake reappeared from the darkness. "The tunnel leads to a cavern where people are gathering. There's a natural stone outcropping of sorts that will offer us a vantage point we can observe from. This walkway is recessed beneath a rock shelf of sorts, which will give us cover."

"What are they doing?" I said.

"Not sure yet, but it's definitely Gehenna."

"How're you so sure?"

"You'll know when you see it," Drake said.

"What are we waiting for?" Jae said.

Drake stopped him. "We're gonna pray first." We bowed our heads and Drake whispered. "Father, what lies beyond this room is pure evil that is in direct opposition to you. Guide our steps, Lord. And all the people said?"

The three of us whispered, "Amen."

Drake led us using the monocular with me holding his belt and Jae holding mine. No sooner had we started this human train than a passive light entered the space. Drake put away the monocular and got on his knees. We followed his crawl towards an entrance that led onto an outcropping of rock that overlooked a massive lit cavern. He stopped us and pointed to a sensor mounted on the ground similar to the one we had seen earlier. Drake took out the same small device and deactivated the sensor the same way.

We crawled from the tunnel onto the outcropping where we sat just under the height of a rock. To our right and left the stone balcony of sorts continued in a semi-circular path above, and around, the perimeter of the cavern. The area smelled of smoke, spices, and some other aromatic incense. Drake motioned for us to look out each side of the boulder we hid behind. Jae took the left with me on the right and Drake facing the direction we came from. He handed the monocular to Jae who clicked off the night vision mode. He scanned the area and exhaled like he wanted to whistle. He handed the device to Drake who handed it to me.

The cavern was massive with a ceiling at least forty feet high. It was lit with dozens of oil lamps, candles, and torches making it about as bright as a cloudy late afternoon. Stone benches were placed in random patterns along the floor. At least two dozen figures dressed in hooded black robes wearing domino half masks stood, or sat, below us. Some of the masks were faces of demons while others had long beak-like noses which portrayed a human-animal hybrid.

To the left and below, black velvet curtains ran half the length of the circular cavern. Where the curtains ended was a darkened tunnel exit directly opposite us. I assumed it led out of the cavern and up to Gaspar Schultz's building. Just to the right of the tunnel exit was a shadowy room with stone tables where several robed figures lay on top of one another engaging in some sort of satanic orgy. Shouts came from onlookers inside the space, many of whom drank from stone chalices. At the edge of that room a young boy in a loin cloth beat on a drum. He looked drugged and moved the drum sticks up and down like a zombie. One of the closer robed figures drank from their stone chalice. A moment later they dabbed their mouth with a handkerchief leaving a deep red stain on the material.

Their cups were filled with blood.

TWENTY-ONE

I scanned back and forth until I found the source of the drink. Below us to the immediate right was an upside-down crucifix carved into the stone wall of the cavern. Thin dark lines of blood trickled down the front and collected in a large stone basin at the bottom. Robed figures dunked their chalices into the stone bowl like they were at a costume party, getting another cup of punch. I followed the trail of blood back up above the inverted cross to where it disappeared into the darkness. Switching the monocular to night vision I looked higher to find the remains of three half-naked young children who lay on a flat stone altar of sorts. IVs attached to their arms hung over the side allowing the blood to flow down the face of the stone into the satanic punch bowl below. All three were lifeless.

I fell back against the rock, terrified I was going to give our position away were I to vomit. Over the past few years, I had seen what I had thought was the worst evil man could conjure up. I had no words for what I had just witnessed. Drake placed a hand on my shoulder as if to ask if I was *okay*. I shook my head back and forth with a tear falling down my cheek as if to clarify that, *I was not okay*. He took another look with the monocular and saw what he had missed earlier. He handed the monocular to Jae and held up three fingers to signify to look in the direction of three o'clock. Moments later the three of us sat with our backs against the rock, silently praying.

A hush fell over the crowd below. I turned to see ten armed men enter from the opposite tunnel into the cavern, dressed in robes. Each wore the same full-faced red demon mask but with different facial expressions. One mask was a smile, another was angry, with others showing joy, surprise, disgust, and tearful laughter. The setting looked like it was from a gothic horror movie set in the 1800s, but in their hands were very real twenty-first century AR-15s.

"Quiet!" one of the armed men shouted.

The young boy drumming stopped. A final masked figure dressed in white entered the hall. Once inside he dropped the hood and removed an animal mask, revealing an old man with white hair and wrinkles covering his face.

Drake mouthed the words, *Gaspar Schultz*.

Jae and I continued to look at Drake for direction. He motioned for us to stay put.

"All of you may remove your mask and hoods," Gaspar said with an eastern European accent, and a phlegmy hoarse voice that sounded like he had just smoked a pack of cigarettes.

As the crowd removed their masks and hoods I scanned back and forth to see if I recognized anyone. There were one or two familiar faces I couldn't quite place, but most I had never seen before. The majority of the people were elderly, with a near perfect male to female ratio. All of them were Caucasian.

"Welcome to our decade of decadence," Schultz said.

The crowd cheered and started to chant a word in another language I didn't recognize. As the cheering continued, I picked up a woman refilling her chalice at the blood punchbowl. Jae and Roger seemed to notice Margaret Schilling at the same time I did. She looked up for a moment as if she knew we were there, before she rejoined the group. Both Jae and Roger had the same disgusted expressions on their faces. I couldn't comprehend how Mrs. Schilling could belong to a group like this. A group whose leader was responsible for the death of her only son.

"I am in touch with some of you throughout the years," Schultz continued, "but most of you I only speak through proxies." He turned to one of his armed underlings. "Is there anyone missing?"

Someone in the crowd with a French accent mentioned a family name I didn't recognize.

Another person from the crowd answered, "His

fidelity was in question and was dealt with accordingly."

Schultz raised his hand. "Then let us get the meeting underway."

Everyone knelt before the bloody inverted cross. It was then I noticed something above the blood, the cross, and dead children. In the flickering lamp light near the roof of the cavern, was the carved face of some hideous creature. The genuflecting crowd one-by-one prostrated themselves. Long moments of silence passed before moaning filled the cavern. It was like they were doing some chant to try to get in sync with one another, or some demonic force. A few minutes later, Schultz was helped up by a robed man next to him. The crowd followed.

Schultz cleared what he could from his phlegm. "Every one of you received from this group every-thing you have ever wanted, be it power, wealth, influence, and comfort. There is not one person here whose net worth is under four hundred million Euros. Every one of you who live abroad arrived here on private jets. Every one of you has access to the cleanest medicine, and best doctors on the planet. Is there any material need I have not met from anyone here?" There was silence. "Anything?" Schultz repeated. "Mention it to me now and it will be granted. Miss Roth, did your daughter receive that kidney we harvested for her?"

A late fifties female spoke from the crowd. "She did, grand cleric, and has recovered."

"Good. Now let us move on to the focus of this meeting." Some of the robe figures sat on the stone benches while others chose to stand. "As you know our roots lie in old Europe and go back to the Middle East, but our twenty-first century battleground is in the United States. This is why I moved Gehenna here decades ago from its previous location in Bucharest. Regardless of how you feel about this place, if a global change is going to happen it must start in the most powerful, and influential, country in the world. Currently that is the United States.

"Only a few of our sponsored candidates in the United States Congress won seats during this last election, and our candidate lost the White House. The hopes we had of terraforming the world into a progressive utopia have been delayed." Hisses erupted from the crowd but stopped when Schultz raised his hands. "There is no doubt this current administration will have the ability to name multiple supreme court justices, which will further slow our work. Times are extreme, and we must employ extreme measures. Some of you have asked when, and how, we would act. Decades ago, I planned for every possible contingency." Gaspar Schultz paused as if he were a stage performer trying to build to a crescendo in his speech. "This week I will launch Operation Mercury which will change the landscape of this country overnight."

"How?" one person shouted.

"Where will it be?" added another. "Wallstreet?"

Schultz smiled. "Why, here of course. Look around you." Dark curtains were removed along the left side of the cavern by guards to reveal stacked crates with the words *HVAC* stenciled on them. Before anyone could pose a question, Gaspar said, "I assure you these crates do not contain heating and cooling equipment. Shipments with the words explosive written on them tend to attract attention."

Laughter and shouts erupted from the crowd. Someone asked if they were nukes.

"No," Schultz said. "But when I'm finished, we will have enough explosive to take out much of DC, including the White House. When I constructed the building above us decades ago, I designed, and planned for it, to be used as a weapon for a desperate time such as this. Throughout the exterior of the building are hollowed out sections where we will plant these explosives. Mixed in with the stucco exterior are fragments of metal that will add to the destructive force of these explosives. Once all the pieces are in place, this building will act like a hundred-foot tall claymore mine and take out at least a one square mile radius including the White House. Furthermore, within the exterior stucco coating is a chemical that, when it becomes dust turns into a poison which will travel for miles, killing anyone who breaths it in."

"This is brilliant," someone shouted.

"My building on Wall Street was built the same way decades ago and, depending on the results of this operation, may be set-off to cripple the financial market."

"You're a genius," someone said.

"Many of you," Schultz continued, "have connections and influence in the media, and must tell your people to report this explosion as a drone strike from a terrorist group overseas. I'm waiting to hear back from a few middle eastern leaders to find out which one won't assist in funding some of our future missions. At which time we will pin the false flag attack on them. The time for meeting in the dark is almost at an end. After Operation Mercury, we will appear in the daylight like the god Mercury to deliver news to the masses and to usher in a new... world...order!"

There were cheers and clapping which stopped when Schultz raised his hands yet again. "I've been in touch with Speaker Kelleher who is at a safe location offsite. I assured her that when this operation is complete, she will be the first female president of the United States. I have contacts in the US military who will back her and enforce Martial Law. Now, you may ask questions."

"When will this happen?" someone said.

Schultz turned to a man behind him. "My son Adrian will explain."

An early forties, dark-complexioned man placed his hand on Schultz's shoulder. "Thank you, Papa," he said in a similar European accent, "and thank you all for being here. The attack will happen within seventy-two hours, a week at the latest. Once all the explosives are in place on the upper floors of our building, we then confirm the president and vice president are in town before activating the bomb."

Schultz spoke again. "Once we take control of government you will all have a role to play in our new world order. Whatever idea you have of wealth and power will be dwarfed. Your families will thrive beyond your wildest dreams." He raised his hands again and shouted, "Prepare yourselves."

There were more shouts and applause.

Once it died down, Adrian added, "If you have homes nearby, you must have your family go on vacations for the next week. Move assets offshore. And relocate valuables out of state. You have been warned."

Schultz stepped back in front of his son. "Now mingle and enjoy each other in every way possible. We will talk more later."

There was more clapping, with many people running up to kiss Schultz's hand like he was a deity. Schultz walked over to Margaret Schilling and took her by the hand into the back alcove. Other couples followed. A line started to form around the blood punch bowl. People scraped the bottom with their stone chalices trying to get at the last of the innocents' blood.

Seeing this, two of the armed guards guided the zombie-like drummer boy over to the bowl. One of the guards produced a bone knife from under his robe. In one motion he leaned the boy over and slit the child's throat, allowing the blood to refill the bowl. The drugged child didn't flinch. After long moments, the boy started to shake. The guard stabbed him in the back and through the heart with the knife to stop the trembling. Seeing this, I started to rise with the intention to fire upon everyone in the room, but Drake and Jae both pulled me back down.

Drake motioned for all eyes on him. He drew a diagram in the dirt in front of us. I was to crawl down the right side of the stone precipice we were on, which had a direct line of sight towards the lower exit out of the cavern. My job was to keep people from leaving. Jae was to go down the left and do the same. Drake motioned for Jae to be careful and drew a stairwell in the dirt as if to remind him his side had a stairwell which led from the lower chamber up to our stone balcony.

The time for research and meetings was over. I wanted to act. As if Drake read my thoughts, I saw him switch his rifle from semi to full auto. He grabbed my chin in his hand and forced me to look at him. Nothing was said but his eyes pleaded with me to trust him, and that we would avenge the boy who was just murdered. These people were more demon than human and had to be kept from escaping back into the world where lawyers and disinfo handlers could manage any crisis.

Jae switched his M27 to full auto as well.

I crawled off to the right and Jae did the opposite,

leaving Drake in the middle. I made it around the semicircular outcropping and came to rest against the side of the stone altar. To my right just above my head was the flat stone platform where the three dead children lay. I snuck my rifle just over the rock outcropping ready to fire. Unlike Drake and Jae, I left my rifle on semi auto. In a moment I would shoot, and kill, other human beings. I wasn't afraid to do the job, but I was terrified that in my wrath I might enjoy it.

A quiet moan, just above a whisper, shook me out of the angry fog. I rose just above a crouch and looked upon the three children. Two of them were pale, lifeless, but a young girl no older than six looked different. I gasped when I saw her chest rise.

She was alive.

Any second Drake and Jae were going to unleash a fury of gunfire. I had to get them to hold off so I could grab this girl. I rested my rifle against the rock outcropping and did the only thing I could and stood up. It was dark where we were in this upper area of the cavern. Anyone below would be hard pressed to see my dark form against the edge of the stone platform, but I hoped Drake and Jae would see me and hold off. I waited a few seconds before I climbed up on top of the platform and kept as flat a profile as possible. I took off a glove and reached over to feel for a pulse on the two far children. Both were cold and dead. I reached for the young girl and felt a weak pulse. I pulled her to me and removed the pic line from her arm which had been draining her blood. I noticed a kink in the line which must have reduced the blood flow and kept her alive. Below, informal conversations continued around the blood punch bowl. I placed a small rock over the IV line to keep it in place on top of the platform so it wouldn't fall down and attract attention. As I lowered the girl down, the IV line slid out from under the rock and fell off the platform.

There were a few gasps from below with someone shouting the words, "Look. Up there!"

In the next instant the sound of gunfire exploded throughout the cavern. I pulled the unconscious girl down behind the rock outcropping as bullets ricocheted off stone above and behind me. The familiar sounds of automatic M27 rifle bursts joined in from Drake and Jae's positions. Seconds passed and screams from below mixed in with the gunfire. I cradled the girl in my arms the way I once did my infant son after he was pronounced dead. Regardless of what happened, I had to rescue this girl. For me, the entire mission now coalesced around this child.

There was a lull in gunfire in my direction as Jae and Drake drew off the enemy. I made the decision to leave my rifle and crawl along the ground, dragging the girl behind me. There was a lot of dirt but also sharp pebbles which I knew would be cutting into her flesh, but I had no choice if I wanted to stay below the height of the rock outcropping. From the sound of gunfire Jae and Roger seemed to be in sync.

As one would pause to change a magazine the other would continue firing. I made it back to Drake with the girl. He dropped down behind a boulder and changed a mag with the dexterity of a young athletic soldier.

"This girl's alive," I shouted over the gunfire thundering around us. "You gotta get her out of here. She's lost a lot of blood and has been drugged."

Drake glared at me as if I were asking the impossible. Only to a man like Roger Drake would falling back to a safe area during a firefight be considered a sacrifice. He knew there wasn't enough space for me to crawl past him with the girl and that I'd have to stand up to step over him. I pushed the girl along the dirt into his arms.

"Get her to the pool, stabilize her, and come back," I said, crawling back towards my rifle before he could debate me.

I made it back to the rifle and checked it before popping my head above the outcropping. Below robed figures lay in incongruent patterns, blood pouring from death shots from Drake and Jae. A few individuals had tried to escape back through the tunnel entrance but were cut down by Jae. The majority of the crowd had retreated back into the safety of the antechamber orgy room. Two guards had turned over a stone bench in front of the space for protection. They fired up in Jae's direction and to where Roger had been moments earlier. Unbeknownst to the two men their left side was exposed to me. I rose on my knees, took a breath and fired two shots. A moment later the two men lay dead or dying. Jae had moved farther down the line allowing him to guard the stairwell while having a clear line of sight of people trying to sneak out the tunnel exit. Each time someone stuck their head out from the antechamber room Jae fired off several rounds, forcing them back inside.

I crawled back to where Roger had been. Behind me was the tunnel we entered from. I could see the faint light from Drake's flashlight bouncing around as he rushed back towards the direction of the pool of water with the girl. If we didn't make it out of the cavern, then that poor girl would be recaptured. A flash of fire exploded somewhere beneath me as an oil lamp was hit by a stray bullet. Another lamp nearby was hit, but this one didn't explode. Instead it drained burning liquid onto two bodies below. One of the robed figures wasn't quite dead. They wriggled and screamed in agony as they burned to death. A sympathetic shot from Jae finished this guy's immediate suffering.

Four armed men burst from the safety of the back antechamber, unloading with AR-15s in Jae's direction. Jae ducked down while I fired, hitting one of them. The remaining three hid behind an overturned stone bench within the main cavern. They reinforced the barricade with another stone bench, blocking my line of sight. One of the three peeled off towards the tunnel exit, trying to go for back-up, or more weapons. I clipped his leg just before he got out of range. He fell but continued to crawl out of sight. The other two behind the overturned bench were joined by four more men who all fired in my direction. I fell back and changed mags. Jae re-engaged from his spot and some of the firefight left me to re-engage him. I moved positions again, this time crawling back towards my original position near the altar. This movement would continue to confuse the enemy. I hoped Jae followed my lead. I rose and continued to fire but didn't have a good angle. Suddenly, one of the men behind the barricade threw something up and over the outcropping where Jae was.

I screamed, "Grenade!"

There was a deafening explosion where Jae had been. I dropped on my hands and knees, crawling back towards Jae's direction. About halfway to Jae I rose and fired towards the hidden group to keep them pinned. I found Jae lying face down covered in dirt. He shook his head, causing dirt and debris to fall off. I propped him up, his back against the rock outcropping to protect him.

"You okay?"

He gave me the thumbs up and I handed him his rifle.

I changed my rifle to full auto, and without looking, fired over the rock outcropping in the random direction of the group of men. I crawled down the line a few feet and stopped to make sure Jae was right behind me.

"Stay with me," I said, peering out of a crack between the rock.

The men were now barricaded on three sides behind stone benches.

"What's the plan?" Jae said, breathing heavy.

"Not sure."

Jae peered out. "If they can lay down enough cover fire from their position it will allow everyone in that back chamber to waltz out the exit behind them to safety. We gotta do something."

My dad's warnings floated back about the severity of what I was getting into. I wished he were with me, and could use his precision shooting, even if he only had his flintlock rifle. Then I remembered what he recently taught me about hunting with a flintlock.

"I'm gonna bark 'em," I said.

"What are you talking about, bark 'em? That some white thing?"

"Just be ready."

I switched back to semi auto and reached over the ledge. It would take the men behind the barricade only a second or two to pick up our new location. I aimed and fired two rounds, hitting an oil lamp hanging behind them. A wave of napalm like fire exploded into the area the men had barricaded themselves into. Five flaming robed bodies jumped out from the safety of the space. Jae fired off a burst, hitting four targets. I fired twice hitting the fifth individual on the second shot.

"Good job," I said, looking at Jae. He smiled; blood covered his bright teeth. He started to cough up blood.

I dropped my rifle and checked him over. "You dummy," I said. "You didn't tell me you were hit with that grenade."

I checked him over and felt a large wet spot of blood under his left armpit, where the side plate of the vest ended. Jae was trying to say something, but I ignored him. He coughed up some blood and spoke again, forcing me to lean in closer.

"Brandon—"

"Don't try to talk, brother."

"There were six," he took a breath and repeated, "There were six."

I realized what he was saying. There were six men behind that barricade, but we only shot five. One had snuck out while we crawled to our new position. Either he scurried out the cavern exit, or up the stairs towards us? Jae's eyes went wide as if to warn of something from the direction we came from. I turned and saw a flash of fire and felt like a truck hit me in the chest. I fell back and heard another shot go off before everything went dark.

TWENTY-TWO

I LOST CONSCIOUSNESS FOR ONLY A FEW SECONDS BUT awoke disarmed and being dragged. It took all my strength just to take in air. Whatever armor plating Jae had put in my vest worked, but it felt like I still might have a cracked rib. I was dragged down the rough stone stairs into the cavern. The area was smoke-filled, and the sound of the firefight seemed to still echo off the rock walls. The horrid scent of burning bodies made breathing even more difficult. I looked right and left but didn't see Jae anywhere. Robed figures cried and tended to the dying.

The voice of Adrian shouted, "There was another soldier with them. Go look up top."

The sound of two sets of boots ran past me up the stone stairwell. I was dropped at the feet of someone. All I could see was the bottom hem of a white robe.

The phlegmy voice spoke to me. "Brandon Hall, born April twenty-four, Nineteen eighty-one. Served one tour in Afghanistan. Almost died once while overseas. Follower of the false Messiah, and husband to Annie, father to Emily and Addison. A cattle farmer and part time private investigator, and it appears, hired soldier of fortune."

With each tidbit of information Gaspar Schultz mentioned, my stomach turned more. Behind Schultz the remaining guards kept some of the unharmed Gehenna members from leaving for some reason. Maybe they wanted to make them watch my execution? I stood up, undoing my vest, and letting it fall to the floor so I could breathe easier. I had no need for it any longer. Behind Schultz stood Margaret Schilling. Her eyes were fixed on me. Her beauty had all but evaporated. In its place was a grotesque disgusting human. A demonic woman who let her only son be killed by a group she belonged to. Slowly, her neutral demeanor turned into a smirk as if she had been waiting for this moment.

"It's nice to finally meet you," Schultz said, walking around me bobbing his head like he was inspecting every inch of my body.

"The feeling's not mutual."

After a moment he said, "It is a shame what happened to your cattle. Who would do such a thing?"

"Go to hell."

He stopped in front of me and looked at my chest. After an awkward pause he poked it like I was foreign to him. "Interesting," he said, continuing to walk around me. "You know I've been trying to kill you for some time, but it's like you've been protected by the supernatural. After the AFA raided your property I was shocked you survived. Then, when you stumbled across Jeb Lawson and his brother in the Dismal Swamp, I hoped they would do the job."

"Sorry to disappoint you."

"But what you don't know is I sent an employee to dispense with you a few months back. He was supposed to run you off the road and make it look like an accident, but he had a heart attack as soon as he entered your town."

"Sad for you."

"This man was thirty-three years old, a former CIA assassin, ran triathlons, and the epitome of health. It's impossible you made it through that gauntlet." Schultz stepped back. "Needless to say you fascinate me at how the supernatural is at work in your life."

"God has a way of doing that for his children from time to time."

"Maybe," Schultz coughed before opening both hands up like he was welcoming me to his home. "Yet here you are delivered right to me where I can slit your throat."

"If it's God's will."

He smiled and drew closer. "Do you think it is His will, Brandon Hall?"

"I kinda hope not."

Schultz laughed. "In another life I would have liked you. We might have even been friends."

"I don't think so," I said, stepping closer. Two men grabbed my arms, holding me back.

"You're over ninety. Your days are waning. What do you hope to accomplish?"

"Technology will extend my life and transhumanism may take it further if not indefinitely. Regardless, I'm here to usher in another."

"I know your boss' name, Schultz. I read the book and I know who wins in the end."

Schultz laughed again. "So you say. Now may I offer you a drink?" He held out a hand and someone gave him a goblet of blood. He took a sip and smiled, blood trickling down his chin. He saw the disgust on my face. "Vampires are on to something," he said.

Schultz took another sip and pushed it against my lips. I closed my mouth tight. He seemed frustrated he couldn't get the blood into my mouth and grunted like an angry animal before pouring it over my head. The warm liquid felt like syrup. The lifeblood of innocent children was being poured over me from an unholy sacrifice. Their very essence. Children who were alive just a short time earlier. I thought of my son Jonah and the blood around his wounds when I held him last. I started to weep and everyone around me laughed. I could hear Margaret's cackle above the others.

"Is the great warrior for God afraid, is he?" Schultz mocked.

My rebuttal was to quote Romans Fourteen. "Every knee shall bow before Him."

"I have enjoyed our parlay," Schultz said, "but it must come to an end." He turned to his son. "Adrian, kill him slow and video tape it, so I can watch it over and over. Every time I watch one of His soldiers die it brings me such a joy."

I struggled, but the two men held me fast. A third man produced a palm sized camcorder. Margaret Schilling walked up and took the camera from him. "Let me be the one to tape this."

Schultz nodded. "Well done Miss Collin."

"How could you belong to a group responsible for killing your son?"

"This group, and its mission," Margaret said, "are greater than any offspring I could produce."

"You're sick!"

Schultz held the hand of his dying comrade. For a moment he seemed sympathetic and motioned for a guard to come over and help. Schultz rose and the guard fired off a round into the dying person's head.

"Adrian," Margaret said. "I'm ready whenever you are."

Gaspar Schultz's son walked forward with what looked like an old-fashioned shiny barber's straight razor. I shut my eyes and prayed for strength to face death head on. The immediate panic and fear left, and in its place was a new feeling. Anticipation. I knew there would be moments of struggling, then I would be with my Lord and my son Jonah. Once there, I would have no more pain, no more suffering, and no more sadness.

A boom woke me from the dream. The two men holding me let go and rushed to Schultz's son who was on the ground in front of me, wriggling. Half his head had been blown off. Gaspar Schultz screamed. The old man dropped on his knees and crawled towards his son the way a snake slithers on the ground. The two guards on either side of Adrian didn't seem to know what to do. They raised their rifles up to face me and I dropped onto my knees, giving Drake a better line of sight. A moment later both men fell back dead with two more shots coming from behind me. I knelt there, covered in blood, feeling like I was about to go into shock. A few robed figures tried to escape into the tunnel exit but were cut down, the remaining group fell back into the alcove.

Schultz screamed for help while he grabbed pieces of his son's skull like he could put Humpty Dumpty back together. "Help my son. Help my only son."

"He's gone, Gaspar," I said.

Gaspar Schultz turned to me his eyes black like they were lit with an otherworldly dark fire. The old man rent his bloody robe and screamed like a man filled with a thousand voices. He produced a knife from somewhere under his torn tunic. It had a bone handle and a long dark Damascus blade. He rushed me with drool pouring out of his mouth. I stood up knowing I'd block Drake's shot, but I wanted to handle Schultz myself. Even injured, I would over-power the old man and exact my own form of right-eous vengeance.

I forearm blocked an overhead stab, but Schultz swung with his free left hand and lifted me into the air, knocking the wind out of me again. The strength the man possessed was beyond anything I could imagine. I stumbled backwards trying to take in a sliver of air so I could fight back. He approached with his arms down as if to taunt me to strike. Gath-ering my strength, I punched him in the face, but he didn't flinch. He tried to kick me in the groin which I blocked by raising my left knee. Another left hook from him I shoulder-blocked but the knife came down, tearing through my clothes and cut into my chest. I couldn't understand how this old man was overpowering me? I swung again and Gaspar ducked like a prize fighter. He straight kicked me in the stomach, knocking me down. I could not believe I was going to lose the fight. Gaspar Schultz came up, knife raised. I struggled to take in air, had no strength, nor weapon within reach.

In the end I used the only weapon left to me which should have been my first choice. "The Lord is my strength and my shield."

Gaspar came up short, his teeth bared like a roaring lion. His arm frozen in a striking pose just over my head. He pulled back to strike. A moment later, Gaspar Schultz shuddered as a bullet punctured his chest. He fell to his knees, and yet, rose again moving again to strike.

"Impossible," I coughed.

Schultz was struck again two more times, each time he fell to his knees and rose again. Finally, Drake took a head shot which finished the job.

I fell back into a robed figure who moaned. All around me was blood, smoke, and death. I turned to see Drake up on the stone balcony shouldering his M27. For a moment it looked like he was accompanied on either side by a glowing army. Soldiers from long ago holding swords rather than rifles. They were tall and bright, but a moment later they disappeared into the smoke. I grabbed an AR-15 from the floor and half-crawled towards the stairwell that led back up to Drake. As people tried to peer out from the back room I fired rounds as did Drake forcing them back inside. The group hissed and snarled from the dark space like vipers trying to escape from a burning nest. Drake met me halfway down the steps and handed me an M27. I knew it was Jae's.

"Jae?"

Drake shook his head back and forth, tears pouring down his cheeks. He walked past me towards the back room where the remaining Gehenna were gathered. Someone fired off a handgun from the space, hitting Roger in his plated vest, but Roger Drake didn't flinch or stop approaching. Someone else fired from a rifle and missed. He stepped on, rather than over, the dead body of

Gaspar Schultz and approached the entrance to the alcove. He flicked a switch on his rifle and unloaded into the space at full auto. Drake stopped to change magazines. I heard screams and wails that sounded more animal than human. Reloaded, Drake emptied his last magazine into the space. It was now silent except for the echo of gunfire. The next sound came from the clink of his M27 falling to the ground. Drake removed his sidearm and unloaded it into the space as well. He turned and walked past me back up the stairwell to where I knew Jae's body lay. The smoke and dust were unbearable and only improved when we reached the top where fresh air came in from the tunnel we had entered from. From topside, I continued to scan for any survivors but there was no noise nor movement from the alcove.

Roger Drake kneeled down in front of Jae's body, his son-in-law's eyes wide open. Roger closed Jae's eyes and started to cry. Not the crying of someone mourning the loss of a fellow soldier, but the wailing of a dad over a dead son. A horrific sound I once made long ago over my Jonah. It was a shameless hyperventilating sound like a dying animal. My tears joined with my friend's, but they were nowhere near as powerful. Roger stripped off Jae's gear and started to lift the muscular man up.

I moved to help, but he shouted, "I got this." In one motion he lifted his son-in-law over his shoulder and started to walk back down the tunnel towards the pool of water. As he moved along the tunnel, I heard Roger quote John 3:19 through his weeping. "And this is the condemnation, that light is come into the world, and men loved darkness rather than light, because their deeds were evil. For every one that doeth evil hateth the light, neither cometh to the light, lest his deeds should be reproved."

I took one last look at what was left of Gehenna, hell on earth. To my far right the two remaining dead children lay on the satanic alter. Below, blood, and gore lay everywhere. Fires smoldered on dead bodies creating an unbearable stench. I had no idea what government group, or agency, would come and clean this up. How would it even be reported? Before turning to leave I saw movement from the alcove.

A single female stumbled out. Margaret Schilling limped out from the space barefoot, her robe tattered, and her exposed flesh covered in blood. A bloody stump was all that remained of her left arm. Margaret shuffled up to the crates filled with explosives. She raised her right arm over her chest before dropping it back down to her side. She continued cross her right arm over her chest as if her left hand still existed. She looked down as if realizing she had only one appendage left. I used the scope on the rifle to look closer. In Margaret's right hand was a grenade. She lifted it to her mouth and pulled the pin with her teeth. She turned as if she knew I were there and smiled before dropping the grenade. I turned and fled after Roger.

A muffled boom was followed by a louder explosion. I tripped and fell over something. I took out my flashlight and could see one of the robed soldiers, dead with a fixed blade knife stuck in his head. The tunnel shook dropping rock, dirt, and pebbles around me. Another explosion followed. I caught up with Roger at the pool. In the green illumination of the glow stick light I could see another robed figure face down floating in the pool of water. Roger had taken both soldiers out quietly, and without firearms. The man never ceased to amaze me.

Roger sat next to the pool with Jae sprawled out in his arms. The young girl we rescued rested inside a wrapped emergency mylar blanket next to him. Her color had improved but she was still unconscious from the loss of blood and whatever drug they used. The tunnel rumbled as more explosions went off, which shook the tunnel and rained down dirt and rock into the pool of water.

"Margaret set off the explosives with a grenade," I shouted. "Get into the water."

Roger cradled Jae's head in his lap, rocking back and forth like a parent trying to calm a newborn. For the first time since I had met him, my friend looked old and frail. "I'm not leaving my son-in-law?"

I picked up the living child, keeping her wrapped in the mylar blanket and handed her to Roger. "Take the child. Cover her mouth and nose and swim fast."

"But—"

"I'll take Jae. Just go."

The entire tunnel shook as if it was going to

collapse. Looking back down towards Gehenna the tunnel started to brighten. Fire and flames were approaching.

"Go!" I shouted.

Drake cradled the young girl and dropped below the surface of the water. I dragged Jae's body into the water and dove behind him. Suddenly, the dark water above lit up as flames covered it like talons of some fiery monster trying to grab us. The water temperature went from frigid to lukewarm. I couldn't imagine the amount of heat that was produced from the explosions. I swam hard dragging Jae behind me. Halfway through the underwater tunnel, rocks dropped around us blocking the way I came. My lungs were on fire, but I continued to pull Jae. More rock fell around me. I prayed the exit would remain open. After long moments I came up on the other side, gasping for air. In the dim green light of the glow stick I could see Roger checking the little girl's vital signs. She was on her side coughing.

"She okay?"

"I think so. She swallowed some water." Roger waded into the water to help drag Jae out.

On shore I checked the little girl over and tightened the emergency mylar blanket around her. She coughed some more, spit up water, and opened her eyes. She tried to say something, but I couldn't make it out.

"Don't talk, sweetie. You're safe now."

"Are you an angel?" she whispered.

I smiled. "No, but I am a dad with two little girls, and I'm here to protect you. Is that good enough?"

She smiled and passed back out as if talking used up all her energy. I checked her pulse and her vitals were weak but steady. Drake rested with Jae's head in his lap. Behind us the water started to boil, and I could feel heat emanating from the rock wall. Had the underwater tunnel not been there to act as a barrier we would have been roasted alive.

"Roger, I have an adrenaline shot in my IFAK pack. Maybe I could—"

"No," he said. "Only use the adrenaline shot as a last resort." He picked up his cell from our pile of helmets and night vision goggles. "Get up to the surface tunnels and you should be able to reach Vanessa who can send help. Take the child."

I took out my pen light, picked the girl up and started off. After a few yards I realized Drake hadn't moved. "You coming?"

"I'm not leaving Jae."

I looked down at the girl in my arms. "I'll be back. I promise."

"I know you will," he said.

I climbed the ladder back up to the tunnels under Dupont Circle careful to keep the girl balanced over my shoulder. I was glad she was unconscious as the past few minutes might have scared her to death. I started to weep again for my lost friend. Jae was now with our Lord and would soon meet my Jonah. Why had God spared me and not him? It was a question I knew would plague me for the rest of my life. I got topside and rushed back through the old vending area. The creepiness of the space no longer scared me after what I had just seen. I opened the steel door into the outside tunnel and dialed Vanessa.

She picked up on the first ring. "Daddy, I've been trying to get ahold of you—"

"This is Brandon. Don't talk. Just listen. I have a young girl about age six that needs medical attention immediately. She's lost a lot of blood. I'm at our drop off location in the tunnel."

"On it," she said, typing away. "Is Daddy okay?"

"He's fine," I said, hanging up before she asked for further details about the mission and her husband.

A cop pulled up and flashed his lights. He must have seen my fatigues and empty sidearm holster and got out of the car with his gun drawn. "Place the child down and raise your hands over your head."

"Listen to me. You're about to receive a call to come to this location," I said.

"Place the child down and raise your hands," he repeated.

The radio on his shoulder chirped and the operator called for all units to descend on our location to pick up a young girl from an undercover government agent. The cop acknowledged the call, put his gun away, and approached me.

"This girl's been drugged and lost a lot of blood," I said, handing her to him.

"Where were you?"

"Under Dupont Circle," I said. "Long story."

Suddenly, the ground shook. In the distance I could see the banking building owned by Gaspar Schultz shake and quiver as if it knew its master was dead. A moment later the building collapsed upon itself covering over the sins of Gehenna.

The cop shouted, "What the—"

I grabbed him by the arm. "Listen to me. Get that girl out of here now! Then get on your radio and keep everyone away from six sixty-six Tartarus Lane. The building's exterior was laced with poison."

I started back towards the tunnel entrance under Dupont Circle and called Vanessa again.

"I'm monitoring what happened," she said.

"Schultz's building exterior was laced with poison. Call Vice President Prince and let him know. Everyone should stay in their homes and EMTs should have hazmat gear on for the next twenty-four hours."

"Got it," she said. "Where's Jae?"

EPILOGUE

Schultz's building imploded instead of exploding, and very little of the poison embedded in the structure was released. Police were able re-route the minimal traffic in the area due to time of night. Only a few local residents with respiratory issues had to be treated. The next day government agents evacuated Schultz's Wallstreet building and started the immediate process to seal the exterior stucco so it could then be demolished.

Four days later, Jae's funeral was held at his church. It was standing room only. Vanessa was inconsolable as she stood before the open casket that had to be custom ordered to fit Jae's frame. Annie and I stood in the back of the church. At Arlington Cemetery Jae was given full military honors. There were a lot of confused expressions on people's faces. Everyone knew Jae had left law enforcement and did

contract security work, but the honor burial revealed
there was more to his job than what people realized.
Rain poured most of the day but slowed down by the
end of the funeral. Roger and Claire held Vanessa up
like she was a cripple without the use of her legs. The
flag from over the casket was reverently folded by
two honor guard soldiers, however when they
finished, neither soldier handed the flag to Vanessa.
Normally, one of them would whisper in her ear
about the President's appreciation for her husband's
service, but the soldier holding the flag stood back.

The cemetery soon cleared of people, and the sun
crept out from behind a massive cloud. Annie went
back to the Jeep to wait for me. I stood about ten
yards back praying as I watched the Drake family
kneel on the hallowed ground where Jae, along with
countless other soldiers, were buried. I wanted to go
up to join the family, and allow my tears to mix with
theirs, but it wasn't my place. Over the next few
minutes, I watched as the pall bearers got into their
hearse and drove away.

In their place, secret service agents appeared as if
from the ether. They were dressed in sharp black
suits and dark sunglasses. From somewhere close by
I heard the quiet putter of a finely tuned diesel
engine. A limousine slowed to a stop. Agents
surrounded the car, with one opening the rear
passenger door. Vice President Prince stepped out
dressed in a black suit and walked over to the
gravesite. The soldier holding the folded flag handed

it to the Vice President who continued on to the Drake family. He knelt and spoke into Vanessa's ear. Her crying continued as she took the flag and hugged Vice President Prince. He stayed with them kneeling in the wet grass for a few minutes. Eventually, all of them rose. They each gave the Vice President a hug. He now cried along with them, and it looked like they were consoling him. Before leaving, he turned to me, nodded, and touched his right hand over his heart.

A week later the first load of Black Angus cattle showed up at our farm. I leaned against the split rail fence with Dad, watching the eight beautiful animals graze.

"This is fitting," he said.

"How so?"

"After the biblical flood, the entire world was repopulated with eight people." Dad placed one of his massive hands on my shoulder. "Patience, hard work, and trust in God. We'll be okay."

Annie came out of the house with Emily and the baby. "You ready?"

"Give me a minute," I said, stretching in preparation for a trail run through the farm. My cell rang. The ID came up as *unknown* which either meant an annoying robocall, or Drake. "Brandon Hall speaking?"

"How's my brother doing?" came Drake's voice.

"Forget me," I said. "How are you doing?"

"I'm recovering."

"Vanessa?"

"She'll never be the same," he said, his voice cracking.

"No, she won't ever be the same," I said, thinking of my recovery from the loss of Jonah, "but she will heal."

"Good point," he said. "How's things on the farm?"

"Gonna be busy soon."

"I wanted to let you know that girl you rescued, fully recovered and was returned to a very grateful family."

"Praise God," I said, knowing somewhere under the rubble of Gaspar Schultz's building were two other children who would never be reunited with their families.

"The Vice President tasked me with re-building a new team. Vanessa's out for the time being until after the baby's born, so I have a spot for an analyst, and a couple agents all of whom I'm gonna pluck from the tree rather than the barrel. I'm on a plane right now heading to the West Coast to interview graduates from a recent BUDS boot camp."

"You got anyone in mind for the analyst?" I said.

"Not yet. Why?"

"I know of a lady in Alexandria about to graduate from Georgetown law who wants to get into government work."

"Text me her information."

"Will do."

"I wanted to let you know I have at least one opening for a NOC."

"NOC?" I said.

"It's a CIA term," Drake said. "It stands for *Non Official Cover*. Traditionally, someone in the business world whose day job allows them to float in and out of industries and countries where they can help us out. A part time spook if you will. I'd like to offer you the job?"

I chuckled. "I'm a farmer."

"I know. You'd be the first NOC in US history with that background, but I trust you."

Emily approached pushing a jogging stroller with Addison in it. Even though I was back on the farm, I still felt homesick. I never wanted to leave my family, or the farm, again.

"I appreciate the offer," I said, "but I'm gonna pass. I've had my fill of action for several lifetimes."

"At least think about it before you say no."

Emily hugged my leg. "C'mon, Dad."

Annie came up and mouthed the words, *Who's that?*

I mouthed back, *Drake*. "I'll talk it over with the boss, Roger, but I'm sure she'll say no."

After I got off the phone Annie said, "I'm afraid to ask what that was about?"

"I'll tell you later."

After the jog we all showered and piled into the Jeep. A short while later we pulled up to Toller's log cabin in Halifax. His golden retriever played outside with his seven-year old son, Max. Emily exhaled in the backseat at the sight of the dog as if she were jealous. I wanted to remind her we could get another dog, but knew the time still wasn't right.

Amber Schilling, the senator's last remaining child came outside with Tollers carrying two bags. With long auburn hair and an enormous white smile, she was a younger, taller version, of her mother.

Tollers shook my hand. "Gonna have your hands full with this firecracker."

Amber rolled her eyes. "I wasn't that bad, was I?"

"I'm just kidding." Tollers looked at his watch. "Gotta head into work and fight the bad guys." He gave Amber a hug and walked off towards his sheriff's cruiser, His son and dog chased after Tollers, as if trying to convince him to stay and play.

Amber turned to me and shook my hand like a professional. "Are you sure it's okay if I stay with you guys for the summer?"

I took her bags and started to load them into the Jeep. "As long as you don't mind a boring farm and a guest suite in the barn that's not quite complete."

"I think I'll enjoy the break," she said. "I have people calling me every five minutes."

"That's sweet," Annie said.

"It's not what you think, Missus Hall. I stand to inherit a lot of money. Dad and mom's estate will be tied up for months in probate, so I'm both homeless and broke for the time being."

"Well you're more than welcome to stay as long as you'd like," I said.

"Thanks, Mister Hall."

"Call me Brandon," I said. "You'll meet Mister Hall soon enough. He's a lot older and grumpier."

Amber smiled and looked down. "You're the only person on the planet my dad trusted."

"Speaking of trust," I said, handing her a check. "This is the overage from the contract job I did for your dad. I don't feel comfortable taking it. It's more than enough to cover you for the summer in case you didn't want to stay with us and wanted to travel Europe or something."

Amber started to cry.

Annie placed her arm around Amber. "Are you okay, sweetie?"

Amber nodded and turned the shoulder-hug into a full-blown bear hug which seemed to unleash a torrent of tears. Tears that had built up for the loss of two parents and a brother. Emily came over holding the baby, and Amber's tears stopped.

"Could I hold her?"

Annie took Addison from Emily and placed her in Amber's arms. A smile formed on both Amber and Addison's lips. As Amber rocked my daughter back and forth, I could see a nurturing side that I had never seen before in Margaret Schilling. I would do everything in my power to protect Amber Schilling from the truth of what her parents' marriage was like, and what her mother was into.

In the Bible, the character of Joseph was put through a gauntlet of trials, which God turned around and used for good. It was a cosmic painting that only made sense when the painter finished His masterpiece and signed His name at the bottom. The people who died with Gaspar Schultz thought they were about to usher in a new world order, but the Almighty had other plans. In their hubris, Gehenna believed their demonic lair was a safe bunker, which ultimately turned into their tomb.

The Schultz's building was bulldozed over, and Gehenna was never discovered. Someone in the media concocted a story about a gas leak causing the explosion. Only alternative media news sites questioned the narrative. In the end, old world families whose net worth in the billions were swept under the rug of history. The bad guys lost that round, but at a heavy cost. No one would know about Jae's sacrifice other than me, the Drake family, and Vice President Prince.

I took comfort in the fact that this wave of evil had passed, but also knew this malevolence would slither back to its home and take on a new form under a new name. Another globalist would arise to take on the mantle formally held by Schultz, and they would recruit like crazy. In times past, I had been anxious knowing that evil did not sleep, and it was always at work in the world. However, another force was also at work, and this force was not equal to, but far greater. I read The good book cover-to-cover and knew how the story ended. Tough times were coming, but we were promised a day when there would be; no more death, neither sorrow, nor crying, neither shall there be any more pain: for the former things are passed away.

There truly would come a day when we would see a happily ever after.

A LOOK AT ANGELS & IMPERFECTION BY DAN ARNOLD

JOHN WESLEY TUCKER IS NEITHER AN ORDINARY DETECTIVE NOR AN ORDINARY MAN.

Private Investigator John Wesley Tucker is hired to do a routine background check for a wealthy oil man, an aspiring politician. His investigation is complicated by his involvement in other cases and events which may be tied to a person associated with his client.

His partner, Christine, finds herself struggling to come to grips with her own ideals and beliefs. She and John are being followed by members of an unknown agency. When they learn there is a connection between the agency and Christine's former boss, all the disparate threads are woven together into a tapestry of death.

John and those around him will be led into a trap from which few will walk away.

A fast-paced, contemporary detective thriller with action, intrigue and a spiritual twist!

AVAILABLE NOW ON AMAZON

THANK YOU

Thank you for taking the time to read *Beneath DC*. If you enjoyed it, please consider telling your friends or posting a short review. Word of mouth is an author's best friend and much appreciated.

Thank you.

John Theo Jr.

ABOUT THE AUTHOR

John Theo Jr. received a bachelor's degree in psychology from Salem State University, and an M.F.A. in Creative Writing from Pine Manor College in Chestnut Hill, Massachusetts. For almost two decades his diverse writing portfolio included roles as a movie critic, a magazine freelance writer, and a college professor where he taught screenwriting.

John grew up in the suburbs north of Boston where much of his youth was spent buried under stacks of comic books. He latched onto any story involving far off places and fantastical characters. Years later he realized the novels and movies that impacted him on the deepest level were ones with a spiritual component. In hindsight, he realized that his youthful obsession with these stories was, in fact, a longing for the Divine.

Today, John Theo Jr. writes novels from a Christian perspective. Like the stories of his youth, John enjoys tales with an otherworldly component to them as well as a good measure of action, adventure, and romance.

Made in the USA
Middletown, DE
20 January 2023

22669053R00213